SUSPICIOUS MINDS

A HIP-SWIVELING COLE RAMSEY MYSTERY

PAUL BISHOP

WOLFPACK
PUBLISHING
— EST 2013 —

BOOKS BY PAUL BISHOP

Fey Croaker Series

Croaker: Kill Me Again

Croaker: Grave Sins

Croaker: Tequila Mockingbird

Croaker: Chalk Whispers

———

Hot Pursuit

Deep Water

A Bucketful of Bullets

Lie Catchers

Nothing But The Truth (Almost)

Fightcard: Felony Fists

Fightcard: Swamp Walloper

Suspicious Minds

Paperback Edition
Copyright © 2018 (as revised) Paul Bishop

Wolfpack Publishing
6032 Wheat Penny Avenue
Las Vegas, NV 89122

wolfpackpublishing.com

Paperback ISBN: 978-1-64119-386-3
eBook ISBN: 978-1-64119-383-2

AUTHOR'S FOREWORD

Some books are just plain fun to write. This book was one of them. *Suspicious Minds*—a crazy Elvis conspiracy novel with a character—Cole Ramsey—who stepped onto the page fully formed. However, while a book may have been a blast to create, it still may not find a home in the world of traditional publishing. When I first wrote *Suspicious Minds*, Elvis had not made any appearances in a fictional format, and while the manuscript received very positive editorial comments, no publisher offered to take a chance on it. *Suspicious Minds* became what is known as a *trunk novel*, a finished manuscript a writer hides away in a trunk for another day.

Sometimes, parts of a trunk novel are cannibalized by the writer and dropped into other novels. In a different form, the finale of *Suspicious Minds* morphed into the finale (without the Elvis's) of my novel *Chalk Whispers*.

But I continued to have a special affection for Suspicious Minds. Earlier this year, I took it out of the trunk and back into the light of day. I went through the manuscript with an editorial eye honed by the many other novels I'd written since. When I was done, I felt positive *Suspicious Minds* would deliver to readers as much fun as I had writing it. I am grateful to Wolfpack Publishing for seeing the same potential in *Suspicious Minds* as I did.

Paul Bishop
    Los Angeles 2018

SUSPICIOUS MINDS

PART I

1977 THE KING IS DEAD

CHAPTER 1

MARCH 23, 1977
ST. LOUIS CEMETERY NO. 2
NEW ORLEANS, LOUISIANA

EVEN BEFORE HE TURNED THE BLACK DEA SEDAN through the cemetery gates, Lew Sutton knew his partner was going squirrelly. Gordon Fontaine hated all drug dealers, but he was obsessed with Zachary Arceneaux. Lew could feel trouble brewing. It always did when Gordy was around.

"Are you going to be a good boy?" Lew asked, as he stopped the car next to a curb overrun with crab grass. Worn and discolored headstones tilted at higgledy-piggledy angles around them.

"If I was going to be good, would I even be here after getting chewed out by our boss for the disturbance I caused last night at the rosary?" Gordy was slumped down on the passenger side of the car with his feet up on the torn and battered dashboard. He wore dark glasses and a loud Mexican guayabera shirt. The shirt hung out over his jeans to hide the gun on his hip. Two toothpicks moved cynically back and forth across his lips. Gordy's version of cool.

Lew chuckled. "I thought I was going to have a heart attack when you started to haul the body out of the coffin and had to be restrained.

"And a fat lot of help you were. That was no cadaver in that coffin. At least it wasn't Arceneaux's cadaver."

"Come on," Lew implored. "Arceneaux is dead. You saw the body at the viewing last night. Let it go, man. Don't let him ruin your career from beyond the grave."

Gordy shot upright in his seat. "He ain't dead. If that body we saw last night was any waxier, it would have had a wick in it. You saw it yourself—the body was sweating."

"You've told it all to me before." Lew put up a hand to interrupt. "Dead bodies don't sweat, but wax ones do."

"Nobody twisted your arm to make you come here today," Gordy said. "The director is after my badge not yours. If you want to split and go chase street junkies, drop me off here." Gordy started to get out, but Lew reached across and grabbed him by the shirt collar.

"Don't screw with me." Lew hauled Gordy back into the seat. "We've been partners a long time. I wanted to put Arceneaux away as much as you did."

"Nobody wants Arceneaux as bad as me."

"There you go with that present tense stuff again. The man is dead. Gone! Finito! Crossed over to the other side! He's on a cruise down the River Styx!"

"In a parallel universe maybe, but not in this world. I'm telling you Zachary Arceneaux is alive! I can feel it."

Lew threw up his hands. "Next, you'll be telling me Jimmy Hoffa is still alive."

"I bet you bought all that crap about Paul McCartney being dead. Play *Abbey Road* backward and you can hear, *Paul is dead, Paul is dead*. What a load of crap!"

"Gordy, we saw the body!"

"We saw *a* body. It wasn't Arceneaux's."

Zachary Arceneaux was known in New Orleans as King Cajun. His organization ran drugs through the Louisiana bayous and swamps with the ease and viciousness of a gator running down its prey. The Mississippi River had become Arceneaux's personal drug artery to the rest of the country.

Arceneaux was a merciless, sadistic taskmaster with a finger in every profitable pie—prostitution, gambling, politicians, real estate, and every other hydra-head of corruption. Drugs, however, were his power base. Anyone who threatened his drug monopoly felt the bone crushing bite of King Cajun.

Gordy's father, Max Fontaine, had been caught in Arceneaux's jaws.

Fifteen years ago, Max Fontaine had been the Drug Enforcement Agency's top undercover agent. His job had forced him to be away from home a lot. Since Gordy's mother died in labor, this meant Gordy was left with an aging and childless aunt and uncle. Gordy didn't mind. He idolized his father, and his aunt and uncle were good to him.

As Gordy grew up on stories of his father's exploits, he came to believe Max was invulnerable—a champion more interesting than any comic book superhero.

When Max told his son he was going undercover in the bayous, Gordy figured it was another routine assignment. Max would be gone for a few months then return with another batch of thrilling tales. This time, though, things were different. Max didn't come home. When Arceneaux chewed Max up and spat his tattered body out on the shores of the Mississippi, Gordy's future became locked in. Arceneaux was going to be taken down, and Gordy was going to do it.

Trading on his father's old contacts, Gordy joined the Drug Enforcement Agency as soon as he was old enough. His abrasive personality did little to endear him to his DEA peers, but his impressive arrest record kept his career on track.

For the past ten years, he had been playing gator and mouse with his father's old adversary. And as the mouse had been about to turn the tables, the gator had been declared dead.

But Gordy was convinced the gator was only playing opossum.

"We going to do this, or what?" Gordy asked.

"Sure," Lew said, putting the car into gear.

Gordy slumped down in the car seat and returned his feet to the dashboard. He adjusted his one-way aviator sunglasses, a thin smile running across his lips.

The DEA sedan moved farther into the cemetery.

Around the next bend, the two agents could see a huge crowd of mourners gathered on a grassy knoll. The area was better tended and less congested with headstones than the other areas of the cemetery. The day was hot and sticky, but the mourners all wore long dark coats.

"Disgusting," Gordy said. "King Cajun even gets a burial plot in the middle of the ground reserved for families and descendants of the city's founding fathers."

"Perhaps it's appropriate," Lew said. "This city was founded on vice, so Arceneaux's legacy certainly fits."

There was a line of black limousines parked along the curb below the grave site. Uniformed chauffeurs lounged against bumpers or huddled in small groups. Aside from the clustered chauffeurs, other hard-looking men stood in pairs at strategic points.

Lew pulled the DEA sedan to a stop at the opposite curb. The radio under the dash crackled, and several of the chauffeurs turned in the agent's direction.

"Looks as if we're expected," Lew said.

Gordy shrugged. "Thank you, Captain Obvious. After ten years of being Arceneaux's personal pain in the butt, we've earned the right to front row seats." The twin toothpicks traveled rapidly back and forth across his lips as he spoke.

Lew nodded in agreement. "Arceneaux was livid after we took down his last five shipments. He went berserk taking his organization apart looking for the source."

"We had him," Gordy said. "He was going down for the long fall, and he knew it. I've waited years to slap the cuffs on him, but when I finally get him pinned down..." Gordy's voice trailed off with a sound full of choked emotion.

"Arceneaux up and dies of a heart attack." Lew finished his partner's sentence. "Inconsiderate of him."

"Don't make fun of me, partner. There's no justice if

Arceneaux is dead. Death is too good for him. He deserves to be put away in a hell hole of a jail. A place where he could end up as desperate as all the runaways he hooked on junk and put on the streets to peddle their asses."

The two partners sat watching the scene in silence. A Catholic priest was intoning low mumbles over the grave.

"What do you want to do?" Lew asked, eventually.

Gordy flipped the toothpicks out of his mouth and put his feet down. "Why don't you start by getting the license plates off all the cars in the funeral party? It might be interesting to see who's who."

"What are you going to do?"

Gordy opened the passenger door and started to slide out. "It's cool," he said. "I'm simply going to pay my last respects."

Taking out a pocket notebook, Lew exited the other side of the sedan.

Physically the two DEA agents were total opposites. Lew was tall, slender, and dyspeptic looking—like a constipated Japanese crane. He was all elbows and knees, angles and bones. His casual clothing hung on him like Goodwill castoffs, and his lightweight black jacket did little to hide the bulge of the 9mm automatic he carried in a worn shoulder holster.

By contrast, Gordy was a five-foot six bantam rooster. He'd only made the DEA's height requirements by taping flesh colored foam wedges under his heels for the entrance physical. He was neat and confident. His full black hair flowed in deep waves across his skull. He was the same age as Lew, thirty-one, but looked ten years younger. It wasn't because Gordy looked twenty, but more because Lew was not aging gracefully.

They were a good team because Lew was in awe of Gordy's ability to never be at a loss for what to do or say next. Gordy, however, had his share of detractors in the agency—old partners or supervisors who despised his cocky attitude and king-size ego. Whenever the booze began to flow at agency parties, everyone knew who was being talked about when *Walking Small* was mentioned.

While trying to keep one eye on Gordy, Lew began to write down license numbers with the stub of a pencil.

"What the hell are you doing, buddy?" asked a chauffeur, watching Lew bend down behind one of the limos for a closer look.

Lew flashed his DEA identification like he was trying to hold a vampire at bay with a silver crucifix.

"Don't you guys ever take the day off?" the chauffeur asked. "Ain't you got no respect for the dead?"

Lew fired back a line he'd picked up from Gordy. "Careful or I'll book you for filth and ignorance in the presence of a federal officer."

The chauffeur held up his hands in a placating gesture. He wasn't being paid to handle cop grief. That job was reserved for the hardmen who were dotted around the cemetery.

CHAPTER 2

ON THE OTHER SIDE OF THE GRASSY KNOLL, WHERE THE mourners had gathered to see Arceneaux put to his final rest, was a higher rise. A small pathway, barely wide enough for a car, led to the top of the second rise and then down again on the other side. At the crest, a lone limousine sat overlooking the funeral ceremony.

In the rear seat of the limo, a dark man of sixty-plus years old sat in the back staring intently out of the side window. He had a face like a bowl full of elbows, all knots and cheekbones. He wore an expensive blue pin-striped suit with a white carnation attached to the stylishly narrow lapel.

Across from the dark man, one of the two men sitting on the limo's jump seats eyed the older man surreptitiously. He figured the price of the silk tie tucked into the pin-striped suit would equal about a month's worth of his own GS-12 government salary.

"I told you he would be here," the dark man said in a gravel voice. He pointed out the bulletproof glass of the window to where Gordy was advancing on the funeral party. "He's going to interrupt the best part. You told me he had been controlled. I want him stopped."

The young man who had been figuring the price of the tie grabbed a two-way radio from the floor below him and began to talk rapidly into it.

Two of the hardmen near the grave each put a hand to their ear, looked around with slitted eyes, spotted Gordy, and began moving toward him.

Gordy saw them coming and slowed his advance.

"You're out of here, Fontaine," the first hardman said as he approached.

"You and what two armies?" Gordy asked, a cocky smile slapped across his face.

"These two," the hardman said. With his right hand he pulled back his sport coat to reveal a gun in a shoulder holster. "Army number one," he said. With his left hand he fished out and flashed a set of credentials. "And army number two."

Gordy squinted at the government pasteboard and the crackerjack prize badge the hardman was showing. "The FBI?" Gordy said in mock awe.

"I'm Special Agent Jordan," said the hardman. "And this is Special Agent Lambert." He indicated the second hardman, who had moved up behind him. "We've been told to escort you from the area."

Gordy shook his head thoughtfully. "Why do you guys always have to say you're Special Agents? Why not just Agents? Are there Not-So-Special Agents? And special or not, what are FBI agents doing playing security guards at a drug king's funeral? Has the world gone mad? Clearly, there's something going on. And I'm going to prove it."

Catching the agents off guard, Gordy faked a move to his left then dodged back to his right. When Jordan reached out to grab him, Gordy kicked the FBI agent hard in the shin and savagely pushed him backward into Lambert.

Jordan, sarcastically nicknamed *Lucky*, cried out as both agents crashed to the ground in a tangled heap. Gordy ran by them and up the grassy knoll to where the casket was being lowered.

Heating Jordan's shout, Lew Sutton looked up from his license gathering. He saw the two men sprawled on the ground and knew his partner had irretrievably blown things open. When Lew saw a half dozen other hardmen converging on Gordy, he started running in the same direction. Gordy was his partner, and come hell or high water, you always had your partner's back.

Gordy shoved his way through startled grave-side mourners. He stopped beside a small winch, which was lowering the casket. "Federal officer," he said. He waved his DEA credentials about while trying to find the off switch for the winch. "I want this coffin opened now!"

"Please," said the shocked priest. "This is a funeral. Show some respect in the presence of God."

"Listen, padre," Gordy said, turning toward the priest. "God wouldn't waste his time showing up at a funeral for Zachary Arceneaux. This piece of dog excrement you think you're burying isn't worth pissing on. But don't worry because Arceneaux isn't even in this fancy box."

The coffin was suspended over the grave by two nylon lowering bands controlled by the winch. After securing the winch, Gordy stepped over to the coffin. He knelt on the turf next to it.

The burial box was an ornately worked piece of art. Fashioned from hand rubbed teak, it was bejeweled with intricate sterling silver handles and overlays. Gordy reached out and began to unscrew the silver angel-shaped wing nuts that secured the lid. The mourners at the grave side began to wail and moan. None of them, however, wanted to interfere with the madman in their midst.

"Please stop," the priest implored again. Anger at Gordy's blasphemy suffused his face with color. Swirling his robes around him, he grabbed Gordy's shoulder and tried to pull him away from the coffin.

Gordy, knowing he didn't have much time, turned from his efforts to undo the coffin lid, pulled his gun off his hip and pointed it at the priest. "Back off, padre. This is the last time I'm going to tell you."

Shocked beyond belief, the priest backed away. Gordy returned to his precarious balancing act over the coffin and began unscrewing angels again. They seemed to be multiplying.

Looking around him, the priest spotted the quick release button on the winch. Placing his hand together, he closed his eyes and quickly mumbled the final lines of the grave side service. "Ashes to ashes. Dust to dust. May this body be received into the loving arms of our heavenly and most merciful father. Amen." The priest's voice rose loudly as he intoned the final word.

"Amen!" responded the mourners in unison.

Gordy was removing the last of the angel-shaped wing nuts, leaning fully across the coffin lid to do it when the priest hit the winch's quick release button. Gordy and the coffin disappeared into the grave like a spooked rabbit down a hole.

The muffled thump of the coffin as it hit the dirt six feet below acted like a signal to the mourners. The grave-side onlookers suddenly energized, shucking off their long black coats to reveal beautiful multicolored clothing beneath.

Brass instruments appeared as if by magic, and the sounds of cool Bourbon Street jazz pierced the shimmering heat of the day. A drum picked up a back beat and the mourners began to dance. Moving their sinewy bodies to the fast-paced music the close-packed revelers hugged each other in celebration of the dead's departure for a higher plane—a tradition older than jazz itself.

In their enthusiasm, several brightly clad women hindered the progress of the dark suited FBI agents attempting to converge on Gordy. Swept up in the dance, the agents tried to get clear, but it was like swimming against a red tide.

Inside the open grave, the lid of the coffin had bounced clear and was resting upright on one edge. Gordy hadn't been so lucky. He was lying half-on and half-off the exposed corpse. Blinded by swirling dust and earth, he pushed out a hand for leverage. His fingers slid across the wax on the corpse's face. He yelled out in horror as the features of Zachary Arceneaux were wiped away to reveal the dead face of another man underneath. The corpse wasn't Arceneaux's. But it was still a body. A dead one. And Gordy wanted to get as far away from it as possible.

Searching for his gun, which had bounced away from him in the fall, Gordy stood up sputtering and swearing. Even standing on the corpse, his weight crushing the brittle bones beneath him, Gordy's head barely rose above the grave mouth. He grabbed the sides of the hole to pull himself out, but the loose earth kept falling in on him.

Finally, using the lid of the coffin for a boost, Gordy rolled out onto the cemetery turf. All around him, the legs of dancers swirled and kicked to the beat of the jazz filling the air.

———

"I WANT HIM DEAD! Do you hear me? Kill him!" The dark man in the back seat of the limo screamed at the two FBI agents sitting across from him.

The smoke black window separating the front seat from the rear of the limo slid silently down. Senior FBI Special Agent Dwayne Bowman sat in the passenger seat next to the liveried driver. Bowman was wearing a ten-year-old suit. It had been out of style since he'd purchased it at a J.C. Penney's two-for-one clearance sale. In his thirty-five-year career with the bureau this was the most distasteful assignment he'd ever pulled. He turned in to look into the back of the limo.

"The FBI is not in the habit of murdering other federal law enforcement officers, Arceneaux. This whole scenario of indulging your whim to attend your own funeral is a stupid waste of taxpayer's money. You're a scuz-bucket of the first order and should be treated as such."

Arceneaux turned his piercing blue eyes on the older agent. "Nobody talks to me that way. You will pay for your insolence."

"I'm not one of your flunkies, Arceneaux." Bowman was unfazed even though his younger counterparts had turned pale under their tans. "You came to us, remember." He pointed a thick, scarred thumb in the direction of the debacle by the grave side. "Gordon Fontaine may have the personality of a proctologist's exhibit, but he's a hell of a cop. He destroyed your empire, forced you into a corner, and survived your assassination attempts long enough to convince a Grand Jury to indict you."

Bowman chuckled ruefully. "You had two choices—go to jail or turn State's evidence. So, you came to the FBI because you couldn't go to the DEA and watch Fontaine wallow in his triumph. The witness protection program is too good for you. We should have let you go to jail instead of setting up this elaborate con job."

Arceneaux was on a slow boil. "Your superiors seem to think the information I can provide them with is worth the effort. They'll hammer you for talking to me this way."

"What are they going to do?" Bowman asked. "Delegate me to assignments where I have to protect sheep-dip like you?" He brought out and lighted a thin cigar, blowing smoke in Arceneaux's direction. "What you don't understand is the Bureau director and I have a lot in common. We're both as high as we're going to go on this job. I'd never make a good area supervisor anyway. I couldn't take the operations."

"Operations?" queried one of the younger agents in

surprise. He hoped to be promoted in the very near future.

"Didn't they tell you during the academy at Quantico?" Bowman asked seriously. "Before anyone can become an area supervisor they have to have their spine sucked out. And if you get promoted any higher, then you have to have a plate glass window installed in your stomach, so you can see where you're going with your head up your ass." Bowman broke out in peals of laughter.

———

GORDY FELT a hand grab at the back of his neck. He rolled away and kicked out catching Agent 'Lucky' Jordan on the shin again.

"Look for yourself," Gordy yelled at Jordan. "That isn't Arceneaux in the coffin!"

Other FBI agents had surrounded the grave mouth. They were all facing outward to keep back the reporters and photographers who were covering the funeral.

The revelers who had been so mournful at the start of the funeral were forming themselves into a conga line. Hanging onto each other, they began to wind their way through the headstones and out of the cemetery to continue the wake elsewhere.

"You're under arrest, Fontaine," Jordan said. He was still bent over rubbing his shin. "You're going to lose your badge behind this."

"Arceneaux is not dead!" Gordy screamed at the man. Several other agents began to move toward him. Gordy began rapidly backing away from the grave and started up the second grassy knoll toward the limo. Jordan and the others began to chase him.

Seeing the limo at the top of the second knoll, things suddenly became clear for Gordy. Instinctively, he knew Arceneaux was inside the long, black vehicle. With speed born of desperation, he started to run.

In the limo, Bowman saw Gordy coming. He spoke rapidly to the driver. "Get us clear."

Arceneaux watched Gordy run toward the vehicle. All his anger toward the relentless DEA agent welled up inside of him. Arceneaux would kill the little man if he had to pull the trigger himself.

Depressing the electric window button with one hand, Arceneaux used his other hand to grab the gun of the young agent next to him.

Gordy saw the limo's window slide down, revealing the face of the man he'd hated for so long. He saw the gun in Arceneaux's hand as it stuck its ugly snout out of the window and spat fire. Stone splinters exploded from a headstone directly in front of Gordy, but before he could react he was tackled from behind as the gun fired again.

"Stay down," Lew Sutton shouted at his partner, his hands wrapped around Gordy's knees. Though he appeared long, lean, and awkward, Lew Sutton could run like the wind. He'd passed Jordan, Lambert, and the other agents in pursuit of Gordy like they were running in quicksand.

Another hand appeared in the window of the limo to grab at the gun, but not before it fired again. The shot went wide of Gordy and Lew, but 'Lucky' Jordan stumbled and fell as the projectile slammed into his thigh.

"You've got to give it up, Gordy," Lew said.

"Lew," Gordy was desperate, "Arceneaux is in that limo." He pointed at the rapidly disappearing vehicle.

"You need help, Gordy," Lew said. "Arceneaux is dead."

"Lew, they're going to put me away for this. You have to help me."

Lew looked at the rapidly approached FBI agents. One of their own had gone down. It was clear they thought Gordy had fired the shots.

"Please, Lew?"

Lew released Gordy's legs, and the two men stood up. Lew had his back to the onrushing agents. "One chance," he said to his partner. "Punch me and run. And God go with you, buddy."

Gordy didn't hesitate. He delivered a roundhouse punch to Lew's jaw, sending the skinny man reeling down the hill.

"Strike!" Gordy yelled as Lew crashed into the FBI agents, knocking them to the ground like a scene from a Keystone Kops' movie.

Gordy hit his afterburners and began running for his life.

CHAPTER 3

JUNE 26, 1977
MARKET SQUARE ARENA
INDIANAPOLIS, INDIANA

ELVIS FELT A TINY BEAD OF SWEAT ROLL DOWN HIS forehead. It left a trail of salty damp before the miniature river emptied into his right eye. Gingerly, he flicked at the affected eye with the tip of a finger as he tried to remove the sting without smearing the carefully applied makeup.

Outside the dressing room door confusion reigned. Elvis thought it sounded like the call to Armageddon. Nobody seemed in charge. Nothing was happening as planned. Orders were screamed with no apparent response. Unidentified crashes sounded as if the arena was being demolished. It never ceased to amaze Elvis that the end product of a concert—the glittering, polished performance—never revealed the true nature of the production's chaos.

Indiana was known for the high school basketball

tournaments held every year in the same gigantic arena now rocking with the anticipation of Elvis' appearance. The basketball championships were the only other event which could be depended upon to pack the house the way it was tonight. Thousands of people sweated and fought to endure the Indiana humidity to get a glimpse of the King of Rock-n'-Roll.

Elvis often wondered why someone would pay money to sit in a seat so far back and so high up in the balcony you couldn't tell who was on stage. Yet the people who sat there would tell all their friends the next day how exciting it had been to see Elvis in person. He might not understand them, but Elvis still loved those people. They were his fans. They had made him what he was, and he owed them, but sometimes the price of their adoration was high.

The Market Square arena was designed to accommodate all types of entertainment. One night the floor would be a frozen hockey rink, the next a basketball court. Tonight, it was a humongous concert auditorium for him alone. There might be thousands of fans, hundreds of roadies, tens of musicians and backup singers, but Elvis would still be alone.

For Elvis the thought of being alone on stage brought back boyhood memories of being an outcast at school, how alone he'd always felt. He was different then and now, the loneliness ever present. Even surrounded by thousands of screaming, adoring, worshiping fans squirming in their seats or dancing in the aisles, Elvis felt alone.

Momma was the one who made him feel wanted and whole. She had been gone a long time, and he missed her so much, but he gained strength knowing, believing, she was in heaven watching. No matter what mistakes he made in the past in his career, his marriage, or anything else, Momma would always understand. She loved him unconditionally.

Alone in the dressing room, the anticipation of the coming performance grew unbearable. Elvis catapulted out of the soft armchair to pace the small room like a caged animal. He felt better standing. When he sat, the extra weight he was carrying made his clothes tight and uncomfortable. Bulges appeared where they were not wanted. He thrust the factor of his weight from his mind. Even though he felt repulsively fat, he had to go on and entertain.

The concerts were what brought in revenue these days. The old records weren't selling, and there were no new recording contracts on the horizon. No matter how much he wanted to shut himself away, being a recluse was not an option.

As he continued to pace, Elvis tried to loosen up his stiff muscles. His muscles had once responded instantly. Now they felt like overstretched rubber bands. He avoided mirrors whenever he could. From his face to his gut, everything was sagging. His color was bad. He had a tough time looking himself in the eye when he washed or shaved. But there was a pill to sooth this anxiety.

The doctors had a pill for everything. There was a pill to make you sleep, a pill to wake you up, a pill to make you happy, and a pill to make sure you weren't too happy to work. The pills were a nightmare, a death-trap. They were no longer temporary medication, they were a necessity of life. His life.

His mind, like his body, was tired. The stress of celebrity life had taking a heavy toll. He'd thought the death threats were as bad as they could get. He was a constant target for everyone from jealous boyfriends and husbands to terrorists and kidnappers. However, events had proven him wrong. A husband and father had far more to lose than a man alone.

The burden weighed heavier as Elvis's star grew brighter. When you became a superstar, the dangers and risks increased a thousand-fold. It didn't matter if you were an ex-husband now, or even if your daughter didn't live with you. Your ex-wife and daughter were always going to be targets of opportunity. Two years earlier there had been a genuine attempt to abduct his family, but the bravery and fast action of one man had foiled the kidnappers.

Other pressures also weighed heavily on Elvis. The people who were close to him kept getting in trouble, always relying on him to bail them out. He was carrying the whole world on his shoulders. Even now, one of his nearest and dearest was so deep in the swamp, Elvis didn't know if he could save him. He didn't know the first thing about offshore banking, or money laundering, or how it had all led to extortion.

Elvis shook his head to clear the fog. He had a show to do. Above everything else, he was a performer. He might not be able to control his own destiny, but he would be true to the millions of fans who stuck with him through good times and bad.

Stretching out his arms, he dropped into a half

crouch and gyrated his shoulders the way he would on stage. He went through a series of half-hearted karate moves. How deadly he used to be. Today, it was simply an expected part of the act. Part of the legend.

There was a knock on the dressing room door.

A voice called out, "Hey, El. It's show time!"

The tension tightened in Elvis' stomach, becoming almost unbearable. With effort, he forced his personal problems back into their mental Pandora's Box. He opened the dressing room door to find two of his body-guards waiting. Elvis smiled with false confidence as they wrapped a cape around him, attaching it to snaps on the shoulders of his white, rhinestone jumpsuit. He stripped the glasses from his face with a flourish and shoved them into a pair of eagerly waiting hands.

One of the bodyguards checked the slim gold watch on his left wrist. The watch had been a gift from Elvis and was worth more than any car the bodyguard had ever owned. The hands on the watch face showed 8:30.

"I'm ready, boys," Elvis said quietly. No trace of the turbulence in his mind could be found in his hand-some countenance. Elvis was all business.

"Time to TCB, El?"

"That's right," Elvis replied in his distinctive mellow Southern drawl. "Time to take care of business."

Standing back stage, the orchestra sounded deaf-ening as crescendos increased with the imminent arrival of the King. The huge brass section started to gain momentum as it increased its volume. The noise of the crowd became a pandemonium as the fans were caught up in the moment, transformed into an immense, pulsating throng of humanity.

The Joe Guercio Orchestra built the anticipation higher and higher with the notes of Strauss' *Also Sprach Zarathustra*, better known to the fans begging for Elvis as the theme from Kubrick's film *2001—A Space Odyssey*. The crowd squirmed in their seats like killer dogs on long leashes keeping them out of reach of the mailman's legs.

The announcer's voice cut like a thunderbolt across the arena. "Ladies and gentlemen...ELVIS!"

CHAPTER 4

THE CROWD SHOT TO THEIR FEET CHEERING AND screaming. Surrounded by the intensity of the action, Gordy Fontaine was jostled from side to side. He tried to scramble to his feet. The ticket scalper had ripped Gordy off for a hundred-and-fifty bucks for a seat midway back in the auditorium. Even standing on his chair, Gordy had a tough time seeing Elvis glide onto the stage, grab the microphone, and rip into the velvet notes of the first song.

Flashbulbs were popping like strobe lights. Elvis struck a pose, his right hand flailing the air, his left leg moving with a life of its own, his supreme self-confidence and legendary animal magnetism flowed out of him in waves that broke over the audience. Time was reversed, and everyone in the room was instantly seventeen years old again.

Gordy felt the passion of the crowd squeeze his heart like a giant fist. He'd first met Elvis when the King walked into the Miami DEA office wanting to help clear up the drug problem in the music industry.

Since then, Gordy had become friends with Elvis. He'd worked off-duty as a bodyguard for him and seen him perform a dozen times. However, the emotion generated by Elvis in concert never failed to overwhelm him.

Gordy looked bad. He'd lost weight and his face had hollowed out. There were dark circles under his eyes, and he'd developed a slight tick along his right cheekbone. Three months on the run does strange things to a man.

The FBI wanted Gordy, and they wanted him immediately. Lew Sutton had not been able to convince them the bullet that smashed Lucky Jordan's thigh, had been fired by someone in the limo. The FBI investigators called the limo a phantom, a figment of Lew's imagination created to cover for a partner who had gone rogue.

The DEA was not in a position to argue the case. Gordy's actions at the cemetery and his obsession with Zachary Arceneaux were an embarrassment. They disowned Gordy quicker than a dollar whore trying to earn a hundred bucks.

A felony warrant had been issued charging assault on a federal officer. The warrant bore Gordy's name in big black letters accompanied by a slightly blurred photograph. Any kind of rogue was dangerous, but a rogue cop was the most dangerous rogue of all. The FBI was not going to cry in their beer if Gordy insisted on being brought in feet first.

Gordy and Lew knew the truth, but they were small voices screaming into the vacuum of the universe where there was no sound. Gordy chose to run and run hard. He knew Arceneaux was alive. It was why Gordy had come to see the King of Rock and Roll.

Nobody sits at an Elvis concert. Everyone in the arena was on their feet bouncing, screaming, and carrying on. Many of the predominantly female fans were crying. Gordy shook his head in wonder. Elvis was a bona fide living legend.

The superstar's voice moved easily into a trio of his standards, *Little Sister*, *Teddy Bear*, and *Don't Be Cruel*, before sliding into the heart rendering emotions of *Release Me*, *I Can't Stop Loving You*, and *Bridge Over Troubled Water*. The crowd went wild.

On stage Elvis could feel the throb of the music rushing through him. The crowd was hidden by the blur of the spotlights, but the power of their love electrified his being. There was nothing outside of the music and the moment.

The crowd was swaying gently, mesmerized, completely under Elvis' spell. Taking advantage of the lull brought on by the slower songs, Gordy pushed his way toward the stage. He had a definite objective in mind. Unlike other law enforcement officers, FBI agents were not allowed to work off-duty. However, Gordy didn't want to take a chance on being recognized by any of the local cops who were moonlighting as security at the concert. He'd been running too long and too hard to be tripped up by some rookie trying to earn a couple of extra bucks for his truck payment.

In three months, most normal folks would have forgotten a face they'd seen once on the wall in the post office, but cops were different. A cop's life could depend on whether he recognized a wanted felon on the street from a set of bad mug shots shown at roll call a year earlier. Cops liked to go home at night, so they developed long memories.

Gordy knew most of the cops hired as extra security were stationed backstage and outside of the concert site. It was one of the reasons he'd paid a scalper for his ticket—to get inside the arena and not be spotted lurking outside.

After meeting at the DEA office, Gordy and the superstar became friends. Elvis was an easy man to like, and he was fascinated by cops and their world. Elvis invited Gordy to one of his concerts. While there, Gordy had been in the right place at the right time to stop the ugly abduction attempt, which could have had stunning repercussions. In the aftermath, Elvis asked Gordy to help tighten up his security services. As a result, Gordy knew how he could get to the King while putting himself at minimal risk.

At the right side of the stage there was a short set of stairs leading down to the arena floor. A bodyguard with a shock of tightly cropped, sun bleached hair stood at the bottom with his arms folded. He had a craggy face and was casually chomping on an unlit cigar. He was facing the crowd.

"Hello, Whitey," Gordy called out over the music.

The bodyguard turned toward him with a scowl. He took a hard look at Gordy, his eyes probing against the glare of stage lights. A smile sprung to his lips.

"Is that you, Mr. Fontaine?"

"As ever was, Whitey."

When Gordy had earned Elvis' gratitude, he'd also saved Whitey North's life. To stop giving anyone else ideas, the whole attempted kidnapping had been kept out of the papers, which was difficult when you were dealing with a figure like Elvis. So, Whitey owed Gordy big and Gordy believed he could trust him.

The two men shook hands.

"Why didn't you let us know you were going to be here? We would have left a ticket for you." Whitey had to place his mouth close to Gordy's ear to be heard. "You could have come backstage. El would love to see you."

Gordy glanced around. The action had quickly become a habit—like a driver checking his mirrors. From Whitey's positive response, Gordy figured the bodyguard hadn't heard about his troubles. Although intense, the fed's search for Gordy had been low profile. Gordy was banking on this—hoping Whitey would think he was still with the agency.

"I need to talk to El in private."

"Now?" Whitey looked horrified.

Gordy almost laughed at the thought of trying to stop the concert, so he could chat with the King. "After the concert," he said. "I'd like to meet him in the limo."

"I don't know, Mr. Fontaine."

Gordy put a hand on the bodyguard's arm. "This is agency business," he lied. "Top secret. You know El is going to want to help."

Whitey still looked dubious.

"Didn't I save your butt two years ago," Gordy pushed. "This isn't a big thing I'm asking."

Whitey nodded. "Come on." Turning, he led Gordy up the stairs and off stage right. Whitey paused once, to send another bodyguard to take his place, then led

Gordy out the stage exit to Elvis's waiting limo. As soon as Elvis was finished with his last song, he would be whisked from the stage, into the elongated Mercedes, and immediately driven away to escape the loving, but dangerous throngs of adoring fans.

Whitey talked briefly to the driver and then opened the back door for Gordy. When Gordy was seated, Whitey stooped to stick his head inside. There was a look of concern on his face when he spoke. "I know how much El appreciated everything you did for him—stopping the kidnapping and rearranging the security and all. But please don't ask too much of him, man. He's talking about getting out—just disappearing. Crazy talk. He's tired, man. Real tired. You know what I mean?"

Gordy smiled. He felt tired himself. "I know what you mean," he said truthfully. "If El goes along with what I have in mind, he'll get all the rest he needs."

CHAPTER 5

GRACELAND MANSION
MEMPHIS, TENNESSEE

Fats McCorkle felt naked standing in front of the television camera. His heart was pounding, and his mouth was so dry he felt his tongue was going to shrivel up and die. The microphone kept slipping in his sweating palm. He wondered briefly how much worse things would get once the cameras were turned on.

This was the rotund reporter's first experience before the uncompromising eye of the television camera, and he was scared to death. With all his heart, he wished he was back in the depths of the radio broadcast room where his mellifluous voice had made him Memphis' most popular drive-time disc jockey. Everyone would agree putting Fat's in front of a camera was not a good idea, but circumstances weren't normal.

Fats winced as the spotlight on top of the remote camera came to life. He tried to adjust his eyes while bringing the hand-mic to his lips.

"Ladies and gentlemen, grief is rampant in the streets of Memphis and across the nation." Fats' voice had a mellow huskiness, assured and soothing. "Sources from inside Graceland have confirmed our worst fears. Elvis Presley is dead. The forty-two-year-old King of Rock-n'-Roll died of a massive heart attack in his bedroom early this morning." Fats paused dramatically, making eye contact with viewers across the nation. He felt the emotional shock of the news he was relaying surging up inside of him. "The King is dead and there is pandemonium in front of the gates at Graceland." Fats unsuccessfully fought down a sob. "We will bring you more details when they are released. This is Fats McCorkle, The Voice of Memphis, reporting to you live from Presley Boulevard for WMBC Action News."

The camera continued to roll as tears welled up in Fats eyes and flooded down his chubby cheeks. Choked with emotion, he was unable to continue.

Fats had been called to the scene by the WMBC news team when rumors of the tragedy leaked. The move was facilitated as the corporation that owned WELV—the *All Elvis, All The Time* radio station—also the WMBC television affiliate.

Aside from being the premiere Memphis area radio personality, Fats was an expert on Elvis. He was also the last local DJ to be granted an interview with the Graceland phantom. Elvis was more than simply Fats' job. The King was Fats' obsession, and the death of The King was a staggering blow.

Thousands of people were lining the streets and sidewalks around Elvis's famous home. Public displays of grief were evident everywhere. Local residents had been unexpectedly caught in the middle of their morning routines. They were surprised and shocked to see people carrying picnic baskets full of food and drink. It was as if the death watch had turned into a family outing. As more and more people flowed into the area, it was as if the whole of Memphis was gradually turning out.

Racked with emotion and grief, Fats tried to get a grip. Even with the insecurities he harbored over his weight, he had always wanted to make the transition from radio to television. It was ironic the death of his idol provided him with his big chance. He had to control himself. He couldn't blow this opportunity. It was a gift the King had literally died to give him. A high price to pay.

Clutching the microphone tightly between his sausage-like fingers, Fats pulled it away from his face and pressed it against his chest. Tears still flowed freely down his cheeks like a spring rain shower.

"Cut! Cut!" yelled a voice from behind the camera. "Come on, Fats. Stay with us, babe. We're going to be here for the duration on this thing. You gotta' help us sell it."

Sell it? Fats shook his head. Was television news what he really wanted? You didn't have to sell the death of a legend. Today would be like the day when John Kennedy was assassinated. There wasn't a man, woman or child in the nation who, twenty years from now, wouldn't remember where they were when they heard the news the King was dead.

Fats' real name was Lawrence Aloysius McCorkle.

He shot to prominence on the radio after years as a mid-western stumble bum, whose one claim to fame was that he knew all the words to every song Elvis had ever sung. In his own mind, Fats envisioned himself as sharing a parallel, if less glamorous, lifestyle with his idol.

Like Elvis, Fats had been rejected by his peers. He was a misunderstood kid who never seemed to get an even break. During high school, Fats would run home to escape the teasing of his classmates by losing himself in his collection of Elvis records. Over and over, he would practice announcing the songs as if he were playing them to a rapt audience over the radio waves. The beauty of radio was nobody could see you. It didn't matter if you were fat, or ugly, or uncoordinated. You could be whoever your voice said you were. And Fats' deep voice said he was slim, good looking, and as smooth and rich as chocolate syrup.

As the years passed, Fats' voice became his calling card. From boiler rooms all over the mid-west, he sold everything over the telephone from aluminum siding to gold leaf bibles. Working the telephone, Fats could sell the Golden Gate Bridge a hundred times a day.

He eventually graduated from the telephone to the radio. Along the way, he lost a wife and gained a hundred plus pounds. The scales currently flirted with the three hundred mark. When WELV in Memphis announced their intention to change to an *All Elvis, All the Time* format, Fats was a natural. As one of the foremost authorities on Elvis, Fats parlayed his knowledge of the King and his own voice for all they were worth.

Now, with Elvis' death, Fats was living every radio

announcer's fantasy—a shot on network TV. But Fats knew that this might be his last stand. Without Elvis, his own professional existence was in jeopardy. In the excitement and tragedy of the moment, Fats had forgotten his large, pear shaped physique would be there for all the audience to see. The thought of the possible ridicule burst out of his subconscious and he felt sick to his stomach.

He had to go on. He had to do this for the King.

An assistant director popped up next to the director and whispered in his ear. He'd been on the phone with the studio. The live broadcast had flooded the station with calls. Viewers were wracked with grief, but they were responding in droves to Fats' genuine display of emotion. The assistant director relayed the orders from the station director. "Home base says let him cry."

The director shrugged. "They want it, they've got it."

"Fats," the director called out. "Let's put a couple more shots in the can for broadcast later. Give us something with *pizzazz*. Make us feel the great loss. Oh, and keep the waterworks going."

Pizzazz? Make us feel the loss? What was the matter with this man? Fats wondered how anyone could become so jaded. He decided he didn't care. If the network was going to take the chance on his Elvis expertise outweighing the sight of his three-hundred-pound frame, he wasn't going to let them down. The show would go on, and Fats would do Elvis proud.

"Move to your left so we can get the front gate behind you," the director ordered.

Fats moved in response to the command. He was only slightly piqued when the cameraman snorted when checking his viewfinder. Fats realized it would be tough to get both him and the gate in the shot. Behind him, he knew the outline of Elvis' guitar on the Graceland gates would be peeking over his shoulder. It gave him an eerie feeling—as if Elvis himself was watching over him.

The director said, "We have speed. And action."

Fats brought the microphone closer to his lips again and steeled himself. "This is Fats McCorkle, the Voice of Memphis, coming at you from the front gates of Graceland, Elvis' Memphis home, where thousands of fans have gathered in disbelief." Once into his stride, Fats gained confidence. "The news of the Memphis Monarch's death has catapulted the entire city into a state of anarchy. Shops close to Graceland have been doing a booming business with throngs of people flooding Elvis Presley Boulevard, and more turning up every minute."

The camera panned to pick up the circus of humanity growing to monumental proportions. The unwinking eye recorded the arrival of the state police as the Memphis police department was unable to cope with the near riot conditions.

Spotting a middle-aged female sobbing and wringing her hands, Fats moved toward her. Behind him, the camera team fell into line.

"Excuse me, ma'am. I'm Fats McCorkle from WMBC TV. I'd like to get your reaction to the death of Elvis Presley."

Fats extended the microphone in her direction.

"I know you," the woman said. "I'd know your voice anywhere. You're on the radio."

"That's right, ma'am. But we're on television now. Could you tell me how you feel about Elvis' death?"

The woman turned to the camera and primped her hair. "Are we really on the TV?"

"Yes, ma'am. Now about Elvis?"

"It's simply horrible. I refuse to believe it. God wouldn't take such a beautiful man away from us so young. There has to be some kind of mistake." The woman began to cry. Her emotion washed over onto Fats. Tears began to form again in the corners of his eyes.

Before the moment could become too maudlin, the woman stopped her sniffling. "There. Did I say the right thing?" she asked. "Did I give you what you wanted? Do you want to do another take? I was an actress in high school, you know."

Fats moved away before he became angry.

"Wait," the woman called after him. "What channel is this going to be on?"

The director next pointed Fats in the direction of a seedy looking character who had been flitting in and out of the crowd for the past two hours selling everything from unauthorized Elvis t-shirts to fake gold chains sporting TCB and Jesus charms.

"Excuse me, sir," Fats placed his considerable bulk between the man and his next potential customer. "Can you tell me what your reaction is to the death of Elvis Presley?"

"I didn't know Elvis Presley, so I can't say I'm too upset by the whole situation." The man spoke in the staccato patter of the quick buck salesman. "I'll tell you one thing though, it's been real good for business."

Fats was taken aback. "Do you think what you're doing is exploiting a tragic event?"

"Not really," the man said, as he raked in twenty bucks and handed over two t-shirts to a woman who had found a way around Fats. "I'm selling the same stuff I've been selling since I started this gig. The only difference is, it's selling a lot better since Elvis is dead."

The man's total disregard for human passion left Fats speechless. He wanted to terminate this interview even more than the first. A commotion in the crowd gave him the break he needed. As the cameraman and the director rushed off to cover it, Fats was pulled along in their wake.

A man was running through the crowd like his pants were on fire. He pushed people aside like a car speeding through a wheat field. He was waving a state of the art camera over his head as he ran.

"It's a hoax," he yelled as he neared Fats and the camera crew. "Elvis isn't dead! I've got the pictures to prove it!"

Behind the man, two hard-looking government types in suits were hot on his heels.

Fats stepped in front of the hard men. Bodies collided, but Fats was an immovable object. The wind was knocked out of the government men, and Fats took advantage of the situation to thrust the microphone in their face.

"I'm Fats McCorkle, WMBC TV. Can you tell us what this commotion is about?"

Caught off-guard, one of the government men replied without thinking. "Chased that moron out of the back of Graceland. He jumped the wall and lost us

in the crowd. He must be one of those scandal magazine reporters. If I ever get my hands on him, I'll..."

"What about his claims the King is not dead?" Fats
interrupted.

The hard-looking man's words were lost in the roar
of a helicopter taking off from the rear of the Graceland
grounds, beating and bullying its way into the
Memphis sky like a giant, angry insect. Tilting slightly,
it slowly rose then gained speed and disappeared into
the afternoon sun.

———

ON THE DAY ELVIS DIED, Fats had been an immediate hit
with the network audiences. Stuffed into a chocolate
brown tweed suit, with tears covering his shiny, apple
sized cheeks, he had looked like a disconsolate teddy
bear. The viewers had taken him to their hearts. By
popular demand, he was called back to handle the
color commentating duties on the day of Elvis's funeral.

The scene in front of Graceland was almost a replay
of the day of Elvis's death. This time, though, the
hordes of mourners seemed more orderly. It was as if
the realization of their idol's death had beaten them
down. A line to view the body snaked from Graceland's
front door, through the gates of the mansion, and
forever down the street. Dignitaries, movie stars, and
commoners all waited together to pay their respects to
a king. Not any king, but the *King of Rock-n'-Roll*. Elvis
Presley. The champion of the little guy.

There was something different about Fats. His dark
brown suit was well cut, hiding some of his girth. His

hair had been cut and styled. He'd also lost weight since the day of Elvis's death. His personality had changed, too. He was more in command. More forceful.

Pallbearers slid the casket into the hearse and closed the door. Fats moved in quickly, catching one of them by the arm.

"What will it be like now Elvis is gone?" he asked in a rush of air.

The man eyed Fats sorrowfully. "It'll be real hard comin' here anymore," he drawled, "knowin' El won't be around givin' orders and tellin' jokes n' all."

"I guess you were pretty close to the King?"

"Y'all could say that, me bein' family." The man suddenly choked with emotion. "El always was takin' care of family."

"There are rumors the family is dissatisfied with the job done on Elvis' body by the undertakers. Could you comment?"

The man wiped his eyes. "Far as the makeup goes, I didn't think the body even looked real—more like a wax dummy, or a shop mannequin. And I'd sure like to know what the coffin was made from because it weighed a ton."

Fats thanked the man and turned back to the camera. He forced a single tear to roll down his face. "This has been Lawrence McCorkle reporting live from Graceland for WMBC TV." He gave a dramatic half sob. "Back to you in the studio."

Fats—no, Lawrence—McCorkle was definitely on the network fast track.

PART II

1996 PRETENDERS TO THE THRONE

CHAPTER 6

APRIL 1, 1996
WEST HOLLYWOOD SHERIFF'S STATION
WEST HOLLYWOOD, CALIFORNIA

DEPUTY CLAYTON MAHONEY was having a hard time being civil to the strange man who was standing in front of the lobby desk at the West Hollywood Sheriffs' station. Clayton had twenty-three years on the job and figured he shouldn't have to put up with this kind of aggravation anymore.

"But I really am Elvis Presley," shouted the disreputable man who'd wandered into the station half-hour earlier. He and Clayton had been arguing ever since.

Clayton curled his lip and snarled back. "If you're Elvis Presley then I'm Tinker Bell. Go buy yourself some blue suede shoes and get out of my station."

"But, officer—"

"Deputy," Clayton interrupted automatically.

"Deputy," the man started again. He was swaying, almost out on his feet. "I know how weird this sounds, but if you get hold of Gordon Fontaine at the Drug Enforcement Agency, he'll confirm my story. I have important information for him."

"Why don't you call him yourself?" Clayton asked.

The man turned out the pockets of the dingy, ill-fitting jumpsuit he was wearing. "Because I haven't got change for the phone. Please hurry. They're sure to know I've escaped by now."

"You've escaped all right," Clayton said, then heard the radio in the Watch Commander's office blare.

"Ninety-five Adam, handle. Ninety-four, assist. Two-eleven, there now. Eight-seven-two-five Santa Monica Boulevard. Shots fired. Man down. The location is Joe's Jiffy Liquor. Tag is twenty-six."

Clayton moved immediately away from the front desk and stuck his head inside the Watch Commander's office. Seeing it was empty, he moved through to the main station hallway. "Hey, Lieutenant!" he yelled. "There's a robbery in progress at Joe's Jiffy again. There are only two available units." He paused for a second. "We've got shots fired and bodies dying!"

Typical slap-head lieutenant, Clayton thought to himself. Never around when you needed him, and always there when you didn't. The radio continued to blurt information as Clayton suppressed his contempt for the Sheriff's Department supervisors.

At 6'2" tall with a rock-hard belly, Clayton Mahoney was a caricature of a middle-aged, cantankerous street cop. Ever since he'd been injured in a shoot-out with two hardened ex-cons trying to rob a bank, Clay had been assigned to desk duties.

It frosted his chestnuts the department's doctor wouldn't clear him to return to full duty status. He was tired of handling the human cast-offs who floated into the West Hollywood station lobby to wash up on the front desk. If he had to wipe the noses of incompetent watch supervisors much longer, he'd be ready for the rubber gun squad.

As a desk officer and watch deputy, his functions were to keep the Watch Commander apprised of all incidents, to assist in assigning calls to West Hollywood units, and to maintain liaison with the dispatch center.

"Where the hell is the lieutenant?" He shot the question toward his younger desk partner, John Hara.

"Isn't it time for his regular constitutional?"

Clay turned back to the hallway and cupped his hands around his mouth. "Somebody get the lieutenant out of the can," he yelled. "We've got blood on the streets!"

A voice came from somewhere down the hallway. "Damn it, Mahoney, I'm coming." Lieutenant Mike Gavin was zipping up his pants and tightening his belt as he hustled down the hall. Gavin was the Watch Commander, the ranking OIC on the graveyard shift, but Clay Mahoney made him feel like a rookie failing probation.

"Glad you could make it, sir," Clay said. He had a stump of an unlit cigar clenched between his front teeth. "Sorry to disturb your time on the porcelain throne. I'm sure studying for the captain's exam is more important than any little emergency."

"Knock it off, Mahoney. And get that cigar out of your mouth. Tell me what's going on without the sarcasm."

Clay sucked the cigar stub into his mouth, chewed it up and swallowed. He grinned like a Cheshire cat.

"I hope you choke on it," Gavin told him, disgust written on his face.

Clay got serious. He liked yanking Gavin's tail, but he was concerned for the deputies responding to the hot call.

"Robbery in progress at Joe's Jiffy. Shots fired with bodies down. Ninety-five Adam is handling with Ninety-four assisting. It's five a.m., all other units are tied up, and there is some yoyo in the lobby claiming to be Elvis Presley."

By now everyone in the station was aware of the robbery at Joe's Jiffy. Deputies, who were in the station booking prisoners, left their charges handcuffed to benches, and rushed out to back up the assigned units. Detectives arriving early for day shift shoved guns into their waistbands and jumped into the back of any unit leaving the station.

Everyone knew what it was like to roll on a hot call by yourself. Two one-man units were insufficient to handle the danger level of the call, and when a deputy needs back up, sheriffs ride in hard. Until the situation was resolved, every doughnut spot in the area would be left unprotected.

For long minutes, Lt. Gavin and Clay watched over the control center in the Watch Commander's office. They listened as units reported arriving at the scene of the liquor store robbery.

Clay called the fire department to get a paramedic unit rolling.

A description of the suspects and their vehicle was broadcast over the radio by Ninety-five Adam. The two suspects fled the scene in a late model powder blue Mustang, but a third suspect was barricaded in the liquor store.

One of the responding sheriff's units spotted the Mustang blowing a red light and the chase was on. The hounds after the fox. The pursuit lasted five minutes at speeds exceeding the safety factor offered by city streets. Finally, the Mustang ran off the road, crashing into a telephone pole while trying to take a sharp turn at sixty-plus miles per hour. The only thing left of the two suspects in the crushed front seat were catsup stains and calcium deposits.

"Notch one up for the good guys," Clay said. He was an ardent believer in swift justice.

John Hara, who was also standing in the Watch Commander's office, turned to look through the one-way glass separating the office from the front desk area. "What's with the old guy in the lobby? He looks in bad shape."

Both Clay and Lt. Gavin looked up. The man, who had been talking to Clay before all the excitement was leaning on the front counter to stop from falling down. His head hung, and his disheveled hair had fallen forward to cover his face.

"Is he the guy who said he had information about Elvis?" Gavin asked.

"No," Clay said as if he were talking to a slow three-year-old. "He's the moron who walked in here at four thirty this morning claiming to be Elvis Aron Presley."

"Is he?" asked Gavin, looking shocked. "Did he have any identification?"

"Lieutenant!" Clay went ballistic. "Elvis has been dead for almost fourteen years. If he'd told you he was John Fitzgerald Kennedy would you have asked him for I.D., or would you just call in the guys with the white coats?"

Gavin returned his gaze to the lobby. He guessed the man's age at sixty to sixty-five. If the guy wanted to be Elvis or Kennedy, or anyone else, it didn't matter to him.

He didn't want this guy getting sick or, worse yet, dying in his lobby. Things could be sticky if someone higher up found out this citizen had been left standing in the lobby for over an hour. Gavin didn't need a screw-up happening on his watch. It was a blot that could shoot down his promotional hopes.

"Mahoney, I want you to find out what assistance this citizen needs. Get him a cup of coffee and a sweet roll from the lunch room. Take care of him."

"Yeah right, Lieutenant." Clay rolled his eyes at Hara. "I'll get on it as soon as we finish wrapping up this robbery caper."

"You obviously do not understand the big picture here, Deputy. We do not leave citizens in our lobby for hours without finding some way to assist them. I will monitor the mop up of the robbery call. You will take care of Mr. Presley."

Clay went from ballistic to orbital. "We've still got a barricaded suspect holed up at Joe's Jiffy! Do you really want me to leave the console in the middle of all this to talk to some Wee Willy Winky who thinks he's Elvis?" Clay was bellowing like a bull trapped outside a cow pen.

"Mahoney, this department operates pretty efficiently even when you're not around. I'm capable of manning the console."

"Lieutenant?" John Hara interrupted the argument. "Ninety-five Adam is requesting additional units at the scene, and I have Lieutenant Tyler from Special Enforcement Bureau on the line. He wants to know if we want a SWAT team."

Clay interrupted before the lieutenant could speak. "Tell Ninety-five help will be there as soon as we finished solving the mystery of Elvis' death."

"Mahoney! Get out there or I will initiate a personnel complaint."

Clay's face was beet red and both of his enormous hands were clenched into fists. He took a step toward Gavin. As he was about to make career mistake number six hundred, he was magically restrained by a gentle, but firm, female hand on his arm.

"Whoa there, big fellow. Cool out. I'll talk to Elvis with you. After all, my brother would love his autograph. When he realizes Elvis is still alive, maybe he will get a real job instead of wasting his time impersonating the King."

Clayton looked at Deputy Joella Garner. Despite his inbred obstinacy, he'd never been able to resist anything she told him to do.

Joella was assigned as a day watch detective. She had been passing the watch commander's office when she heard the commotion. She and Clay had been in the academy together and on-again-off-again lovers for years. She'd been saving Clay from his temper for as long as she'd known him.

Clay took a deep breath and followed Joella as she gently tugged him away.

Gavin watched them go. He hoped the stand-off at the liquor store didn't last too long. He needed to get to the locker room and change his pants over for a pair without brown stains. Clayton Mahoney terrified him.

CHAPTER 7

On the short walk to the lobby, Joella was glad she had been able to stop Clay from doing something stupid and save Lt. Gavin from total embarrassment. Clay had made enough bad decisions in his career. He certainly didn't need to make another one this close to his retirement.

Joella automatically brushed down the wrinkles in her white blouse and made sure the badge on her belt was prominently displayed. She'd been married to another sheriff's deputy, but the union had been a disaster. Ever since divorcing him she'd put all her efforts into her job. She was considered the best detective on the squad.

"Excuse me, sir," she said brightly to the man leaning on the front counter. "I'm Deputy Garner. We're sorry you've been kept waiting, but there was an emergency. How can we help you?"

"Ma'am, I know how hard this is going to be for you to believe, but I am Elvis Presley. I need to get in touch with a DEA agent named Gordon Fontaine." The man's voice held a soft southern drawl. It had a familiar deep resonance, but that could have been wishful thinking.

Joella glanced at Clay. He glared but moved away without arguing. He knew what she wanted. At the other end of the front desk, he picked up a phone and began dialing.

Joella smiled again at the man. "If you are Elvis, and I'm not saying you're not, where have you been for eighteen years? And what does the DEA have to do with it?"

The man shook his head slowly. His eyes were sunk in their sockets and looked slightly wild. Joella figured he was coming down from a drug high.

"I'm going to have a hard time convincing you I'm not a nut without going into everything that's happened. If I tell you what's been going on since my death was faked, you'd have me put away before I was through the first few months." The man swayed on his feet.

"Do you want to sit down?" Joella asked in genuine concern. "Can I get you a cup of coffee or something to eat?"

"My stomach is real jumpy from the stuff they pumped into me. I don't think I could keep anything down. Thanks anyway." The man smiled, a slightly twisted combination of lips and teeth setting his dark features alive.

Joella felt ghost fingers race up her spine. Goose pimples sprang to life on her arms. She stared intently at the bone structure of the man's face. Could it really be true?

"There is one quick way to wrap this up," she said.

"How about letting me take a set of fingerprints for comparison? Elvis had his taken when he went into the Army. They'll still be on file."

"No, they won't," the man said.

"What do you mean?"

The man shook his head. "It's complicated. They would have disappeared after my death. The same as the death certificate, the autopsy report, and other documentation. The people involved in this have powerful connections."

Before Joella could say anything more, Clay broke into her concentration.

"There's nobody named Gordon Fontaine working for the DEA," he said. "I talked to the local office, and they checked with their headquarters unit."

"There has to be..." The man's voice interrupted insistently and then trailed away.

"Gordon Fontaine isn't on the DEA's payroll," Clay said firmly. He stared at the man, daring him to challenge him again. Then a light seemed to dawn across his face. "Wait a minute," Clay said. "I get it. This is an April fool's gag, right?"

"What are you talking about?"

"It's April first, and I can smell an April fool's set-up a mile away. You did a hell of a job, pal. You had me going for a while, but the jig is up. Who sent you? Was it Jenkins at communications? No, wait. I bet it was Charlie Blythe over at Firestone. He owes me one for sending the stripper to his wedding reception last month."

"What do I have to do to convince you?" the man

interrupted angrily. "Put my collar up and sing a couple of verses from *Hound Dog*?"

"Couldn't hurt," said Clay smugly.

Joella reached out to steady the man.

"Knock it off, Clay." Her look singed Clay's hair. "I'll handle this."

"Whatever you want, but this guy is pulling your leg." Clay walked away laughing. "Don't say I didn't warn you." When he'd taken two more steps, he turned back. "You know what Elvis would be doing if he were alive?" He began rapping his knuckles on the desk top. "He'd be knocking on his coffin lid saying, *let me out of here*." Clay laughed uproariously and walked off.

"Jerk," Joella said under her breath. She turned back to the man who claimed to be Elvis. He still gave her goose bumps.

"I don't think you're going to get much help or sympathy from official channels," she said. "Your Gordon Fontaine doesn't seem to exist. You say there are no fingerprints on file for comparison. You have no identification of any kind." She shook her head. "I'm sorry, but you have to see it from our side. If you persist, I'm afraid somebody will suggest locking you up on a seventy-two hour hold for mental evaluation."

"I understand," the man nodded sadly. "But I don't know how I can go on."

There was something about this guy. Joella had talked to hundreds of *5150's*—crazies. This guy didn't fit the mold. She made a quick decision.

"This is going to sound as weird as you saying you're Elvis. But, I've got a kid-brother who makes a living as an Elvis impersonator. He's a cool guy and he'll find a place for you to stay until we can get to the bottom of this. I'll give him a call. Okay?"

The man sighed in resignation.

Lieutenant Gavin stuck his head out of the watch commander's office. "Wrap it up, Joella. It's hitting the fan at Joe's Jiffy. I need you out there."

Joella grabbed a piece of scrap paper and a pen. She scribbled a number then dug into a pocket for change.

She thrust the items at the man. "Call my brother. His name is Cole Ramsey."

"Joella!" The lieutenant yelled again.

"Thanks," the man said. "I won't forget your kindness."

The last glimpse Joella had was of his profile as he slipped a quarter into the lobby pay phone. Shadows highlighted the planes of his face and hid the wrinkles. For an instant, he could have been twenty years old instead of in his sixties. *Holy Hell...* The light changed, and the illusion passed.

CHAPTER 8

RING! RING! RING!

Rolling over, Cole Ramsey threw off the light sheet covering his naked form and snaked an arm out to grab the phone. Still fuzzy with sleep, he knocked the instrument off the upside-down planter barrel, which acted as his nightstand. Keeping his eyes closed, he groped around on the floor until he snagged the phone cord. He hauled the receiver in hand over hand like a fisherman trying to pull in a lobster pot.

"Hello," Cole croaked into the mouthpiece. His voice was spent and full of sleep. He cracked an eye lid open, propped himself up on an elbow, and stared at the luminous glow of the clock radio.

6:00 a.m.

Good grief, he thought. He'd only gone to bed two hours earlier. He normally didn't know this time of day existed.

"Is this Cole Ramsey?" a soft voice inquired.

"Yeah. Who's this?"

"Sir, your sister told me to get in touch with you."

Cole sat bolt upright in bed. He was suddenly wide awake. Ever since his sister became a sheriff, he'd had nightmares about receiving this kind of call. "Is she okay? What's happened?"

"Your sister is fine. I've just been talking to her."

There was something familiar about the voice coming down the phone line. It had an interesting lilt Cole had heard before.

"Who is this?" Cole impatiently asked again.

"Sir, this is Elvis calling."

———

THE DRIVE from Santa Monica to West Hollywood took Cole thirty-five minutes on the congested early morning surface streets. For some reason he didn't yet understand, he'd agreed to meet this Elvis character at Hot Cross Buns, a small pastry and coffee spot near the West Hollywood Sheriff's station. Cole sometimes met his sister there for a quick snack when she went off-duty.

Cole considered the situation might be an elaborate practical joke—especially since it was April Fool's Day. It wouldn't be the first time his sister, or one of his many acquaintances, had pulled a fast one on him because of his identification with the King of Rock-n'-Roll. He couldn't help his knack for impersonating the King, or if people were willing to pay to see him do it. However, the voice on the phone had held a deep note of desperation. Cole's instincts told him the intonation was too real not to be true.

After hanging up, Cole rolled his lanky 6'1" frame

out of bed and rummaged around in the laundry scattered hither-and-yon. Eventually, he'd uncovered a pair of clean blue running shorts, which he slipped into sans skivvies. Worn espadrilles found their way onto his hard-calloused feet. A sweatshirt with the sleeves cut off and the neck band torn out topped the ensemble. On the front of the sweatshirt was the faded outline of the Greenpeace logo and a picture of baby seals being clubbed to death. Cole believed in causes.

His living space, the third floor of a small commercial building over a converted recording studio and a restaurant, was an artist's dream. In the high ceiling above him, canted skylights diffused the morning sun through a northern exposure. A wide expanse of strip framed windows on one wall let in more light and overlooked the carnival activities along Santa Monica's Ocean Avenue.

Another wall was plain plasterboard, providing the static canvas for a living and ever-changing mural. Paint was not Cole's primary creative outlet, but when the mood took him, he could be lost for days transforming the loft with Bohemian fervor.

The floor furnishings were a hodgepodge of cast-offs and 50's avant-garde antiques, more evidence of Cole's eclectic tastes. Most of the pieces had been scrounged, recovered, bartered for, or received as gifts from friends who admired his collection. An ancient Coca-Cola bottle machine stood next to a vintage Wurlitzer juke box. The juke played nothing more recent than 45's from '65.

In a corner there was a coffee shop booth complete with Formica table. Next to the booth were a small refrigerator, a huge commercial oven complete with stove top, and two deep stainless-steel sinks. A long bar mirror dominated the space above the cooking facilities.

The only partition Cole had allowed to invade the vast floor space was hiding the commode and shower. A claw foot porcelain tub had been jerry-rigged into service, but it sat on the hardwood floor in plain sight outside of the bathroom.

Clothing and bric-a-brac were draped and scattered everywhere. Posters and notes covered the plasterboard walls. Some had been painted over, blending into Cole's living canvas. Newer ones awaited their opportunity to be turned into art.

A Martin acoustic guitar, a Fender Stratocaster, a Kustom P.A. system with the traditional tuck and roll upholstery, three Fender amps, and two synthesizers stood in the middle of the room. Surrounding them were stacks of records, tapes, sheet music, and magazines.

In front of Cole's musical tools were a pair of metal, shell-backed patio chairs. They were placed on a small round mat near an old Philco black-and-white television. Bent rabbit ears stood on top of the oversized TV console. A further tour of the room revealed a lightning yellow surfboard, a boogie board, and a pair of swim fins propped up on the railing by the entry stairway. Above the collection hung a gigantic, unframed, black velvet portrait of Elvis.

Cole's presence in the building was through the blessing of his father, who owned the building. The ground floor was leased by a retired English policeman who ran a restaurant called Copper's. Cole had carved out a niche for himself in the building. A space where he was free to express himself and find sanctuary from those who disapproved of his lifestyle. Money was made to be spent. He refused to grow up. Refused to give up or compromise his dreams. His mother blamed herself for his frame of mind, believing she let him overdose on Peter Pan as a kid.

Cole's car was a further statement. It was obvious perhaps, but then Cole didn't march to a different drummer, he boogied with a whole different orchestra.

Cruising down Santa Monica Boulevard with the rag top down, he stretched his arm out along the back of the wide bench seat. *Only in California*, he thought, *could you start the day off by having breakfast with a dead legend*. He pushed a tape into the dash deck and pumped up the volume. The loud opening notes of *Heartbreak Hotel* turned heads in his direction. Smiling, Cole covered his eyes with a pair of Wayfarers.

If you are what you drive, Cole was a '62 pink Cadillac with elongated tail fins and more chrome than a first-year orthodontic patient. Cole had salvaged the Pink Madam from a wrecker's yard after months of searching. Months of restoration and scrounging for parts transformed the car into the condition it now enjoyed—original with essential modifications. It took a lot of cash from one-night gigs in smoky dives and Sunday afternoon wedding receptions to keep the Pink Madam in Bondo, parts, gas, oil, and tires.

Cole drove past Wilshire Boulevard, heading through Beverly Hills in the morning bumper to bumper traffic, then spurted out into West Hollywood.

As he pulled up in front of the Hot Cross Buns Deli & Bakery, a car pulled away from the curb directly in front of the establishment. Cole had a knack of always being in the right place when it came to parking spaces. He'd never had to search for one in his life. He could drive into the busiest parking lot in the city on Christmas Eve and a spot would open up as if by divine providence. He never thought about it. It just happened.

With typical show-off cool, he parked and hopped over the car door without opening it. He ran a hand through his ragged surfer blond hair and strolled into the small eatery.

Inside, a half dozen tables were crowded near the front window. They were occupied by the usual business commuters or West Hollywood *WAMs*—waiters, actors, models—on their way home after a night in the fast lane. Nobody looked like Elvis.

"Cole! How come it's been so long since you come to see me? Don't you love me anymore?"

Cole waved at Nikki Bonaducci who stood behind the deli counter dishing out pastry and cappuccino. She was plump, fiftyish, with drop dead bedroom eyes, and a Gibson Girl pile of jet black hair.

"I do love you," Cole said. "But you're far too much woman for me, and Aldo would skin me alive if he caught us together."

Nikki let out a girlish laugh. which brought a smiling Italian man out of the back area.

"I thought as much," Aldo Bonaducci said when he spotted Cole. "You're the only one who makes her laugh that way." The man stretched out his hand and Cole shook it.

"I see you're still pushing health food," Cole said.

Aldo gave an all-purpose Italian shrug. "It pays the bills. What can I tell you? I'm not their mothers."

"Stop jawing and get back to work," Nikki told Aldo with mock gruffness. "Leave me to my lover, old man."

Aldo shrugged in resignation, but his eyes were sparkling. He retreated to the back room with a wave. The thought of Nikki taking Cole as a lover seemed to amuse him

Cole smiled at Nikki. "Can I have a large orange juice and a bran muffin, please?" Feeling foolish, he looked around again to make sure Elvis hadn't walked in. "Has anyone been asking for me? He tried to sound casual"

"You mean like the police, or your sister, or somebody else?"

"I mean like this morning. I'm supposed to meet somebody here."

"What does this person look like? A woman?"

Cole shook his head. "Not this time."

"What does this person look like?"

Cole hesitated. He didn't want to be the brunt of a joke.

"What's the matter?" Nikki asked.

Cole dropped his voice to a half whisper. "I know this sound weird, but he would like Elvis would if he were alive today."

Nikki laughed until she shook, making customers look over at her

"You are a funny boy, Cole. You have Elvis on the brain." She placed his order on the counter. Cole made to pay, but Nikki waved him off. "After the performance you put on at my daughter's wedding, you know your money is no good here." Nikki leaned across the counter, giving Cole a quick kiss on the cheek. "Go look for Elvis."

Cole gave a mock salute and a cocky grin before sliding into a chair at one of the recently vacated window tables. His knack also extended to seating in restaurants.

An hour later, his table was scattered with muffin crumbs and two empty orange juice glasses. He was tired, ready to give up. Clearly, the phone call was a practical joke.

In his imagination, Cole could hear some cop saying, "Hey, Joella, is your brother still doing his crazy Elvis impersonator act? It's April fool's day. Let's phone him and make out it's Elvis calling."

Cole could see his sister willingly playing along. She never understood why he would never get *a real job*. Hanging out on the fringes of the music business, waiting for a break to make him a star, was not what Joella considered a responsible way to live.

Cole had been a surprise, late-in-life, pregnancy his parents saw as a rejuvenating blessing. Joella had always resented their liberal approach to Cole's upbringing, especially when compared to their expectations for her. Cole knew she loved him, but there was always a tender rift between them.

Cole cleared his angry thoughts. He stood up, blew a kiss in Nikki's direction, and walked outside to his car. There were tickets on the windshield of the cars in front of and behind the Pink Madam. Curiously, the windshield of the Cadillac was virgin glass even though it had been parked longer.

Cole hopped in and settled behind the Pink Madam's steering wheel. He noticed his heart rate was accelerated. He'd allowed his insane and impossible dream of meeting his idol to make him vulnerable. He shivered his entire body, trying to clear cobwebs. *Come on, man*, he thought. *What's the matter with you? Elvis is dead.*

CHAPTER 9

DESPITE BEING CONVINCED HE WAS THE TARGET OF A prank, Cole was reluctant to leave the area. He glanced up and down the sidewalk looking for anyone resembling The King.

This is ridiculous. He was overtired, that was the problem. He'd done an all-night session in the record studio below his pad, working a gig for Sunray Records. Sunray was a sleaze outfit. They advertised in the back of music magazines, promising to put your words to music, cut a half dozen copies, and make you an overnight song writing star.

In reality, Sunray waited until they had a pile of notoriously bad lyrics—lyrics people had pinned their hopes and five hundred bucks up front. Sunray then applied the lyrics to one of six basic melodies, and production-lined them into record grooves. Cole and several other musicians picked up beer money playing the exhausting sessions once a month. Sunray hadn't produced a hit yet.

The Sunray gig took its toll on Cole. Despite his

sister's belief he was a lovable flake, he was serious about his craft. However, he couldn't pick and choose his gigs. At twenty-two, his uncanny ability to mimic Elvis Presley was a blessing and a curse. He was struggling to have his own musical voice taken seriously, but his best regular gig was as Elvis at a twice a month dinner theater revue called *Legends Alive*. He picked up additional cash winning Elvis impersonator contests up and down the state. Sunray loved his Elvis croon, constantly encouraging him to exploit it for their midwest and southern customers.

Cole put the pink Madam into gear and drove five blocks to the West Hollywood Sheriff's station. He found a parking spot smack in front of the lobby doors, levered himself out of the driver's seat, and slid over the car door.

In the lobby, he spotted a desk officer he knew and asked for his sister.

The officer picked up a phone and punched a number. "Joella," he said when the call was answered. "Elvis is at the front desk to see you." He began to laugh and hung up. Cole smiled tolerantly. He was used to this type of abuse. Everyone thought they were a comedian.

A minute later, Joella came into the lobby and found Cole staring at a board of wanted posters. She gave her brother a hug. There was a wino sitting on one of the lobby's wooden benches. Joella recognized him as Duster Haywood, one of the local street people.

"Are you going to listen to me?" Duster asked when he spotted Joella. "I got some information to sell."

"Duster, when was the last time you had a meal?" Joella asked him.

Duster put on a thoughtful expression and tried to think back. Joella sighed. Reaching into her back pocket, she produced a five-dollar book of McDonald's coupons. She extended them to Duster who looked at them suspiciously.

"Take them, Duster," Joella said. "If I give you cash, you won't buy food."

"Yes, I will, missy," he said, giving her a gap tooth grin.

"Take 'em or leave 'em," Joella said.

Duster grabbed the coupons. "I ain't selling you my information. I want real money for my information."

"Come back when you've had breakfast and we'll talk about it." Joella said.

Duster always had information to sell, most of it worthless. He was a regular at the station—tolerated because he was harmless, and because, like a stray cat, he wouldn't go away.

Duster grumbled and began gathering his bagged belongings.

"Nice class of friends you keep," Cole told his sister.

"Did Elvis call you," she asked, giving him another hug.

"He called," Cole said with a sigh. "Which one of your pin head buddies was it?"

"What are you talking about?"

"Enough is enough, Jo. It's over. Hardy-har-har, you got me."

"Wait...The guy who said he was Elvis called you, right?"

"Yeah."

"Did you meet him? What did he say?"

"You know he didn't show."

Joella put her hand on Cole's arm. "I'm serious, Cole. This was no joke. There was a guy in here this morning who said he was Elvis Presley. He was trying to get in contact with a DEA agent named Gordon Fontaine, but DEA denied his existence."

"Why have him call me?"

"We had a barricaded suspect situation. Everybody was too busy to take the guy seriously. I talked to him briefly and there was something about him—some kind of honesty that made you want to believe him. I told him to call you because I thought maybe you could help him. Nobody here seemed to give a damn."

"Standard operating procedure."

"Cheap shots?"

"They're the only kind I can afford."

Joella glared. Cole waggled his eyebrows.

"Don't give up your day job to become a comedian," Joella said.

"I don't have a day job," Cole replied.

"Did this guy call you or not?" Joella asked in exasperation.

"He called, but never showed at Hot Cross Buns to meet me. Did you see him leave?"

Joella shook her head. "Everyone was either running out to the field or handling the communications console."

"You're sure it wasn't some kind of joke?"

"I'm not saying the guy was Elvis, but I don't think it was a complete put-on."

Cole knew his sister was being truthful. "I'll drive around and see if I can spot him. What was he wearing?"

Joella described the station's early morning visitor, then Cole gave her a quick hug and promised to meet her soon for dinner.

Joella watched her brother's lean frame glide through the front doors with the grace of carefree youth. She shook her head in wonder.

Outside on the pavement, Cole heard someone call him.

"Hey—You."

Cole saw Duster had followed him out of the lobby.

"Heard you talking to the lady cop. You want to know what happened to the guy who was in the lobby this morning."

"You saw him?"

"Ol' Duster sees everything goes on around here. They should pay me to act as security."

Cole looked at the disreputable bum and wondered how Duster ended up this way. It didn't dawn on Cole that Duster's clothing was in better shape than his own. However, the difference was, Cole wore his outfit by choice.

"Do you want to know about him or not?" Duster asked again.

"Sure."

"I ain't no free information service."

Cole dug out a couple of dollar bills and offered them to Duster.

Duster scoffed. "I ain't no charity case either, son. I

give good value for money. You want the information you're gonna need a few more dead presidents."

Cole replaced the two ones with a five, which Duster snapped up.

"I saw the guy in the industrial strength jumpsuit come out the station." Duster's voice was a whisky rasp. "He started walking, but a black stretch job pulled up beside him."

"A limo?"

"Ain't I talking plain enough English for you?"

Cole nodded encouragingly.

"The guy in the jumpsuit started to run. These three big guys got out the back of the limo and started to chase him. The guy in the jumpsuit floored one of them with some kind of karate kick, but the other two guys wrestled him to the ground. Another guy got out holding a straight-jacket. They used it to hog-tie the poor guy, then threw him in the car."

"What happened then?"

"What do you think happened? The limo took off outta here like a scalded cat."

"Did the limo have any special markings on it?"

Duster's eyes gleamed with greed. "I told you Old Duster sees all." He snapped his fingers at Cole.

Reluctantly, feeling like he was being taken for a ride instead of the guy in the jumpsuit, Cole pulled out another hard earned five.

Duster did a disappearing act with the bill.

"I got the license plate of the limo." Duster paused significantly.

"You've also got all the cash I'm going to give you," Cole said.

Duster shrugged philosophically. "The license was easy to remember. It was personalized—*GLITZ 8.*"

"Glitz Limos," Cole said immediately. "I see them all over town."

Duster shrugged again. "If I'm lying, I'm dying."

"We all are," Cole said. He hopped into the Pink Madam.

"There's one more thing," Duster called after him. "The guy in the jumpsuit was a dead-ringer for Elvis."

CHAPTER 10

CRUISING IN THE PINK MADAM, COLE struggle to believe he wasn't being played for a chump. Even Duster the wino could be one of Joella's vice cop buddies in full costume. But, if Duster was a vice cop, why would he give up the limo's license plate? If it was a joke, then what was the punch line?

Cole grumbled and angrily swerved the Pink Madam into a wide U-turn, interfering with traffic in all directions. Backtracking two blocks, he pulled into an empty parking space in front of a liquor store. He jumped out of the Caddy and slid up to a pay phone near the entrance.

A tattered phone directory was attached by a short wire to the booth, making it awkward to thumb through. Struggling with the book, Cole flipped through the pages until he found Glitz Limousine Service. There was a phone number inside a red-ringed, mid-sized ad, but no address. Cole figured the number would be the dispatch office, but it might be all he needed. He shoved a quarter in the phone slot and dialed the number.

"Glitz Limousine Service, this is Randy." The voice on the other end of the line was male and pure California surfer dude. Cole thought it was possibly a Teen-age Mutant Ninja Turtle moonlighting as the recep-tionist.

"Good Morning," Cole said, getting ready to lie through his teeth. "This is Deputy Garner with the Los Angeles Sheriff's Department." He didn't give a second thought to taking his sister's name and rank in vain. "There was a hit-and-run accident today involving a postal jeep and a black sedan. The mail carrier in the jeep was injured. He told us the driver of a limousine saw the accident and called an ambulance on his car phone. However, he didn't wait for the police to arrive. We'd like to talk to the driver to find out if he can tell us anything about the suspect." Cole was pleased with his story. "The mail carrier didn't see the license of the hit-and-run driver's car, but he did see the limo's license plate—*GLITZ 8*. Which brings me to the reason I'm calling you."

"Why?" asked Randy from the other end of the phone.

Cole pulled the receiver away from his ear and stared at the mouthpiece as if he couldn't believe the question. He put the phone back to his ear. "Let me give it to you in words of two syllables or less. I need the name of the guy driving your limo with the license plate *GLITZ 8*."

There was a pause as if Randy was thinking it over. "Who did you say this was calling?"

Cole gritted his teeth. It was a good scam, but it was being wasted on a guy who if you blew in his ear would thank you for the refill. "This is Deputy Garner with the LASD."

"LASD?"

"The Los Angeles Sheriff's Department."

"Hey, that's really cool, dude. What's it like being a cop?"

"Frustrating."

"Whoa, dude, like, what kind of gun do you carry?"

"A forty-four Cro-Magnum. I also drive one of the new cop cars with the side-ways Porsche engines."

"Awesome."

Cole figured he better give Randy a nudge before any more brain cells died. "What about the driver of *GLITZ 8*?"

"Sorry, dude, but that sled is already rented out."

Cole felt like reaching through the phone lines and beating Randy's brains out, but it was obvious someone had beat him to it. "I know the limo is rented. I want to know who rented it."

"Oh, that's cool, dude. I'll look it up."

Great, Cole thought, as he hung on the line. Perseverance is everything.

"I found it, dude," Randy said when he came back. Cole was grateful he hadn't been disconnected. "We leased the sled to the Elysian Corporation 'cause their ride is in the shop."

"Where does this Elysian Corporation hang its hat," Cole asked.

"What hat, dude?"

"The address," Cole said with soft tension in his voice. "What is the Elysian Corporation's address?"

"Be cool dude. It's written down right here. 1368 Stadium Way. Hey, that's near Dodger Stadium. Do you think they could get me tickets?"

"You never know your luck, dude," Cole said and hung up.

Back in the Pink Madam, Cole turned the engine over and pulled into traffic without looking. A bus squealed its brakes sending passengers in all directions. Cole punched up the tape deck again. Elvis' throaty roar gave voice to *Little Sister*, and Cole sung along with the same timber and natural timing.

On the drive to Dodger Stadium, Cole knew he had to play the hand out. He never could leave well enough alone.

Surface streets took him to the Santa Monica Freeway. The east-bound fast lane took him through downtown LA and shot him onto the old Pasadena Freeway. Five miles farther, he switched freeways and took the Golden State north to the Stadium Way off-ramp.

The Pink Madam purred up the hill toward Dodger Stadium. Cole knew the Los Angeles Police Department's training academy was located somewhere nearby on what had been the site of the 1932 Olympic village.

The surrounding area, known as Elysian Park, was a large oasis of green in the heart of LA. It connected with Griffith Park a few miles to the north. Joggers were everywhere, along with bike riders and race-walkers. Cole wondered if the Elysian Corporation was connected to the park administration, or if the two were even associated. Either way, it was tough to see any connection to Elvis.

Following his nose, Cole drove slowly up a long hill, bore to the left when the road split. He started looking for address numbers as various, widely separated, buildings began to pop up deep within the park setting.

He didn't need the numbers to find his destination. There was a large sign attached to artistically twisted and imposing iron gates. The gates were attached to an eight-foot-high stone wall around the interior complex.

Stopping next to the sign, Cole smiled ruefully. He got the joke now. Randy back at Glitz Limousines must also have been briefed by Joella. He should have figured it out earlier. Surely nobody could be as dumb as Randy.

Joella had known Cole wouldn't be able to resist tracking down Duster's big clue. She had him figured as a prime April fool, and he'd bought off on it hook, line, and *singer*.

It seemed a lot of trouble for nothing, but cops had a weird sense of humor. Joella said he was obsessed with Elvis—crazy obsessed. And now she'd pulled this stunt to push her point. The lettering on the tastefully designed sign spelled out the joke.

ELYSIAN SANITARIUM
ADMINISTERED by the Elysian Corporation
ADMITTANCE BY APPOINTMENT ONLY

THE WILD GOOSE chase had ended at the gates to a high priced loony bin. His sister was about as subtle as a rock slide.

CHAPTER 11

THE CROWD WAS ELECTRIC. EVEN OFF-STAGE IN THE wings, Cole could feel the animal energy, and it was all directed at him. Nothing had ever happened like this before—at least not with the savage power it was generating now.

The audience was chanting for him, *"Cole! Cole! Cole!"*

Not for Elvis, but for him.

He turned slightly to look at Slam Wheeler, Clyde Hardin, and Garret Ladd. They were his back-up musicians—Slam on bass, Clyde spilling riffs on an old Fender guitar, and Garret pounding out the back beat. All three were clustered closely behind him.

"They want you bad, boy," Slam said. "We playin' it solid tonight."

Cole still couldn't believe it.

The gig at the Appaloosa Club in Santa Monica was unusual. Normally, as part of *Legends Alive*, Cole and his back-up crew were one of three Elvis impersonation acts. Cole played the young Elvis fresh from the early Sun

Record recording sessions. Eddie Wyatt portrayed the leather clad Elvis from the 1968 comeback, followed by Dan Holliday with the flashy big finish as Elvis in Vegas. It was a good presentation, but it was an ensemble production and Cole often felt lost in the shuffle.

Jerry Tilghman, the manager of the Appaloosa Club, caught Cole's act at a *Legends Alive* special performance at Disneyland. When Tilghman was putting together a rock-a-billy night for the Appaloosa, he signed Cole and his crew as a gimmick act.

There had been five acts on the Appaloosa bill. The first three had primed the pump, but Cole—batting fourth in the order—had brought the capacity crowd to their feet. The women had jumped around, and hooted and hollered like hysterical teens. They were enjoying themselves, getting into the act—longing for a man like Elvis to swoon over.

By the time the headliners, Joe and The Cool Cats, hit the stage, Cole had whipped the audience into an unexpected frenzy. The Cool Cats didn't stand a chance. The crowd chilled during a rendition of The Cool Cats' current radio hit *Cool Cat Strut*, and then turned ugly during a plodding cover of Jumping Bill Knox's *Anything You Want*.

Then the chanting started, *"Cole! Cole! Cole!"*

It was slow at first, building from the back of the club and making its way forward, but by the time The Cool Cats were into the middle of their third song it was clear what the crowd wanted—or more precisely who the crowd wanted.

"Cole! Cole! Cole! Cole!"

That was the curious thing, though. They were yelling for Cole, not Elvis. However, it was Elvis—living through Cole—who they wanted to see.

"Cole! Cole! Cole! Cole!"

"You ready to give 'em what they want?"

Cole looked behind him again and found that his crew had been joined by Jerry Tilghman.

"Hey, I'm sorry, Mr. Tilghman. I don't know what started this."

"Then you're dumber than I thought you were," Tilghman said. "You're good, kid, and those people out there are paying customers who want more. Can you give it to them?"

"But what about?" Cole gestured toward Joe and The Cool Cats who were looking more like ragged alley cats.

Tilghman waved a hand at somebody in the opposite stage wings and the power to The Cool Cats shut down. The crowd cheered.

"Cole! Cole! Cole! Cole! Cole!"

Joe and The Cool Cats straggled off the stage with their tails between their legs.

"Screw you!" Joe said, as he shoved his way past Cole. He was a skinny kid with bad acne, stringy hair, and tattoos down both scrawny, exposed arms. His band was only a flavor of the month. There was no way their music had staying power, a fact proved by their performance—or lack of it—tonight.

Cole shrugged and let Joe pass by. He was too stunned by the crowd's reaction to his own performance to take offense.

"What are you waiting for, kid?" Tilghman asked. "Get out there!"

Slam and Clyde grabbed their instruments and, along with Garret, were heading into the limelight. Stage hands quickly broke down the Cool Cats' rig and put Garret's skins back on a raised platform.

Garret picked up his sticks and began to lay down a slow beat. Slam picked up on it on his bass, and Clyde began to strike the cords to 2001 A Space Odyssey—Also Sprach Zarathustra. The tune was out of place for the time frame in which Cole portrayed Elvis, but the crowd cheered and ate it up. The lighting crew began to ad-lib by running several spots quickly around the club over the heads of the audience.

Garret built the music to a climax. There was some laughter from the audience as it was clear the three musicians on stage were having a good time improvising a tongue-in-cheek rendition.

A firm hand gave Cole a push from behind and he popped out from the wings onto the stage. The audience screamed and cheered and applauded even louder.

After one hesitant step, Cole felt himself filling with the fuel with which the audience vibrating. He felt struck by lightning as the sensation ran into the center of his being and then exploded outward flying from the tips of his fingers and the top of his head. He marched forward and grabbed the microphone as if he owned the joint.

Like Elvis before him, he already owned the audience.

"Thank you. Thank you very much," Cole said. The

Elvis drawl slid easily from his lips. It softened and changed some vowels, so the words came out sounding more like, "Thunk you. Thunk you v'ry much."

He was listening to the beat behind him, not sure where the musical rift was going, but knowing Garret would lead him through. A second later, he picked up the rhythm of *Mystery Train*, Elvis' fifth and final single for Sun Records in 1955, and he ripped into the lyrics.

It was a simple song, but Cole milked it for every emotion by singing with an unearthly confidence. The words spoke powerfully through him of every dream, every fear, he had ever had. The crowd went wild. He carried the simplistic rhythms into *I'm Left, You're Right, She's Gone*, and *I Forgot to Remember to Forget.*

There were women—girls again—gathering around the stage, two, three, four rows deep. They were screaming at Cole, swooning. It was as if his act had been expanded to encompass not just his back-up band but the whole club—the audience impersonating Elvis's audience, just as Cole was impersonating Elvis.

There was a brief flare-up in Cole's psyche. A shooting star burning bright with the question of being doomed to forever play the role of someone other than himself. Then it died as he went beyond himself and deeper into his chosen role. His shoulders began to shake, and his leg started to twitch in earnest as he launched into *Baby, Let's Play House*. The crowd was right there with him.

Forsaking the white jumpsuits favored by most players on the Elvis track, Cole wore a gray, loose fitting, sports jacket over a red silk shirt. The shirt was tucked into pleated gray wool slacks, which topped a beautiful pair of suede oxfords. The turned-up collars of both jacket and shirt were the only concession to the classic Elvis fashion. This was the early Elvis, before the glitz, when there was nothing but the man and his music.

Cole's hair was slicked up and darkened it with grease, as Elvis himself had done. The alternating boyish pout and rakish snarl, however, were naturally Cole's, as was the deep smooth voice—a random stroke of genetics that was an amazing mimic of the King's.

The sounds Cole and the band were laying down went straight back to the roots of country and blues—the crossover most responsible for the black/white sounds Elvis created. Cole's voice was filled with cool passion. It was the same sound, the same edgy flirtation with self-parody, that endeared Elvis to his fans. It was the sound of a wink, a shared in-joke, a conceit encompassing the audience. It made everyone cooler together than they were alone.

There were more songs. If *When My Blue Moon Turns to Gold* had them rocking in the aisles, *That's All Right*, reprieved from Cole's earlier set, nearly raised the roof.

The reaction, however, was nothing compared to what happened next.

As if by unspoken agreement, Slam, Clyde, and Garret slid into the opening notes of a song Cole knew well. The problem was, it wasn't an Elvis song. It was a Cole Ramsey song...*Sweetwater Woman* sounded like an Elvis song, but it was pure Cole Ramsey.

Cole was so far into Elvis the *lead-in* to the song threw him for a moment. When he realized what was happening, he turned on the band in a panic. The crowd was grooving to Elvis. If the band broke the connection, the success of the evening could fall down around their ears.

Slam said, "Just do it!"

Without missing a lick, the band regenerated the intro, and Cole had no choice except to follow and sing.

It was quickly clear there was no cause for worry. The audience ate up *Sweetwater Woman* and hollered for more. Cole and the band obliged them by sliding into two further rock-a-billy songs Cole had written.

One Brick Shy of a Load and *Tennessee in My Dreams* were both heavily influenced by the crossover county sound which rocketed Elvis to fame. Even though Elvis had never heard the two songs, let alone sung them, they were still pure Elvis, and the crowd went wild in their appreciation.

Before the notes of the last song were over, two women had climbed up onto the stage and started to rush Cole. Almost dropping the microphone, Cole felt fear in his belly as the women started grabbing at him. The sleeve of his jacket was torn off as he escaped into the stage wings and the club's bouncers moved in to clear the stage. There was pandemonium on the stage floor.

Slam grabbed Cole up in a bear hug. "You were so cool you were hot!"

Jerry Tilghman shook his hand again and again. "There's never been anything like this happen at the Appaloosa. You just made a legend for yourself out there, kid. Listen..." In the pause, everyone could hear the roar and applause of the crowd. "You really turned them loose out there," Tilghman said. "Have your agent call me tomorrow to talk about a return gig before you get too big for me to afford."

Cole smiled weakly. He didn't know what to make of the audience's reaction. Did they like him, or was it the whole Elvis thing? It was truly weird living through a dead man.

————

IT WAS four in the morning before Cole returned to his room over the recording studio. He flopped on to his bed feeling drained and wired at the same time. After leaving the club, he'd driven to the beach. There, he walked up and down the Santa Monica pier trying to calm himself and regain perspective.

He'd tried to call Joella before going out to the gig at the Appaloosa, but she was not home. He'd left a message on her answering machine. He'd told her how he had fallen for her little joke and had ended up at the gates to the Elysian Sanitarium as she had planned. He'd told her to compliment whichever cop she'd gotten to play Duster because he'd done a hell of a job sucking Cole in. The same with the guy on the Glitz Limousines' phone.

Joella thought he was crazy to play Elvis all the time. A waste of his life and talent she said. Cole wondered what she would have thought if she had been at the Appaloosa Club. He shook his head. He wanted to call her, to discuss the success of the evening with somebody who was family.

He looked at his watch—4:30 a.m.

Why not? Joella had given him the runaround the day before. It was the least he could do to get back at her. He bounced off the bed and over to the phone. There was a message on his answering machine. He pushed the replay and heard Joella's voice.

"Cole? What the hell is this message about Elysian Sanitarium?" His sister's voice was full of anger and frustration. "I've never heard of the place. I told you this thing with Elvis wasn't a joke. I've never heard of Glitz Limousines either. If you still think this is a joke, then you better give a call to the morgue because it's where poor Duster can be found. He was murdered this afternoon. Call me and let me know what's going on."

CHAPTER 12

C<small>OLE HAD AN OLDIES RADIO STATION PLAYING SOFTLY AS</small> he eased the Pink Madam to a stop a hundred yards from the Elysian Sanitarium. The car's rag top was down even though the early morning air was filled with a definite bite.

Turning off the ignition, Cole sat listening to the tick of the cooling engine. This was the point of no return. He could stop things now, but if he went any further there would be no turning back.

Joella had not been home when Cole had tried to call her at 4 a.m. He figured either her love life was picking up, or she'd been called out on a case. He'd tried to sleep, but his mind refused to shut down. His thoughts jumped between visions of the Appaloosa Club to his earlier search for Elvis.

The possibility of Elvis being alive was torn out of the supermarket gossip rags. But if Joella hadn't been joking, then something weird was going on—and the trail led to the Elysian Sanitarium.

What if Elvis is alive? The thought wouldn't leave

Cole alone. But if he knocked on the sanitarium's door and ask to speak to Elvis, he'd be locked up quicker than an Amish tourist at a fashion show.

What to do? What to do?

Energy from his stage performance still coursed through his body. It was forcing him to get up and charge ahead. When his emotional high led to the inevitable physical crash, it would be a doosie. Until then, he had to be doing *something*, and Elvis was calling. He made his decision and hoisted himself up over the door of the Pink Madam. Wearing black jeans, a black cable knit sweater, and black moccasins without socks, he jammed the car keys into a pocket.

Feeling as if he were on display, Cole surveyed the wall surrounding the sanitarium. He then walked deliberately up to the huge wrought iron gates barring the entrance. Inside, concrete pillars topped by sculptured gargoyles framed the sanitarium's entrance doors. The building had an ominous presence, as if it were auditioning for the main role in Poe's *Fall of the House of Usher*.

Surrounding the starkly constructed main building were hedges and other greenery. Several tall oak trees and a couple of white park benches added permanency to the scene. A squirrel ran across the neatly trimmed lawn. It appeared peaceful but exuded a sense of unease—a park with an evil attitude.

Nervous someone might really be watching him, Cole shifted his weight trying to decide what to do next. Without any specific plan, he shoved his hands into his pockets, drooped his head in an Elvis-like gesture, and started to walk the perimeter of the wall.

The sanitarium grounds were situated on a corner lot, which pressed into a steep hillside. On the left, the high wall defined the border between the sanitarium and its neighbor, a private hospice. On the right, the wall ran down a short street which dead-ended into the same hillside the sanitarium was nestled against.

From the corner, Cole saw another gate was used for deliveries. As he watched, a truck drove down the street and pulled up in front of the gate. The driver got out and walked to the gate, where he pushed an intercom button planted in the wall. After a few seconds the gate began to swing inward. The driver sprang back into his truck and prepared to drive through.

Impulse took over and Cole sprinted forward as the truck began to pull through the open gate. *Gotta make it,* he told himself, increasing his pace as the back of the truck disappeared.

The sound of the gate closing caught Cole's ears while he was still ten yards away. He reached down for extra speed, but his effort was not enough. As the gate clanged shut, Cole was barely able to stop himself ending up like a bug meeting a windshield.

He turned away and leaned forward to catch his breath, hands on his knees. Behind him, he heard a deep chuckling like water flowing over loose rocks. He turned and saw a slender, stooped, black man looking at him through the black wrought iron of the gate.

"What are you laughing about?" Cole asked. He was peeved he hadn't been quick enough to slide through the gate behind the truck.

"It's no wonder you white boys never win Olympic

sprints," the black man said. "You is all elbows and knees when you run—like a camel with jock itch. You gotta be like a panther when you sprint—smooth and flowing. And you gotta be black."

"I suppose it explains all the black athletes who win gold medals in swimming."

"Where I grew up you got lots of running practice. Weren't much call to swim away from trouble. Anyway, it's hard trying to learn how to swim in the flow from a fire hydrant."

Cole laughed. The black man chuckled again. He was perhaps in his late sixties, but it was hard to tell. His skin was the color of sweet chocolate, but tough-looking like the leather of an old flying jacket. He had thin graying hair mashed down on one side with a bad case of bed head.

"Do you work here?" Cole asked.

"Work here, sleep here, exist here. Ain't been outside in years."

"What do you mean?"

"I mean what I say. This here place is where I was put and where I chose to stay. They lets me work outside, taking care of the grounds and all. Dr. John gives me my dream candy to keeps the nightmares away. I'm happy. Makes no never-mind to me what goes on outside these gates. My whole world is in here."

"You wouldn't want to let me in and show me around your world, would you?" Cole asked.

The black man looked at him with disdain. "Why don't you tell me what you want? I may be crazy, but I ain't stupid. You are stupid, but you ain't crazy. It's why you on the other side of these gates and I'm over here."

"Ouch!" Cole said. He hesitated, not sure how to play the situation.

"Don't be takin' your time making up lies. Just lay it out for old Skeeter in truth and time. I knows you were tryin' to sneak in here when that truck pulled through, and I figure you're goin' to wait until the truck pulls back out so you can try again. However, you ain't gonna get very far once you're inside unless I decide not to rat you off."

"Would you do that to some poor white boy who doesn't know how to run?"

"'Course I would. You don't control my dream candy. Dr. John does. But tell me your tale and, iffin' I like it, then maybe I'll play along."

"Why?"

"Because I'm crazy, you fool. Plus, it sure do get boring around here and you might liven things up."

Cole figured he didn't have much choice. He plunged into the deep end. "Elvis Presley might not be dead. And he might be being held at Elysian against his will. I know it sounds crazy." He said it all in a rush.

The rumbling chuckle echoed out of Skeeter's throat again. He bent in half to slap his thigh. "You might be eating too much sugar cereal, but if you want to find Elvis you sure came to the right place. We got three of them suckers in here along with a Napoleon and two Cleopatras."

"Three Elvis Presleys?"

"That's right. Every crazy honky in the world who mistakes rhythm for soul thinks he's Elvis. When they think it too much, they ends up in places like this. Iffin' all you want to do is meet Elvis then, hell, I'll introduce you to him myself." Skeeter presented his soft chuckle again. "Trying to find Elvis." Skeeter shook his head. "You white folks sure do spend your lives doing strange things."

"It's a living," Cole said, not wanting to explain to a crazy man that he too ran around acting like Elvis. Skeeter would probably die chuckling at the thought.

At that moment the truck appeared on the gravel drive to head out again. Skeeter jerked his hand away and jumped back as the gate began to electronically swing inward.

Cole moved to one side and pressed himself against the wall. When the truck pulled through, he slipped onto the sanitarium grounds before the gate could close. He found himself facing Skeeter. Skeeter suddenly pushed both hands against Cole's shoulders and knocked him to the ground behind a large wheel-barrow-style cart containing gardening tools and a large trash can.

"Stay down there, honky. You want Dr. John and his boys to see you?" Skeeter sounded agitated. "What am I gonna do with you now? Iffin' Dr. John catches me helping you, he'll take away my dream candy for sure."

"Come on, Skeeter," Cole said from his prone position. "You told me you would introduce me to Elvis. I'll play it anyway you want. Dr. John won't have to know a thing. Let me see your three Elvis Presleys, and I'll get out of your hair."

"Don't be wiggling like a snail without a shell. Get into the barrow and lie low."

Cole saw what Skeeter had in mind and quickly complied. With agile body movements, he boosted himself into the cart and lay down on top of a shovel and two rakes. The sides of the cart hid him from casual sight. Skeeter grunted his approval and, picking up the handles of the cart, began to push it toward the main structure of the sanitarium.

The extra weight of Cole's body in the cart didn't seem to bother Skeeter at all.

CHAPTER 13

"WHY ARE YOU IN HERE?" COLE ASKED HIS BENEFACTOR.

"As good a place as any, and I don't gots no problems here? Dr. John takes all my money and I don't gots no problems."

"Dr. John takes all your money?"

"He surely does. But I foxed them. It's all set up legal like, so they only gets a bit every year. Otherwise, I'd be out on my black ass."

"Doesn't sound like a good a deal."

"Because you young enough to deal with problems. You ain't got no dream candy monkey. I don't wants no problems. I just wants my dream candy."

"Then how come you're helping me?"

"I told you before—I'm crazy. Iffin' I wasn't crazy, I wouldn't be here. Anyway, there ain't no poontang worth chasing in this place, so watching you make a fool o' yo'self is the only entertainment I gots."

Skeeter pushed the wheelbarrow into a garden storage shed and set it down. "You stay here a minute," he said to Cole. "I'll make sure Big Melvin isn't about."

"Big Melvin?" Cole asked, but Skeeter had shambled away toward a side entrance to the sanitarium. Cole wasn't sure if Skeeter would be coming back. The old man had it together one minute and was living on planet Zork the next—like maybe Skeeter had been a Hollywood producer in his prior life.

Ten minutes later, Cole was sure Skeeter wasn't coming back. But as he was getting ready to leave the garden storage shed and assault the sanitarium by himself, he heard a low whistling. He poked his head into the open and saw Skeeter signaling him from the sanitarium's side entrance. Cole ran across the open space and through the door Skeeter held open far enough for Cole's slim body to squeeze through.

"Thought you'd forgotten about me," Cole said.

"I'm old and crazy, but there's nothing wrong with my memory. Had to make sure Big Melvin wasn't sniffing around."

"Who is Big Melvin?"

"Don't ask. Pray you never find out."

Skeeter led Cole down a long corridor painted a calming pale blue. There were doors at regular intervals. Most were closed, but a couple were open to reveal empty patient bedrooms.

"Where is everyone?" Cole asked, noticing there was nobody in the corridors.

"This wing is in the breakfast room waiting to gum their oatmeal."

"Are you supposed to be there?"

"Nah. They don't worry about ol' Skeeter. I eats when I wants, and the rest of the time I take care of the grounds. I do a good job so they leaves me alone. Makes the staff and me feel warm and fuzzy."

Skeeter pulled Cole through the maze of corridors. Cole realized he would never have navigated the building without a guide.

"Here we are," Skeeter said, stopping at the beginning of another corridor. "The Avenue of the Stars."

"Is that a joke?"

"It's what we call this wing 'cause everybody on it thinks they is somebody famous. We gots us a James Dean, a Marilyn Monroe, and a Teddy Roosevelt."

"And three Elvis Presleys."

"Delusions of grandeur, every one of 'em."

"Who do you think you are?" Cole asked Skeeter.

"Plain ol' Skeeter Tallman. Gold medalist in the 100-yard dash in the 1936 Olympics in front of God, Adolph Hitler, and the world."

"Didn't Jesse Owens take the gold medal in the hundred in 1936?"

"Jesse Owens ain't crap. I blew him off by a second and a half."

Cole didn't want to get Skeeter mad by arguing with him. It didn't matter much who won the 100-yard dash in 1936. All he wanted to do was find a dead singer. It was a tossup as to who was crazier.

Cole was beginning to feel nervous hanging around.

"Where's the first Elvis?" he asked. He had no idea how to recognize the Elvis his sister had seen, but he had to start somewhere.

Skeeter pointed. "The opening act is right behind door number two."

Skeeter took a plastic key card out of his pocket and pushed it into a slit in the wall near the door.

"Where did you get the pass key?" Cole asked.

"Took it off Big Melvin once when he was whumping on me. It fell out his pocket, and I never told him. I went back later and picked it up. Boy-o-boy, did Big Melvin ever catch hell for losing it. Served his ass right for whumping me. Now, I uses it to get around. Let a few screaming mimies out when no one is looking. Livens the place up, and Big Melvin gets his ass chewed all over again. It purely doesn't pay to mess with ol' Skeeter. You best remember, or I'll run you to ground before you've gone a hundred yards. I tell you I was in the 1936 Olympics?"

"Can we get on with this?"

"Don't you be getting uppity."

"I'm sorry. I don't want to meet Big Melvin if I can help it."

At the sound of his nemesis's name, Skeeter's expression changed. He hurried to open the door. He and Cole stepped inside, the door gliding shut noiselessly behind them.

Sitting in an overstuffed armchair by a barred window was a big man with bushy black hair and mutton chop sideburns. He was fifty-five to sixty years old and was wearing the same style of blue jumpsuit Joella had described. However, Skeeter was wearing the same kind of outfit. Cole figured it was the sanitarium's uniform.

But Skeeter had something else in common with *Elvis.*

"How can this yo-yo think he's Elvis?" Cole asked Skeeter in disgust. "He's black."

"You looking for logic and sanity, then you be in the wrong place."

"Hullo, I'm Elvis Presley," the man said to Cole. He stood up from his chair and extended his hand. The voice was uncanny. If Cole had been brave enough to close his eyes he would have sworn it was the King speaking. Cole looked at the extended hand.

"He won't bite you," Skeeter said.

Cole took the hand gingerly and found his knuckles being ground together. The black man pumped Cole's arm up and down as if expecting water to spurt out of Cole's mouth. "Would you like me to play you a song?" he asked.

"No... Thanks," Cole said quickly, pulling his hand out of hock. "Let's move on," he said to Skeeter.

"Whatever you want, man," Skeeter said. He let loose with his deep throated chuckle. "You should have seen the look on your face. Priceless, I'm a tellin' you." Skeeter slipped the pass card into the slot inside the wall and he and Cole made a quick exit.

Cole put his hand on Skeeter's arm. "No more surprises, okay?"

"I was just funnin' with you. You did say you was looking for Elvis, and that good ol' boy surely do believe he's the King of Rock-n'-Roll. You should have let him play you a song. He rips up a mean six string."

"Further proof he isn't Elvis."

"What?"

"Nothing," Cole said. "Where to now?"

Skeeter led the way down the corridor. He stopped in front of a door with a number eighteen above it. He placed the card on the edge of the lock slit, but Cole stopped him from pushing it home.

"How come all these people are in their rooms?"

Skeeter shrugged like it was common knowledge. "The day is just beginning. Everyone is locked down from last night. We eat breakfast in shifts. Helps spread the staff around. Right now, *A* wing is eating. Soon *B* wing will be released. Then this wing, *C*. It keeps everyone on a schedule."

"How long do we have?"

Skeeter pondered. "About forty minutes."

Cole nodded. "Okay."

Skeeter pushed the key card home and the door swung open.

Another fiftyish man looked up as Cole and Skeeter entered. He was lying on the bed in his pajamas, roused from sleep by the noise of the door opening.

At least this one is white, Cole thought. *Maybe we're finally getting somewhere.*

The man was the right height to be Elvis, and fifty pounds overweight. His hair was receding, but what remained was pitch black, and the sideburns were in full glory. He looked at Cole, his sleepy eyes widening in shock, "Jesse? Jesse Garon? Is it you?" he asked.

Cole looked over his shoulder, expecting to see Elvis' dead, shortly after birth, twin brother standing behind him. There was only Skeeter. Then Cole realized since he too looked like Elvis, the man on the bed thought he was Jesse. Things were getting way weird.

"I'm not—" Cole started, but the man jumped up and grabbed him in a bear hug.

"I knew you wouldn't forsake me, Jesse. I knew you'd come back some day and save me. I've been praying for you, Jesse. I know you'll help me get out of here. My fans are waiting. They need me, but Dr. John keeps giving me pills. They're trying to make me forget who I am, but I still remember. I'll always remember."

"Take it easy," Cole said. He didn't think this guy was the *Elvis* he wanted. His demeanor was not in line with what Joella told him about the character she interviewed. Cole struggled out of the man's grip. He sat down on a hard-back chair, which was the only other piece of furniture in the room.

The man looked at Cole with pleading in his eyes. "Please get me out of here, Jesse."

Cole ran a hand over his face. He sure hoped this wasn't the real Elvis. The guy was pathetic. "How did you get here?" Cole asked.

The man sat down on the edge of his bed. He put his elbows on his knees and supported his chin on his hands. "The whole problem started when mama got sick. You weren't there to help, Jesse, so I had to ask them for help. I knew I shouldn't have done, but I had no choice."

"You asked who for help?"

"Mama was real sickly," the man went on, as if Cole hadn't spoken. "I would have done anything to help her get better. I didn't know what to do until they offered to make her better. I should have known they wanted something in return. But when they told me they wanted to study my voice, I didn't think it would come to this."

Cole was getting confused. "Who are they?" he asked.

The man buried his face in his hands, his voice coming muffled through his fingers and tears. "They took my high notes, Jesse," he blubbered. "They kept them and wouldn't give them back. Mama didn't get any better neither. If mama had got better, I would have let them keep my high notes, but she didn't. Mama up and died, and they kept my high notes. When I told the police what happened, they laughed and asked for proof. Then I was put in here. I been waiting for you to rescue me ever since."

Cole shook his head. "Who stole your high notes?"

"The Atlantians. They took my high notes, got back in their ship, and took them back to Atlantis. And they didn't do nothing for Mama. Atlantis was moved to another planet, you know. That's why nobody has ever been able to find it on Earth."

Cole stood up and moved toward Skeeter. "This is getting too crazy. You sure this guy doesn't work as a story editor for the *Celebrity Tattler*?"

Skeeter plugged his key into the door slot.

"Jesse!" The man made a grab for Cole. "Where are you going? You can't leave!"

"Don't worry, Elvis. I'll be back," Cole said. He wondered how far back he was putting the man's treatment. "I'm going after the Atlantians to get your high notes back."

"But how, Jesse?"

"You let me worry about it." Cole put his hand on

the man's shoulder, pushing him gently back toward the bed. "You stay here and get better. I'll be back soon."

"God bless you, Jesse."

Cole slipped out the door. He stood next to Skeeter, who plugged in his key and the door slid closed. Cole leaned against the corridor wall and closed his eyes. He felt cold and clammy. "Good grief, Skeeter. Are you and I the only sane ones in here?" Cole knew it was a stupid question to ask in a mental hospital, but it came out anyway.

"What do you mean by *we*? You got a mouse in your pocket or something? I'm as crazy as the fruitcake in there—as crazy as the rest of the fruitcakes in here. Iffin' I wasn't, I wouldn't be here. You're the oddball, man. In the land of the insane, is not the sane man crazy?"

"Quit messing with my mind," Cole said. He pushed himself upright. "One more to go?"

"Last Elvis coming up." Skeeter moved down three doors and went through the routine with the card key again. The door swung open and a man with one hand hidden inside his shirt looked out at them. He was naked from the waist down. He quickly covered his groin with a French admiral's hat snatched off his head.

"Oops! Wrong room," Skeeter said. He quickly locked the door again.

"Wrong room?" Cole said. "More like wrong century, wrong continent."

Skeeter moved on to the next door and unlocked it.

A man in a blue institution jumpsuit sat on the bed with his knees drawn up to his chest, his arms hugging them. His face was thin and drawn, but Cole immediately recognized the classic Elvis bone structure. The man was slender, not unlike the Elvis of 1968. His hair was long and disheveled, but it held a deep black luster belonging to a younger man. He was humming softly. Cole listened intently, unexplainable excitement rising in his chest.

"He's humming *I Can't Help Falling In Love*," Cole said to Skeeter.

When he got no response, he turned to see what his companion was doing. Skeeter was nowhere to be seen. However, a hulking mass of a human flesh blocked the doorway. Without a doubt this was Big Melvin.

Cole bolted for the door. He ducked his shoulder, a defensive-end looking to cripple a wide-receiver and drove it into Big Melvin's mid-section.

It was like running into a brick wall.

Big Melvin didn't even step backward. But Cole crumpled to the floor. A huge ham-hock reached down to grab Cole by the scruff of his sweater. He was lifted and shaken like a rag doll. Big Melvin had no difficulty with the effort.

His eyes rattling around in his head, Cole felt close to passing out. The room spun around, and he couldn't focus.

"Enough, Melvin." Cole heard a voice say. The voice was right. It was more than enough.

"Yes, sir, Dr. John."

"Hold him steady."

Cole felt Melvin's other huge, simian hand take hold of him. He felt paralyzed. In his distorted line of vision, a tall slender man with a beak-like face swam into view.

"Mr. Cole. We have been a naughty boy. Almost got away with it, too. But don't worry, we'll take good care of you." There was a tiny prick on Cole's right forearm, the sensation of liquid being injected—and then everything was warm, and safe, and black.

CHAPTER 14

COLE REGAINED CONSCIOUSNESS SLOWLY. IT WAS A LONG time before he realized his eyes were open, but there was no light—none. His head was driving a back-beat to a fast-paced top forty tune. His mouth tasted like a dance floor after an all-night party.

Lying in the complete darkness, he tried to sense his surroundings. Other than the flat hardness beneath him, there was no sensory input to digest. There was only the blackness and the pounding of his head.

He closed his eyes. Darkness. He opened his eyes. Darkness. He wondered if he was dead and in his coffin. The thought scared him into a panic making him fling his arms around in the air.

When he calmed himself, he realized he was laying on a cot with a stiff mattress. The mattress was covered with a coarse blanket, which made his skin itch. *Did you itch if you were dead?* He forced himself to sit up and swing his legs over the edge of the cot. The movement made him cry out as pain exploded in his head. With his legs still dangling over the side of the cot, he lay his torso down again waiting for the nausea to pass.

After a few minutes, which could as easily be a few hours, he felt a little better. He tried sitting up again. He made it with nothing but some residual dizziness.

When he felt well enough, he decided to explore what he was sure was a dark prison cell. What he wasn't sure about was how long Dr. John and his cronies would hold him. He figured they pumped him full of drugs until they decided what to do with him— which could be anything from killing him to doing a kitchen lobotomy and turning him into a permanent patient. He felt a chill as images of Jack Nicholson in *One Flew Over The Cuckoo's Nest* whizzed around in the darkness.

With one hand, Cole felt along the top of the mattress until he discovered it butted against a wall. Leaning over to keep his hand on the wall, he stood up and began to walk around the room using the wall as a guide. He moved slowly, keeping his free hand out in front of him in search of obstacles.

After five steps, he had made his way unhindered to a corner. Making the turn, he took eight more steps to the next corner. Ten more steps to another corner. Eight more steps to the forth corner. Five more steps back to the cot. He sat down. He had bumped into nothing except walls. His heart was pumping madly, and he had to remind himself to breathe slowly.

Standing up with the backs of his legs touching the cot, he put his hands out in front of him and began to walk slowly across the middle of the room. Eight steps later, his fingertips touched the opposite wall. There seemed to be nothing in the room except for the cot and the terrors of bugs, slimy creatures, and the demons his imagination kept concocting.

To keep busy, he made another circumnavigation of the room feeling for a door or light switch. Nothing. The door must be flush to the wall with no interior handle. He made his way back to the cot and curled up in a ball on his side.

He was so scared he thought about sucking his thumb. Then he remembered his mama's warnings about how he might suck his thumb off, and the battles his parents had to break him of the habit. Not wanting to let them down, he kept his digit dry. But It wasn't easy.

The darkness and the residual drug in his body combined to make him sleepy. He dozed off into a fitful dreamscape chasing blue jump-suited figures with long sideburns through dark, never-ending caverns. He could never catch any of them, and there were too many to choose from to chase them all. Elvis, Elvis, everywhere and not a drop to drink. The nonsense rhyme ran through Cole's mind as he twitched in his sleep.

———

"COME ON, WAKE UP!"

Cole heard the voice in his subconscious. It was soft and lilting and he thought again of his mother. She would wake him in the mornings for school by shaking his shoulders, stubborn with sleep, in the same way.

"Ah, Mom, I don't want to go to school," Cole mumbled.

"I'm not your momma. Come on, wake up!" This time the voice was sharper, still soft in lilt, but definitely male.

Cole felt his cheeks sting as they were slapped lightly. He opened his eyes and saw there was light in his room. The door was open, and Elvis was leaning over him. At least it looked like Elvis.

"Hurry up!" said another voice. Cole looked over to see Skeeter Tallman gesturing at him. "Iffin' we wait around much longer Big Melvin gonna catch us fo sure."

Cole sat up on his cot.

"Can you walk?" the man who would be the king asked.

Cole realized he had last this Elvis rocking back and forth on a bunk with his legs drawn up to his chest. It had been right before Big Melvin wrapped his arms around Cole and sent him to Lullaby Land.

"Are you really Elvis?" Cole asked. It was a reasonable question in his mind but said aloud it sounded silly.

"In the flesh. It looks like you came to rescue me, but now I'm gonna be rescuing you."

"Neither of you is going to be rescued iffin' you don't shut your yaps and move your asses." Skeeter was getting agitated.

Elvis helped Cole to stand up. "Ol' Skeeter has a built in Big Melvin alarm. If he says we got to move, then we better move."

"Where were you when Big Melvin was using me as

a squeaky toy?" Cole asked Skeeter as they gained the hallway.

"Survival is the name of the game in this joint. Iffin' you don't know when to get off the stage then you gonna get thrown off. 'Sides, I came back for you, so what are you bitchin' about? You white boys is never happy."

"I'm happy. I'm happy," Cole said.

"Humpfff!" Skeeter snorted.

"And I'm grateful."

"I should think so," Skeeter was beginning to look mollified. "I even served you up Elvis on a silver platter. The only thing missing was an apple in his mouth."

"Thanks, I think." Cole looked at Elvis who smiled almost shyly.

Could he really be Elvis? Right age, right look, right sound. But then didn't Cole have all those things when he was on stage?

"Don't stand there gorping," Skeeter said. "We gots to beat feet."

The strange trio were moving rapidly down the corridor when they heard a shout behind them. Big Melvin was in pursuit.

"Move it!" Skeeter yelled.

Cole was propelled forward as Elvis grabbed him under one arm and began running. Cole's rubbery legs were going in nine different directions at once, but he found the fortitude to keep going when his whole body was screaming at him to fall down.

The gap between the trio and Big Melvin did not grow, but it did not shorten either. Big Melvin was indeed big, but he was not fast. Fortunately, there was no other staff around to assist him.

Skeeter led the way through the labyrinth of corridors until the trio were spat out an unobtrusive side door into the outside air. When Skeeter had hit the slam bar across the door, a siren had blasted, setting off a series of wailings around the complex.

Beginning to recover, Cole shook Elvis's helping hand off his elbow and ran to catch up with Skeeter.

"You'll make the Olympics yet," Skeeter said, as Cole pulled alongside.

"Not if Big Melvin catches us," Cole said, nodding to Big Melvin barging through the exit door after them. "We have to get out of here!"

"Trust ol' Skeeter. He'll see you right."

"I'm sorry I put you in the middle of this."

"Hell, this is the most fun I've had in years. It's worth a couple of electroshock sessions."

"Come on," said Elvis. "Quit gassing and let's put this pop stand behind us."

Running down one side of the main building, Skeeter veered to the right as Dr. John stepped out of a doorway in front of them. The doctor put up a hand like a traffic cop trying to stop a wayward motorist, but Skeeter, Cole, and Elvis kept running.

"My car is on the other side of this wall," Cole said. "Is there a way over?"

"I'll give you both a boost," said Skeeter.

"But how will you get over?"

Skeeter's rumbling chuckle overwhelmed him to the point of slowing him down.

"Are you crazy? I'm not going over the wall. It's an insane asylum out there. I want nothing to do with it."

"What about Big Melvin and Dr. John?"

"You really think ol' Skeeter can't keep outrunning them? I was in the 1936 Olympics, remember? Here, let me show you how I done it."

Skeeter put on a burst of speed. Struggling after him, Cole and Elvis ran in the direction of the perimeter wall. Big Melvin pounded the turf behind them, yelling like a banshee competing with the wail of the alarms.

Skeeter reached the perimeter wall and turned his back to it. Leaning against it for support, he cupped his hands low in front of him. Cole saw what Skeeter had in mind. He gave Elvis a shove forward.

Elvis ran straight toward the thin black man. Without breaking stride, Elvis stepped into the saddle made by Skeeter's cupped hands and was propelled up to the top of the eight-foot-high wall. He scrambled over the top and slid down the other side.

Holding back, waiting for Elvis to get clear, almost cost Cole dearly. Big Melvin was rambling on as if he were a steamroller. He was reaching out to grab Cole when Cole ducked down and swept the back of his leg across Big Melvin's shins. The giant screamed, pitched forward, and crashed to the turf. His mouth filling with grass, dirt, and rocks like the scoop of a dump truck.

Jumping up, Cole sprinted for the wall. Skeeter was waiting for him. He flung Cole high and hard as Cole stepped into his hands. Because Cole was much lighter than Elvis, he took off like a rocket, clearing the top of the wall without touching it.

"Thanks, Skeeter. You deserved your gold medal," he said as he flew into the air.

"If you're lying, you're dying," Skeeter yelled. "Good luck, honky."

It was a long drop on the far side, but Cole landed on the balls of his feet and rolled onto his shoulders. Elvis helped him up and Cole pointed toward the Pink Madam. Together they ran to the car and climbed over the doors. The sweet engine turned over on the first try.

Jail House Rock blasted out of the tape deck.

"One of my favorites," Elvis said coolly.

Cole punched the accelerator and the Pink Madam spun gravel.

———

IN HIS OFFICE, Dr. John Carpenter picked up the telephone and dialed a number from memory. On the other side of the richly appointed room, Big Melvin sat on an embroidered couch with an ice pack to his jaw. On the floor in front of him, Skeeter was struggling within the confines of a straightjacket.

The phone rang three times before it was picked up. "Hello."

"This is Dr. Carpenter. The bait has been taken."

"Did you have any trouble?"

"One of the inmates became involved, but he won't be a problem."

"Are you sure?"

"Nothing a dose of dream candy won't handle."

There was a silence on the other end of the phone as if the situation was being considered from all angles.

"You've done well, Doctor. Your country is grateful. I'll be sure the director knows of your cooperation."

"Thank you. Ahh...About the charges we discussed?"

"They will be held in abeyance."

"Abeyance? I thought—"

"Don't think, Doctor. Just do. As long as you cooperate, you won't need to worry."

The phone line went dead.

CHAPTER 15

COLE SLID THE PINK MADAM INTO A PARKING SPOT IN front of Copper's and slammed the gearshift into park. The car rocked back and forth for a second on worn shocks as the engine died into heat tinkling silence.

Copper's, the pub which occupied the floor beneath Cole's apartment, wasn't open for business, but John Peel, the owner, was outside spraying down the sidewalk. He waved to Cole.

"You hungry?" Cole asked Elvis.

"Very."

"Fancy some English grub?"

"I'm hungry enough to eat anything."

Cole hoisted himself out of the car. He waited for his companion to do the same before walking toward Copper's.

Even if the pub wasn't open, John Peel would feed them. He and Cole were good friends—not related, but still family.

John Peel started Copper's when he immigrated to America ten years earlier. He'd come to California on a vacation to celebrate his retirement from Scotland Yard. He and his wife fell in love with the sunshine and beaches and decided to stay. Immigration had been a tough barrier, but Peel had proved he had enough financial backing to open up Copper's and the bureaucratic red tape was finally cut.

Copper's had been a success from the get go. The Santa Monica area was the bastion of British immigration in California. Peel's bangers-and-mash and fish and chip combinations put the other English-style restaurants in the area to shame. He also pulled a fair pint at the bar and the location had become a favorite watering hole for local cops from the Santa Monica Police Department, the Los Angeles Police Department, and deputies from the Los Angeles Sheriffs' Malibu station.

Peel ushered his two early morning clients into the pub and locked the door behind them. He was never happier than being behind the Copper's grill cooking up an English feast. His father had run a fish and chip shop in England, and Peel believed it was in his blood even though his own first career had taken him in another direction.

The inside of the bar was decorated in an eclectic mix of Victorian motif and memorabilia from Peel's days as a British bobby. There was also a huge collection on a wall of police uniform patches from all over the world. A series of three dart boards and chalk scoring boards dominated another wall, and a long bar yet another.

"Who's your friend?" Peel asked when they were inside.

"John Peel meet Elvis Presley," Cole did the introductions. "Elvis, John Peel."

The getaway from the sanitarium had been a mad dash giving Cole little time to converse with his new companion. If this was indeed Elvis, then Cole was walking around next to the biggest damn story of the century. If his new companion wasn't Elvis, then he was walking around next to a loony who might be an axe murderer in disguise.

"You one of Cole's impersonator friends," Peel said, as the two men shook hands.

Elvis looked at Cole, who hadn't explained what he did for a living.

Peel reached out and turned Elvis' head from side to side. "You look more like Elvis than most of the guys Cole brings around, except you're a little old for this kind of gig."

Seeing Elvis' confusion, Cole thought fast. "If Elvis were alive today he'd be almost sixty. We're adding a *What If?* act to *Legends Alive*. It will present Elvis as he would be today if he hadn't passed on."

Peel shook his head. "Only in America," he said, then brightened. "How about a couple of English hearty breakfasts, then?"

"Sounds great," Cole said. He led Elvis to a small booth as Peel headed for the grill.

"What in the world is going on?" Elvis asked.

"You've been gone a long time, El. A lot of people make a living these days by recreating your act on stage. There are Elvis impersonator acts all over the country. All over the world."

"You, too?"

"Yes," Cole said, looking slightly embarrassed.

"That's awful."

"Don't look at it that way. It's the ultimate in flattery. You're a legend, perhaps even the biggest legend of all time. People who loved you don't want to let go. I hate to say it, but you're worth more dead than you are alive. You're not just a singer or actor anymore, you're big business."

Elvis buried his face in his hands. "I don't know if I can face all this again. It's going to be worse than when I left. Everybody wants, and wants, and wants. They were sucking the life out of me. I might be better off back at Elysian."

"Your fans love you, El."

"I'm not talking about the fans. They were the greatest. I sung for them and them alone. They were everything to me. But there were scum sucking leeches who always wanted a piece of the action. Exploiters who never cared if I was too tired, or too burned out, to sing or act. Take another pill they told me. Get the doctor to give you a new prescription. Something, anything, so they could get what they wanted out of me. It was why I ran when I was given the chance. If I hadn't *died* when I did, I would have been dead soon after I was buried."

Cole didn't quite follow the logic of Elvis' last statement. Before he could follow up, Peel brought plates heaping with breakfast foods. Bacon, English sausages, fried eggs, fried tomatoes, fried bread, and baked beans. It was a cholesterol explosion of British grub to be washed down by mugs of tea strong enough to stand a spoon in.

Elvis ate like a frenzied dervish. Cole did the same.

He didn't know he was hungry until Peel had set the food on the table. Talk was postponed until the plates were wiped clean with slices of bread.

Cole was the first to return to conversation.

"I hate to ask, El, but where have you been for fourteen years and what is going on?"

"First tell me why you were looking for me at Elysian?"

"You first. I already know my story. I'm not convinced yet you are Elvis Presley. The assumption is pretty absurd."

"Until I can get to the man who can confirm everything I say, you're going to remain unconvinced."

"Who is this guy?"

"A DEA agent by the name of Gordy Fontaine."

"My sister told me the DEA said he doesn't exist."

"Your sister? What does she have to do with this?"

While fleeing from the sanitarium, they had simply been two guys on the run from a common enemy. Introductions and stories had not been important.

"Skeeter didn't tell you who I am?" Cole asked.

"The poor confused joker told me there was some guy who'd broke into the sanitarium looking for me. He'd been running a game by taking you to visit the other guys who claim to be me. He was checking you out. Making sure you were cool."

"Why?"

"Because we look out for each other. Dr. John treats Skeeter like a jail trustee. He allows Skeeter to help Big Melvin keep everyone in line using Dr. John's dream powders.

"Skeeter knows I hate the stuff, so whenever he can,

he fakes giving it to me. It gives me a brief respite to figure out how to escape. Now exactly who are you and why did you come looking for me?"

"My name is Cole Ramsey. You called me—"

Elvis looked excited. "Your sister is Deputy Garner?"

"Yes. Joella gave you my number at the police station, but you never showed up to meet me."

Elvis shook his head. "Lord knows I wanted to be there, but Big Melvin and his goons showed up. I put one of them down, but there were too many and I ain't young anymore."

"You look in good shape."

Elvis laughed. All the quality of the south was in the sound. "You mean I look in better shape than I was fourteen years ago—when I was two hundred and fifty pounds of bloated flesh, and so strung out on prescription drugs, I didn't know what way was up?"

"Yeah." Cole looked sheepish, and Elvis laughed again.

"Shows what proper diet, yoga, and isometric exercises can do for you."

"But what about the dream powder?"

"It's a strong sedative to keep the loonies in line. Sends you on a trip through the clouds and keeps all the demons at bay. Nothing like the other stuff I was swallowing by the fistful when the show had to go on."

"How did you end up at Elysian?"

"I promise to tell you, but you're not going to believe me unless I can get to Gordy Fontaine and have him confirm my story."

"Gordy Fontaine doesn't exist."

"Yes, he does. He was one of the DEA's top under-cover agents for years. I helped him several times by making big buys from cats in the music industry. I'd set them up and Gordy and his partner would take them down while they were on their way to me with the stuff. Everybody believed I was taking everything under the sun, so it was easy to get the contacts. Everybody wants to sell to a star."

"My sister told me the DEA was contacted and they'd never heard of Fontaine."

"I don't know what's happened with Gordy since I've been gone, but he had a daughter. She'd be about your age. Her name is Sheila Fontaine. If we can get to her, perhaps she can get us to her father."

"But—"

Elvis put his hand on Cole's arm. "Help me get to Sheila Fontaine, and I'll tell you everything. I'm going to have to convince her, too. I've been living in hell for fourteen years, but I've done what Gordy Fontaine asked me to do. The information I have for Gordy is more important than you can realize. Don't make me explain myself twice. Get me to Sheila and I promise I'll run down the whole shebang."

Cole was silent, looking into Elvis' pleading eyes.

"Please, Cole," Elvis said. "Help me."

Cole stood. "I have to be crazier than Skeeter." He stuck his hand in his jeans for some change. "Let me call my sister."

CHAPTER 16

"Joella! You've got a call on four-one."

Joella didn't look up from the report she was reading to acknowledge the directive. Instead, she snaked out an arm and collared the receiver off the phone on her desk with a set of well-manicured fingers.

"Garner."

"Jo, it's me."

Joella sat up in her chair and riveted her attention.

"Cole! Where have you been? I've been leaving messages everywhere."

"Some detective. Can't even track down your little brother."

"Can't you ever be serious?"

"I can, but you bring out the tease in me."

"The teasing is a defense to avoid giving straight answers."

"I have a mother, Jo."

"She always was too soft on you."

"Please, Jo. I've got plenty of problems without sibling rivalries."

"Are you in trouble?" Jo was anxious.

"I may be sitting on the answer to the biggest hoax since Watergate."

"What do you mean? Does this have anything to do with Duster? You know he was shot in the back of the head execution-style."

"That's awful. I can't imagine why anyone would want to bump off a harmless bum."

"What made you think he was a vice cop who was part of a prank?"

"Because he talked to me outside the station. He hit me up for a few bucks then told me about a guy who looked like Elvis being dragged off in a limousine with the license plate *GLITZ8*."

"And you bought it?"

"Not at first. But I couldn't leave it alone." Cole leaned against the wall of the English-style phone box in the back of Copper's. "I found Glitz Limousine Service in the phone book and called them. I got this ditzy receptionist who told me *GLITZ 8* was on loan to the Elysian Corporation. He gave me the address, but it turned out to be for a private sanitarium. Elvis, Duster, the guy at Glitz—I still thought it was you telling me I'm crazy to do what I do."

"I think you should grow up," Jo said, "but I wouldn't give you that kind of run around."

"I know that now."

"What do you mean?"

"When I heard your message about Duster being killed, I went back to Elysian."

"Tell me you didn't."

"If I did, I'd be lying."

"And?"

"I sort of snuck in—"

"Cole!"

"Hang on—"

"You were arrested for trespassing, right? Where are you being held?" Joella's voice was rising though the decibels.

"Slow down. I'm not under arrest," Cole tried to reassure his sister. "I did get caught at the sanitarium, but it was by some crazy doctor and his trained ape. They drugged me and locked me in a padded cell. Some friends helped me escape."

"You have friends in a loony bin?"

"Long story. I have one of them with me now."

"You're with an escapee from a mental institution? Are you crazy?"

"An odd question under the circumstances."

"Shut up, Cole. Who is this guy?"

"That's the problem."

"Yeah?"

"He's Elvis Presley."

Joella was trying to digest this information when she saw two official-looking men walking across the squad room toward her. She didn't recognize them, but she did recognize trouble.

"You can't be serious about this guy being Elvis."

"You believed him enough to have him call me. Now you're singing a different tune?"

"Because it's crazy. Where has the guy been? What's he been doing since he died?"

"I'm working on the answers. I need you to check something. I know the DEA said this Gordy Fontaine guy doesn't exist, but Elvis is insistent. He says Fontaine had a daughter—"

"Hang on," Joella said, interrupting Cole's flow of words. She covered the mouthpiece of the phone and turned to face the two men now standing in front of her desk. They smelled like feds. It was an odor to which street cops were highly sensitive.

The men rudely staring, letting Joella know they were important.

"Yes?" Joella said, looking directly at the men.

"DEA," The older man said. He was tall and angular, all long bones and sharply angled joints. His suit looked like a costume pinned on a scarecrow. He flashed a badge in a black leather case. "We'd like to speak to you."

"Take a number and stand in line." Joella refused to be intimidated. "I'll be with you when I'm done here." When the two feds didn't move, Joella said, "Have a seat in the interview room." She pointed to the doors of a tiny soundproof cubicles.

The feds didn't move until they realized Joella was going to wait them out. The tall one nodded and he reluctantly moved away, tugging his partner along with him.

"Are you still there, Jo?" Cole was saying when Joella put the receiver back to her ear.

"I'm still here."

"You got me into this thing. Are you going to help or not?"

"I didn't say I wasn't going to help," Joella said. "The DEA is here and guess what they want to talk about?"

"Gordy Fontaine?"

"I'll give you long odds if you want to disagree."

"Not a chance. What do you think is really going on?" Cole asked.

"No idea, but you're going to have to run with it. If I tell anyone I'm investigating the death of Elvis Presley, I'll be on traffic duty before end of watch."

"I understand, but I need help getting a line on Fontaine's daughter."

"What was her name?"

"Sheila."

"Sheila what?"

"Fontaine, I guess. Unless she's married."

"Fontaine would still show up on a DMV printout as an AKA."

"Cool."

"Hold on and I'll check." Joella punched the hold button.

Seeing the tall DEA agent standing in the interview room doorway, Joella waved. "Be right there."

Joella waited for the agent to disappear back into the room before she walked over to a bank of computers. Sitting down, she entered her password then selected the format for the Department of Motor Vehicles driver's license information. She entered the name Sheila Fontaine and waited. The screen spat back three possibles:

CDL: C0566892 Fontaine, Sheila A
DOB: 4/9/32
ADD: 104
CITY: Los Angeles

CDL: X9811628 Fontaine, Sheila D
DOB: 1/29/63
ADD: 28
CITY: Stockton

CDL: A8441287 Fontaine, Sheila L
DOB: 8/18/68
ADD: 148
CITY: Long Beach

JOELLA ELIMINATED the first choice as being too old. The second choice was a possibility, but Stockton was a long way to send Cole on a wild goose chase. Joella selected the third entry. The computer whirled then grudgingly regurgitated the output:

DEPARTMENT OF MOTOR VEHICLES
DRIVERS LICENSE INFORMATION
LAW ENFORCEMENT USE ONLY
UNAUTHORIZED ACCESS TO THIS
INFORMATION IS A MISDEMEANOR
CDL: A8441287
Fontaine, Sheila Lisa Marie
DOB: 8/18/68
Blond / Blue / 5'6 / 122
Address as of 8/18/89: 14897 Seaview Circle, Long Beach 90068
Previous address as of 8/18/1985: 171 E. Spinnaker, NHW 90167

Vehicle Violations:
4/23/9112500(a) VC
Vehicle Plate: ELLVS
Failures to appear: None
END OF MESSAGE

COINCIDENCES HAPPENED, but there was only so much Joella was willing to contribute to fate. The fact this Sheila Fontaine had *Lisa Marie* as a middle name was a clue, but the personalized plate on her vehicle was the clincher.

Joella brought up another computer format and tapped in the letters *ELLVS*. Within seconds the information popped up:

DEPARTMENT OF MOTOR VEHICLES
REGISTRATION INFORMATION
LAW ENFORCEMENT USE ONLY
UNAUTHORIZED ACCESS TO THIS
INFORMATION IS A MISDEMEANOR
LIC: ELLVS
YR: 90
MK: Ford BT Coupe
EXP: 6/93
Registered owner: Fontaine, Sheila L
14897 Seaview Circle, Long Beach 90068

JOELLA HIT THE PRINT KEY, waited for the chatter of the printer's pinwheel to stop, then tore off a copy of the information. She returned to her desk and picked up the phone.

"Cole?"

"Still here."

"There were three possible, but your best bet lives in Long Beach."

"What's your reasoning?"

"A strong hunch. Her middle name is Lisa Marie, and she drives a 1990 Ford with the personalized plate *ELLVS*—El Lives."

"Close enough," Cole said. "Give me the info."

As Joella spoke into the phone, she saw the DEA agents heading back to her desk.

"Gotta go," she said, as the two men drew close. "Call me when you have anything and take care of yourself."

"You too, Jo."

Joella felt the need to say more, but the line went dead. She felt a whisper of premonition. She didn't want Cole to end up like the phone line.

CHAPTER 17

"DEPUTY GARNER!" THE SHORTER OF THE TWO DEA agents sounded annoyed.

"I'm sorry to keep you waiting, gentlemen," Joella nipped the complaint in the bud. "What can I do for you?" She took the sheets containing the information on Sheila Fontaine and laid them on her desk top.

"I'm Lew Sutton," the older, angular man said. He introduced the smaller man as Agent Deke Rivers, and everyone shook hands. "As we said, we're with the DEA."

There was a pause.

Joella jumped in to the lengthening silence. "Am I supposed to be impressed?"

Rivers didn't like Joella's flippant tone. He leaned forward to brace his hands on the front of Joella's desk. "Somebody from this station called our office asking about an agent by the name of Gordy Fontaine. We want to know why." His tone was belligerent. He had bunched his shoulder muscles under his cheap imitation silk jacket to look like a charging linebacker.

Joella laughed. "Where did you get this bulldog?" she asked Lew. "You know we have a leash law in this county. I hope you brought your pooper scooper with you."

Rivers actually growled his displeasure.

Joella spread her hands on her side of the desk and leaned forward to get in Rivers' face. "Back off, puppy dog. You're playing in my territory and I don't want you pissing on the rug. I've been doing this job for too long to be intimidated by some wet behind the ears muscle job. Back off or I'll slam your tail in the door."

Lew hip-checked Rivers back from the desk. "I'm sorry, Deputy Garner. Rivers isn't quite ready to be let loose in polite company."

Joella pushed herself upright. "Get real, Sutton. The good cop, bad cop routine doesn't even work in the movies anymore. Why don't you tell me what you want?" Joella worked up a sarcastic smile. "You know, police working with police. Or is that concept lost on the federal level?"

"Let's start over," Lew said, chastened. "We're interested in why a deputy called our office looking for Gordy Fontaine."

Joella felt her ears burning but fought to keep a poker face. She was aware of the printouts on her desk containing the information on Sheila Fontaine. She didn't know where this interview was going, but things were getting mighty weird. She wished she hadn't put Cole in the middle. He was running around with an escapee from a mental ward who claimed to be Elvis, and now the DEA wanted to know what was happening. Joella didn't know either, but she was sure going to find out.

She spoke directly to Sutton, ignoring Rivers. "Your office said they'd never heard of Gordy Fontaine. Yet they're interested enough to send out two of their best and brightest to ask questions?"

"The agency doesn't like to wash their dirty laundry in public," Lew said. "We like to know who we're dealing with. Would you give out information on an undercover operative over the phone to anyone who asked?"

"No, I wouldn't." Joella sat down in her swivel chair. She gestured for Sutton and Rivers to sit in the two chairs in front of her desk. "But now you know I'm a real cop, tell me about Gordy Fontaine."

"We asked first," said Lew. "Why do you want to know about him?"

"Technically, my deputy asked first over the phone, but I hate semantics. Anyway, you're probably not going to believe my story."

"You'd be surprised," Lew said, smiling encouragingly.

"Elvis Presley strolled into the station yesterday morning looking like he'd been sucked through a garden hose backward," Joella said. "He asked us to get in touch with a DEA agent named Gordy Fontaine." Joella's tone was matter-of-fact, as if dead celebrities walked into the station lobby every day. "Elvis said the situation was a matter of national importance. We tried your people and got stonewalled." Joella shrugged. "The next thing I know, Elvis has disappeared, and I have a dead transient on my hands who told another witness he saw Elvis being stuffed into a limousine."

"Elvis Presley?" Rivers asked in disbelief. "*The* Elvis Presley?"

"The King of Rock-n'-Roll."

"Didn't anyone tell you Elvis is dead?" Rivers looked smug. "You sure it wasn't Buddy Holly or James Dean?"

"Blow it out your sphincter," Joella said without anger. "You asked, and I'm telling you. Don't blame me if you don't like the way it adds up. The guy sounded convincing. He thought this agent of yours could help prove who he was."

Lew chuckled. "I think we can clear this up. Gordy was a good agent. In fact, he was my partner."

"Was?"

"Yes, *was* is the operative term. Gordy flipped out sixteen years ago. He became obsessed with a drug kingpin named Arceneaux. However, before we could bust him, Arceneaux died of a heart attack. Gordy claimed it was a put-up job. He believed Arceneaux was still alive and the heart attack was a hoax. At the funeral, he created an embarrassing scene trying to prove his point."

"Really?"

"It was a mess. Nobody knew how far over the edge Gordy had stepped. He tried to get the coffin open. When he was restrained, he ended up breaking away and shooting an FBI agent by the name of Jordan in the leg."

"Lucky Jordan?"

"You know him?"

"Unfortunately. He's the pompous ass who's now in

charge of the FBI's Los Angeles office. I've had several dealings with him. None of them pleasant. If Fontaine shot him, he must have been trying to do humanity a favor."

Lew laughed. Really laughed. "I'm sorry," he said, regaining a semblance of control. "But your attitude toward Agent Jordan is much the same as Gordy's. He once said the only difference between Jordan and a porcupine is a porcupine is a bunch of little pricks and Jordan was one giant one."

"Gordy sounds like a good man."

Lew sobered. "He was. Now, he's another cretin with a federal warrant for his arrest. His name has a big flag next to it in our department's computers. When your deputy called about Gordon Fontaine, it set off bells and whistles. Being Gordy's ex-partner, I made sure I was assigned the follow-up investigation."

"I don't know what else I can tell you," Joella said. "I'd like to say the whole thing was a hoax, but if it was, I don't know the purpose."

"Are you doing any further follow-up?" Lew asked.

Joella thought of Cole. "I'm too busy to be chasing dead legends who disappear in puffs of smoke," she lied. "I have enough live felons to keep me busy."

"What about your dead transient who told another witness about Elvis being forced into a limousine?"

"The other witness has also disappeared," Joella cursed herself for having mentioned Duster. She didn't like giving free information to the Feds. "But that's nothing unusual. Nobody wants to get involved anymore."

"What was the witness' name?"

Joella wasn't about to roll over on Cole, so she kept on lying. "The witness was another homeless person. He slipped away when nobody was looking. He told us his name was Jon Burrows when he made his statement."

Lew looked steadily at Joella without saying anything. He was trying to read her for hidden motives. "Jon Burrows, huh?" Lew shook his head.

I blew it, Joella thought to herself. He recognizes the name as one of Elvis' favorite AKAs. She internally cursed herself again for not being able to think of anything better on the spur of the moment.

"Can I see Burrows' statement?" Lew asked.

Joella kept her voice steady. "The statement hasn't been written out yet." She was going to play this out and there was nothing Sutton could do about it.

"Can I see your notes?"

Joella forced herself to smile. "I didn't make any notes. I have a photographic memory. Check it out if you want. It's been court validated more than once."

"I'm sure it has," Lew said. He stood up. "You dance well. We'll have to play this tune again sometime."

"Don't bother. My dance card is always full."

Lew turned to his partner. Clearly, the whole conversation between Lew and Joella had gone over his head. Joella gave him credit for keeping his mouth shut. Maybe there was hope for him yet.

"Come on, Deke," Lew said to his younger partner. "It's time to blow this pop stand."

"Hip vernacular," Joella told him.

"All part of the price of the TV generation," Lew said. He shook Joella's hand. "Thanks for your help."

"Anytime," Joella replied.

She watched the two men leave the squad room. She reached for the DMV printouts with Sheila Fontaine's information on them. Her heart bound up into her throat.

The paperwork was gone.

CHAPTER 18

DEKE RIVERS TURNED THE BEIGE FORD TAURUS OUT OF the sheriff's station parking lot and into the flow of traffic. He glared at his senior partner. "Total waste of time. Why did you let her give you such a run around?"

"Deke, you need to save your heavy-handed tactics for the butt-hairs of the world. With other citizens, you'll get further with a sympathetic word and a smile. And badgering another cop is never a good idea. Listen and learn or shut up and drive."

Rivers couldn't let it go. "You old guys think you've got a monopoly on some investigative secret. But you let everyone buffalo you because you're running scared somebody is going to complain about you."

"Your priorities are screwed up. We're public servants, not the other way around. Tell me, what information you walked away with during our conversation with the deputy?"

"There was no information to get. Elvis Presley, my ass." Out of the corner of his eye, Rivers caught Lew shaking his head. "Tell me you came up with some-thing." His tone reeked with sarcasm.

Lew sighed patiently. "Nobody randomly decided to call and inquire about Gordy. There had to be a reason. If you'd have read Gordy's file, you'd know he had strong connections with Elvis."

"That doesn't prove anything."

"But this does." Lew reached in to the inner pocket of his jacket and pulled out the DMV forms last seen sitting on Joella's desk. He was rather proud of himself lifting them without her noticing. A little practiced sleight of hand and misdirection went a long way. "Another investigative technique you need to develop," he told Rivers, "is the ability to read upside down."

"What are you talking about?"

"This is a DMV printout from Garner's desk."

So?"

Lew held the paperwork out. "This printout is for Sheila Fontaine—Gordy's daughter. I spotted the name while you were busy with your macho posturing."

"We could have pulled it out of the computer ourselves."

"Did God not give you brains when you were born?" Lew was getting frustrated. "The information isn't important. What's important is the information was on Garner's desk. If she not involved in this caper, then why is she tracking down Gordy's daughter? And who did she give the information to over the telephone?"

"How do you know she gave the information to someone?"

"You have to open your eyes to be a detective. She was talking on the phone when we arrived. She sent us away while she went over to the computer, printed these pages out, and went back to talking on the phone."

Rivers shook his head as if this reasoning was too much to take in. "What do we do now?"

"Think about it."

Rivers thought. His brow wrinkled in concentration. "We go check out Gordy's daughter and see who turns up to visit her?"

"Perhaps there's hope for you yet."

"But I thought you said Gordy's daughter was too obvious a lead. You said Gordy was too smart to be caught through a family connection."

"The one thing about Gordy you can count on, is you'll never know if what he does is the result of high intelligence or pure dumb luck. He will never do the logical thing. It makes logic for Gordy to stay away from his daughter. But somebody else obviously thinks he's in contact with her. They also believe they have the right kind of bait to get her to lead them to Gordy. I don't care if they're right, but I want to find out who they are."

"You always sound like you admire this Gordy guy."

"I do. He was a great cop."

"Then how come he's on the run?"

"Because his heart is pure."

"How can his heart be pure if he's a crook?" River's voice was agitated.

"On his worst day Gordy Fontaine was worth ten of you. He was my partner when he went off the rails, and I feel responsible for him. I'm getting close to the end of my career, and it's my job to bring Gordy in. I'll do it because I'm the only man he'll come in for standing up. Anybody else will have to bring him in feet first."

"Sounds fine to me."

Lew gave Rivers a hard stare. "Don't push your luck. Don't force me to choose between you and Gordy because you'll lose in a New York minute. Drive the car. Do what I tell you, when I tell you, and you'll live to fight another day."

———

JOELLA HUNG UP THE PHONE. There had been no answer at Cole's apartment, and he was so unpredictable she couldn't think where else he might be. She stood up, adjusted the 9mm Smith and Wesson on her hip, and pulled on a loose-fitting jacket.

She slid her name into the *out* position on the sign-in board. A plainclothes sergeant noticed her leaving.

"Where you headed, Jo?"

"Gotta get a line on my kid brother. As usual he's in trouble over his head." Between Elvis Presley, the DEA, the FBI, and whoever else might be interested, it was big trouble.

"Can I help?" The sergeant had been trying hard to get into her pants.

"Not right now, Vince, but thanks."

"I'll keep it warm for you."

"Don't wait up on my account." She smiled to take the sting out of her words, but she was going to have to do something drastic about the guy soon.

In the station parking lot, she fished her car keys out of her purse. Her plain detective car was a beat up brown Chevy with black-walls and three antennas. It had ninety thousand miles on the odometer, air conditioning that only worked on cold days, and the disposition of a ripped-off whore.

She turned the engine over and crossed her fingers the old rattle trap would make it to Sheila Fontaine's address in Long Beach.

———

"Let's rock-n'-roll," Cole said, as he walked back to where Elvis was still sitting in a Copper's booth.

"Your sister was able to give you the address?"

"I have the address for a Sheila Fontaine who lives in Long Beach, but we don't have much else to go on. The info came from the DMV files." Cole tossed several bills on the table top to pay for their meal.

"Lead on," said Elvis. He stood up and followed Cole out the door. Both men waved to John Peel as they left.

The Pink Madam fired up first time with *Little Sister* blasting out of the cassette deck.

"How much did you tell your sister?" Elvis asked when they were on their way.

Cole looked over at his companion. "Everything. We have a lot of disagreements, but we don't keep secrets from each other."

Elvis shrugged. "I was concerned she may try and interfere. Dr. John has powerful connections. He could bring pressure down on the Sheriff's Department if needed."

"You're walking on thin ice, pal." Cole's voice hardened. "My sister is a good cop. She won't bow down to anyone."

"I didn't mean to offend. I'm concerned people like yourself and your sister might get hurt."

"It's our choice," Cole replied. "But I'm not yet convinced you're Elvis Presley. You've got a lot of explaining to do."

"I'll explain everything once we find Sheila Fontaine."

"You sound like a broken record. If you don't get on with the song when we find Sheila, then this recording session is over, and you can take your fancy dance steps elsewhere."

"Agreed," Elvis said quietly. With a deliberate movement he leaned over and turned the stereo up to a level that made further talk impossible. With the rag top down and *Suspicious Minds* blaring from the speakers, they made the rest of the trip in conversational silence.

CHAPTER 19

WHEN COLE PULLED THE PINK MADAM TO THE CURB IN front of Sheila Fontaine's address, he heaved a big sigh. This caper was beginning to put major stress on his normally upbeat attitude. The Elvis sitting next to him seemed more and more like a figment of his own imagination. The man sat there, a smug smile on his face, looking like an artificially aged picture of the King. The look was right, the voice was right, but the circumstances were odd. And there was something Cole couldn't quite grasp—a feeling of being manipulated perhaps.

Cole felt uncomfortable confronting Sheila Fontaine. How did you walk up to somebody and say, "I know he's been dead for sixteen years, but Elvis wants to say hello?"

Furthermore, Cole didn't feel good about pulling an innocent into the quagmire. However, his other choice was walk away and not look back. But he wasn't built to back off. He had to follow this through.

"What are we waiting for?" Elvis asked.

"I don't know," Cole replied. "Maybe a heavenly chorus announcing the second coming while *Blue Suede Shoes* plays softly in the background."

"I ain't God, son. I'm just a singer who got in over his head."

"Says you." Cole shook his head and climbed over the driver's door. "Come on."

Elvis mirrored Cole's actions and exited on the passenger side.

"On second thought, maybe you should wait here," said Cole. "You might spook her."

"I might give her a shock," Elvis said. "But she knows me, not you. She'll believe a lot sooner if I go with you."

The two men walked up the driveway to the ranch style home. The small front lawn was well trimmed and the house in good repair. The surrounding neighborhood was older but gave the impression of being established as opposed to stagnant or deteriorating. Cole used the big brass knocker on the front door.

After a few moments a feminine voice asked, "Who is it?"

Cole plunged in. "My name is Cole Ramsey. I'd like to speak to Sheila Fontaine."

"You're speaking to her. What can I do for you?"

"This would be a lot easier if you opened the door."

"Easier for you, maybe," Sheila's voice was no nonsense. "What do you want?"

Cole hesitated.

"I'm sorry, I don't do any business at the door with people I don't know," Sheila cut in. "I think you should leave or I'll call the police."

Elvis stepped up onto the porch and stood directly in front of the peep hole. "Sheila," his voice was honeyed whisky, "I know this will be hard to believe, but it's me, Uncle El."

There was silence on the other side of the door. Uncle El, thought Cole, well wasn't that precious. "Uncle El?" Cole asked *sotto voce*.

"I'm an honorary uncle. It's what she called me when she was younger," Elvis said to Cole, then turned back to the front door. "All I ask is take a look at me, Sheila. You'll know it's me. I have important information for your daddy."

"I think you both better leave," Sheila's voice came back through the door. It had risen an octave. "I'm going to call the police."

"No, Sheila, please. It really is me," Elvis tried again.

"I have a gun. If you try to break in, I'll shoot you."

"This is ridiculous," Elvis said.

"It is ridiculous," Cole agreed. "We're scaring her. This isn't right. We better go." Cole tried to pull Elvis away.

Elvis shook off Cole's hand. "Sheila, when you were twelve, I gave you something special for your birthday. It was a huge brown teddy bear."

There was quiet for a moment or two from behind the door, and then Sheila said, "Tell me something everybody doesn't know."

"The bear had a gold chain around its neck with a TCB charm attached to it."

"More common knowledge."

Elvis was hopping around with anxiety. "On the night I gave you the bear, one of his eyes fell out and we

155

sewed it back on together. You got the needle and thread out of a Little Merry Miss sewing kit."

There was silence behind the door, and then there was the sound of locks being turned and bolts being drawn back. Sheila Fontaine open the door and looked out.

Cole thought she was beautiful. Her long face was graced with a model's high cheek bones and framed by a thick fall of rich chestnut hair. Her lips when she smiled were full and lush and peeled apart to reveal small, perfect, dazzlingly white teeth.

"Uncle El? How can it be you?"

"It's a long story, darling, but it's me." Elvis held out his arms and Sheila stepped into them and began to cry.

———

THE INSIDE of the house was as neat and comfortable as the outside. Money used wisely as opposed to lavishly. In the living room, Cole sat in a plump armchair near a matching couch where Elvis and Sheila sat. On a low coffee table there was a silver coffee pot and a half-filled china cup. In the armchair on the other side of the couch was a teddy bear. It was so large it appeared to be another participant in the conversation.

"This whole situation is so confusing." Sheila said, topping up her cup from the silver pot. "I don't know what to do."

"I don't get it either," Cole said. He felt a bit of sympathy for Elvis. Here was a guy used to having his every whim catered. Now, trying to make the biggest comeback of all, nobody was making things easy for him.

Elvis ran a hand over his face. "Let me try again." He plunged in. "Sheila's father was with the DEA. He didn't like the games the DEA and the FBI were playing with a drug dealer named Arceneaux. Gordy always believed in doing the right thing, even if it meant pursuing his own brand of justice. After my last concert in Indianapolis, I found him waiting in my limousine."

"Gordy Fontaine went rogue?" Cole asked.

Elvis nodded. "I was always glad to see Gordy. We'd been friends a long time. Even before he stopped the kidnap attempt."

"You'd worked with my father before?" Sheila asked, even though she knew the answer. It was like she was checking the story against her own memory for flaws.

"Several times. I'd originally approached the DEA because I wanted to do something to help the drug problem in the music industry. Several of the new long hair groups were stepping so far over the line it was destroying many less successful musicians. It was also affecting many of the hangers-on and groupies."

"Come on, El—drugs have always been a part of the music scene," Cole said.

"But what was happening then was an epidemic sweeping the industry. We're not talking a few reefers between sets, or a few of the isolated jazz faces sticking heroin in their veins or snorting cocaine. Drugs were killing the entire music scene. I could see what was happening, and I wanted to do something to stop it."

"What about your own drug use?"

"I never took anything not prescribed for me by a doctor."

"Prescription abuse is okay, but not illegal drugs?"

"Don't be sarcastic. I wanted to help the kids who were going down the drain."

"And your plan was the DEA?"

"They laughed at first, but then Gordy saw a way to use me. I let several undercover guys travel with me as roadies and musicians, and they made several major busts. When we went to Hollywood even the FBI got in on the act. In the movie *Double Trouble*, remember the group backing me up called *The G-Men*? Well, the name was a big inside joke."

Cole and Sheila were silent.

Elvis shook his head in frustration. "I know it sounds like a bad TV movie, but here's the reality. In 1970, I was nominated by the U.S. Jaycees as one of *America's Most Outstanding Young Men* for the work I'd done in drug enforcement. I was a bonded deputy with the Memphis Police. It's on record I went out with them on narcotics busts. I was a member of the California Narcotics Officers Association. President Nixon presented me with my Federal Agent's Badge from the Bureau of Narcotics and Dangerous Drugs—which at that time was part of the DEA. I'm not making this up. You can check all of it."

"But how does it fit into your disappearance?" Cole asked.

"You need to understand what it is like being a superstar. I know it's what you dream of being—what every kid in America dreams of being. But it has far more curses than blessings. So many people are dependent on you—demanding and demanding. And the fans—God bless them—are never satisfied. They always want more than you can give." Elvis took a breath. "The stress was killing me. My weight was blowing up. The doctors were stuffing pills down my throat to keep me going—to keep the money rolling in. I was living the exact narcotic horror I was fighting against."

Elvis paused, remembering.

He spoke softly. "Everybody wanted a piece of Elvis the King. My life was controlled. My health was controlled. My money, my career, my marriage—all of it was controlled. I didn't know how I could go on. Then Gordy showed up in Indianapolis."

"Did you know he was on the run?" Sheila asked.

"I never believed Gordy went rogue," Elvis said with a smile. "Your father was so straight, he made a plumb-line look crooked. He was convinced Zachary Arceneaux was not dead. He believed the FBI had put Arceneaux in the witness protection program for his testimony against other major drug dealers. Gordy said Arceneaux only informed on those drug dealers he considered competition and was running his own drug ring from inside the witness protection program."

"What did he expect you to do?" Cole asked.

Elvis looked pensive. "Gordy knew I was having issues with a shirt-tail relative mixed up in illegal off-shore banking scheme run by an international con-man named Izod Penzon. The FBI wanted Penzon and were running a sting called Operation Fountain Pen to nail him. They wanted me to use Penzon's ties to my relative to help take him down."

"The FBI threatened to arrest your relative if you didn't cooperate?"

"The implication was there. But there was another big problem. If I helped the FBI out, I was going to have to disappear into protective custody for a while until all the loose ends could be tied up. The FBI believed the threat was serious enough to warrant faking my death. It was the only way I could be fully protected from the bad guys and all my fans who would be searching everywhere for me. When it was safe, I would be allowed to come forward and tell the whole story."

"They were going to fake your death over the arrest of one con-man? Come on—"

"It wasn't one con-man," Elvis said. He leaned forward, his expression intense. "It was billions of dollars of drug money being laundered through offshore banks in the Caribbean and Panama. Back then the United States wanted Noriega out of power in Panama. Everything was smiles on the outside, but there was rot at the core. However, nobody wanted to risk another Bay of Pigs fiasco like in Cuba.

"The idea was to close down the independent source of Noriega's wealth by putting Penzon on ice. Penzon was the go-between for Noriega and the drug cartels. If the FBI could bust open Penzon and his criminal organization, they would have Noriega by the private parts because he would have no other source but the U.S. for the money he needed to maintain his power base."

"What does this have to do with my father?" Sheila asked.

"Gordy believed if I took the FBI's offer, I would be

put into the same witness protection program as Arceneaux. He wanted to persuade me to go undercover—to do what the FBI was asking, for me to lead him to Arceneaux."

"Abandoning your career?"

"Until everything was resolved. Then I could make a grand reappearance as an American hero and live up to the awards I had been given. It was a chance to do something for my country."

"The why did you need Gordy to push you into making the decision?"

"Because I didn't know if it was right to involve somebody else in my family—even if they were only distantly related."

"Sounds like your relative was already involved by their own choice."

"Not choice, but out of not thinking straight, and not having the God given sense to stay out of trouble. But I owed Gordy, and when he told me what he wanted me to do, I knew it was the right thing."

Cole nodded. "Let's say I buy this mumbo-jumbo...what happened—why didn't you make your comeback?"

"The answer is tied to why I have to talk to Gordy. He'll back up everything I've told you, but I have to get to him before it's too late."

"Too late for what?" Cole asked.

"To stop Arceneaux. Noriega may be out of Panama, but the FBI never did catch Izod Penzon. He and Arceneaux are scheming to give Panama back to the drug cartels."

"Why not go directly to the FBI? They were the ones who faked your death."

"Because the FBI also faked Arceneaux's death. They think they have him under control, and they won't believe Arceneaux has a plot brewing with Penzon. I have to get to Gordy."

Cole looked at Sheila. "What do you think?"

"My father is obsessed with Zachary Arceneaux because of what was done to my grandfather. As for the rest? I'm just a singer. I don't know about this international intrigue stuff."

"You're a singer?" Cole looked at her in surprise.

"Yes. I play a lot of small clubs, and I've cut a couple of demos. I also recognize your name now. I've caught your act a couple of times at the Palomino. You're good, but I never thought you'd end up on my doorstep."

Elvis interrupted in frustration. "This is important. There are people chasing me. I've got to get to your father. Do you know where he's hiding?"

Sheila looked at Elvis accessingly. Finally, she made up her mind. "Let me make a phone call, and I'll take you to him."

CHAPTER 20

COLE FELT HE WAS IN AN OLD SPY MOVIE. SHEILA REFUSED to call her father from her home phone and insisted on being taken to a phone booth several miles away. There were several perfectly good phone booths close by Sheila refused to use. Her actions made sense when she claimed if the FBI—or anybody else who wanted to capture her father—had a tap on her home phone, they could have also tapped the pay phones close to her house.

Sheila made Cole drive a circuitous route involving cruising through traffic lights as they turned red, random U-turns, and pulling over to the road shoulder to let traffic pass. Sheila took advantage of the Pink Madam's top being down to stare into the sky in case they were followed by helicopter. All the fuss seemed out of a paranoiac's nightmare, but Cole was willing to go with the flow.

For Cole the experience was akin to surfing the tube of a huge wave. He was cut off from outside, totally engulfed in the wave, having no control beyond main-

taining balance and awareness. He would never intentionally step off his surfboard while in a wave tube. The
experience was so rare there was something mystical in
riding the wave until the world of water crashed down
—either wiping out or being shot clear.

Cole knew he had to ride this caper to conclusion.
He couldn't intentionally walk away. He couldn't stop
the Pink Madam and make everyone get out before
driving away into oblivion. He had to stay tubed, within
the rare world of the experience, until it reached whatever resolution it was racing toward.

"Are we done with games?" Cole asked. He zipped
through a yellow light so close to being red it could
have been considered orange.

"I have to be careful. My father has been on the run
for a long time. He hasn't been caught because he's
cautious and smart. The FBI and others have been
trying to get to him through me for years. But his work
is too important for him to get caught because I
screwed up."

"What kind of work? I thought your father was a
fugitive," Cole said. He caught Sheila's wry smile in the
rear-view mirror.

"I'll let daddy explain once we reunite him with
Elvis. I think you'll be impressed."

"I'll believe you for now."

"You can drop us off and we can catch a cab." Sheila
was unknowingly echoing Cole's previous thoughts,
but it sounded suspiciously like teasing.

"I'll stick," Cole said.

"A thirst for glory?" Sheila asked. Again, it was as if
she were teasing him.

"Innate curiosity," Cole replied.

"How about what happens to curious cats?"

"I'll have to watch my tail, but I need to know where we're going?"

"Downtown Long Beach Marina," Sheila said. "Across from Shoreline Village."

———

"THEY'VE STOPPED MESSING AROUND," said a young FBI agent bent over the circular, greenish screen of the tracking monitor. The bright dot near the center showed the location of the Pink Madam in the grid of city streets. The high-tech transmitter attached to the bumper was working smoothly.

"They're getting on the freeway heading toward the ocean." The young agent was athletic and wore an off-the-rack navy-blue suit with black socks and brown wingtips. His shirt was bleached white and fully starched. One collar point was slightly frayed. A thin blue tie completed his official ensemble.

"At last," said Lucky Jordan. He kicked the bureau sedan into gear and took off from the curb with a squeal of black walls. "I'm finally going to get to Gordy Fontaine after all these years."

"Should we call for back up, sir?"

Jordan looked at his young companion. "Weaver, how long have you been out of Quantico?"

Weaver swallowed visibly. "A month, sir."

"Then sit down, shut up, and hang on."

———

"THERE!" Lew Sutton pointed toward the Pink Madam as it raced up a freeway on ramp. Deke Rivers swung the wheel of the beige Ford Taurus in a squealing U-turn to head in the right direction.

"How did you spot them?" Rivers was amazed.

"Eyes in the back of my head," Lew said. "They issue you a set when you promote to GS-thirteen."

When Lew and Rivers arrived at Sheila's address, they had seen the Pink Madam parked outside. Waiting patiently on a side street, the two DEA agents were in a position to start a rolling surveillance.

They were behind the conspicuous Pink Madam when Cole stopped for Sheila to make her call from the phone booth.

"We need extra teams to do this properly," Rivers said, driving past them.

"We're going to do this ourselves. Don't lose them."

The words were prophetic because it was what Rivers proceeded to do. Not once, but twice. The first time, Lew was able to get them back on track after Cole jumped a light. However, the second time, when Cole pulled over to the side of the road, Rivers had been forced to drive straight past. Lew thought they had lost the Pink Madam for good. Professional grid searching and a whole lot of luck had put them back on target.

"Lose them again," Lew told Rivers, "and you'll be staffing a one-man office in Anchorage."

———

BEHIND THE DEA AGENTS' beige Taurus, Joella's brown Chevy sputtered as she accelerated to catch up. She had seen Deke Rivers make his sharp U-turn and wondered if she'd been spotted tailing them. They didn't notice her when they drove past, so she quickly made a subtler U-turn. She was following as the Taurus zipped up the freeway on-ramp.

On the freeway, she saw the bright tail fins of the Pink Madam ahead. She figured Sutton and Rivers would be too busy tracking the Pink Madam to think about checking their own tail.

Upon her arrival at Sheila Fontaine's address, Joella had done a swift reconnaissance. She spotted Lew and Rivers on stakeout. Pleased her instincts had been right, Joella started watching the watchers, satisfied she would be there to help Cole if anything went south. She didn't know what was going on, but she was determined to find out.

As the convoy headed for the docks, Joella knew the situation would quickly be resolved when the freeway ran out at the ocean a few miles away. While driving, she took her gun from the holster on her waist. She used her knees to steer while she checked the round in the chamber and slid the magazine out. When she saw the magazine was full, she pushed it back into the gun butt. She prayed the lucky star Cole had been born under was bright enough to shine on both of them.

Because the docks and piers around the Long Beach harbor supported several large public attractions, the area was clean. The Queen Mary had been given a permanent dock along one of the piers, drawing thousands of visitors a year. Across the street from the Queen Mary, Howard Hughes' Spruce Goose was on display. Around the two attractions, Shoreline Village shops sprouted like barnacles on a ship's hull. There were harbor tours, restaurants, and berths for the Catalina Island ferries.

Cole turned the Pink Madam down Shoreline Drive toward the marina entrance. Near where the Los Angeles River flowed into the Pacific Ocean, Cole could see the impressive lines of the Queen Mary. The ship was festooned with flags and bunting for a special tourist promotion. Cole turned into the marina lot, parking in a conveniently open spot near the pedestrian entrance. He hopped over the driver's door while Elvis held open the passenger door for Sheila.

The marina was packed with hundreds of yachts of various sizes and classes. Many smaller commercial boats were housed along floating slips or moored to buoys. The salt air was intensified by the smell of fish and seaweed. Soft white clouds crept lazily across the blue sky, doing little to filter out the blaze of the sun.

Sheila walked behind Cole and Elvis, as if she expected them to know where to go.

Cole turned to her. "Where now?"

"Uncle El knows," she replied. "He's been aboard *Gator Bait* many times."

Cole looked at Elvis. Elvis looked down and shuffled his feet. "Ah—it's been a long time. I don't rightly remember where she's tied up."

"You don't remember the *Gator Bait*?" Sheila asked. Amazement filled her voice.

"Course I do," said Elvis confidently. "But I'm a little weak on where she's docked."

There was a pause. Everyone stared at each other. The tension level rose perceptibly.

"My father never had a boat called the *Gator Bait*," Sheila said calmly.

"What is going on?" Cole looked from Elvis to Sheila. Neither answered.

If Cole had been a cartoon figure a light bulb would have appeared over his head. "You're not Elvis," he said turning back to the man with whom he had escaped from the Elysian sanitarium.

There was a gun in the phony Elvis' hand. Cole had never thought to search him.

"Hell, son, hasn't anybody ever told you? Elvis is dead."

CHAPTER 21

COLE COULDN'T BELIEVE THERE WERE NO WITNESSES WHO could see what was happening. Sheila, however, had somehow maneuvered the trio down a secluded dock sheltered on either side by large yachts.

The business end of the gun in the phony Elvis' hand pointed into the space between Cole and Sheila. It was an ominous looking blue steel automatic.

"Who are you?" Cole asked.

"You can call me Elvis if you want."

"I've smeared his name enough already." Looking with a more objective eye, Cole couldn't believe he'd been sucked into believing the guy was Elvis. He was ashamed of his own gullibility. *It's amazing how we believe what we want to believe*, Cole thought with chagrin.

"Then call me Rex. It doesn't much matter since we ain't going to be together much longer." The soft Elvis accent had broadened into a harsher twang. Rex moved the barrel of the gun toward Sheila. "Where is your father's boat?"

Sheila laughed.

"I'll shoot him." Rex slid the gun over to point directly at Cole.

"Shoot him," Sheila said. "My father means more to me than he does."

Cole looked shocked. "Wait a second." He could understand Sheila's sentiment. His life might not be important to her, but it sure was to him. "Can we talk about this?"

"You have five seconds to tell me which boat your father is on," Rex said to Sheila. "If you don't, I'll put a bullet in good ol' Cole's kneecap, which will ruin his leg shaking Elvis career. After another five seconds, I'll put a bullet in his groin, and then his stomach, and on up until I put one between his eyes. It ain't gonna be pretty."

Sheila looked at Cole.

Cole looked at Rex.

"One...two..." Rex said with a smile. He seemed to be enjoying himself.

"He isn't kidding," Cole said. He put a big hint of desperation in his voice. Internally he was getting ready to launch himself at Rex. He wasn't going to go down without a fight.

"Three...four..."

Rex's finger began to tighten on the trigger.

Cole dove forward as a shot pierced the quiet of the afternoon. He felt a burning streak lance down his spine as he shoulder rolled and crashed into Rex's feet, knocking him down like a bowling pin.

Rex swung the butt of his automatic, catching Cole a glancing blow across the temple.

Cole's vision blurred. He felt himself beginning to gray out, but he continued to wrestle with Rex, fighting for control of Rex's gun hand.

"Run," he yelled toward Sheila.

Then there was a pounding of feet, and Cole felt Rex stop struggling.

"One move, slimeball, and you'll be decorating the dock."

Cole didn't know if the voice was talking to him or to Rex. He shook his head to clear it, and then felt hands easing him away from Rex. They were nice hands. Gentle hands. They belonged to Sheila Fontaine.

"Are you all right?" she asked with true concern.

"I think so." Cole's vision began to clear. Somebody had a revolver squarely between Rex's eyes. Rex's automatic was lying on the dock. The stranger kicked it into the water.

Sheila held Cole's arm. "Cole, I want you to meet my father...Gordon Fontaine."

"Howdy," Gordy said, busy slipping plastic handcuffs around Rex's hands.

"Don't think I'm not grateful," Cole said. "But didn't you cut things a bit close."

Gordy looked at Cole with a big grin. "You're young and healthy. You'll recover. Anyway, I had to know for sure whose side you're on."

"What are you talking about?"

"I had to know if you were part of this put up caper to catch me, or if you were truly an innocent bystander."

"Gee, thanks," Cole said, with quiet sarcasm.

Sheila lifted the back of Cole's shirt. The burning sensation intensified as the fabric pulled away from the wound. "Nasty furrow," she said, observing the damage caused by Rex's bullet. "You're bleeding, but it's more show than go."

"Thank you, nurse." Cole jerked away from Sheila, pulling his shirt back down. "Will somebody please tell me what's going on?"

Running feet could be heard coming down the dock toward them. Cole and Sheila turned around.

"FBI," shouted Ned Weaver, the young agent who had been tracking the Pink Madam with Lucky Jordan. "Put up your hands!" Weaver had his 9mm extended in the Bureau approved two handed, bent knee shooting position. The problem was the gun wasn't particularly aimed at a specific target.

Lucky Jordan rushed forward and pushed his subordinate off the edge of the dock and into the murky waters. Without hesitating, he used his own 9mm to open fire at Gordy.

Cole reacted immediately. He tackled Sheila, knocking her to the rough wood surface of the dock, rolling over and over until they reached the cover of a tied-up yacht.

Gordy was next to them. He poked his head around the prow of the boat and capped off a round in the direction of Lucky Jordan.

"That's the FBI you're shooting at," Cole yelled.

"Like hell," said Gordy. "Lucky Jordan is bent like a corkscrew. If this was a real FBI operation, there'd be enough brown wingtips on the dock to open a shoe store."

———

WHEN GORDY FIRED BACK at him, Lucky Jordan cursed his impatience at not waiting until he'd had a clear shot. He needed Gordy out of circulation permanently if he was ever going to be safe, and he didn't need any witnesses knowing how it happened. It was why he pushed Weaver into the water.

If his actions were ever questioned, Lucky would say he was pushing Weaver out of the line of fire. Nobody would question him as long as he had the body of Gordy Fontaine as a peace offering. Fontaine was a wanted felon—wanted for shooting a federal agent. Nobody was going to look closely if Lucky brought Gordy in feet first.

Lucky was in too deep with too much to lose. He had to kill Fontaine.

"Jordan...put down your gun." A new voice came from the entrance to the dock. "DEA," Lew Sutton said when he saw Lucky stick his head above a gear locker.

Having followed Cole and company to the marina, Lew and Deke Rivers had seen the situation develop. When the bullets started to fly, the DEA agents took cover behind two wooden stanchions along the edge of the dock.

Deke was confused by the whole situation. But he had enough sense to keep his mouth shut and do what Lew told him. It was obvious Lew knew far more about the situation than he'd explained.

"Screw you," Lucky said.

"You can't kill everybody here," Lew said. "Surrender now."

"You tell him, Lew," Gordy called out.

"Save it, Gordy," Lew called back. "It's time for you to come in out of the cold."

"Not yet. I've got one more chance at Arceneaux, and I'm not going to blow it this time."

"No way," Lew yelled back. "The agency has given you a lot of rope on this. Anymore and you're going to hang yourself. We've got Jordan. Let us take it from here."

"It's my neck, Lew," Gordy yelled. "I'll keep it stuck out."

Lucky Jordan was scared and angry. He had badly mishandled the situation. It had been a brilliant plan to capture Gordy, but it was falling apart. He might still be able to salvage something, if only his freedom. He checked the extra magazines of ammunition attached to his gun belt, then fired two rounds in the direction of Lew Sutton and another round toward Gordy.

A bullet whined off the prow of the boat protecting Gordy, Cole, and Sheila. Gordy could see Rex—the phony Elvis—was trying to make himself invisible behind a wooden stanchion.

"Let's get out of here," Gordy said to Cole and Sheila.

"What do you have in mind?" Cole asked.

"Can you swim?" Gordy asked.

"Does a wet hound dog stink?" Cole replied.

"Cute," said Sheila.

Cole smiled at her. "What me, or the comment?"

"Shut it," Gordy said. "On three, I'll lay down covering fire. Sheila, you and your friend run for the end of the dock and then keep going."

"Keep going?" Cole asked.

"Trust me," Gordy said. "Help will be waiting."

"Will it be who I think?" Sheila asked as she touched Cole's arm as if to reassure him.

"In the flesh," Gordy replied with a smile.

"No way he'd agree to be left out."

"Who wouldn't agree?" Cole asked. Things were getting murky again.

"Trust us," Sheila and Gordy said in unison.

Cole sighed. "You can't get off a roller coaster before the end."

CHAPTER 22

JOELLA BAILED OUT OF HER CAR AS THE FIRST SOUNDS OF gunfire rang out. Quickly, she reached back in and grabbed the radio microphone. Giving her location, she requested back-up from the Long Beach Police. She was out of the sheriff's jurisdiction, but she didn't care. Cole was in trouble, and she wasn't going to let city borders stop her from getting involved. Throwing the mic back in the car, she drew her weapon and ran toward the action.

———

NED WEAVER TOLD Lucky Jordan he'd only been out of the FBI academy for a short time. It had been a lie. Weaver was the Bureau's top undercover agent. His youthful looks were his greatest weapon, causing every villain he pursued to underestimate him.

For five years, Weaver had worked for the Bureau's Internal Affairs Unit. His job was to ferret out the rare rat who slipped through the Bureau's tough screening process, or who rotted in positions of trust. Rats like Lucky Jordan.

For months, Weaver had been working an operation to regain control over drug dealer Zachary Arceneaux. Using the witness protection program as a cover, Arceneaux had ditched his rivals then ditched the Bureau's watchdogs. The pursuit of Arceneaux had led the Bureau to a mole in their own backyard—Lucky Jordan. Weaver had been brought in to nail him.

Pulling his muscled body up a mooring rope, Weaver's was determined to take Jordan down. It was time to get to the bottom of everything involving Arceneaux—and now Elvis Presley. Weaver believed Elvis was dead, but stranger things had happened. If the Cajun Gator Zachary Arceneaux could still be alive and kicking up hell, why couldn't Elvis?

———

LEW SUTTON SAW Ned Weaver stalking Lucky Jordan's blind side. Lew sensed what was happening even without knowing the exact circumstances. It was clear Weaver was going to take Jordan out of circulation.

Lew wanted to help the young agent, but before he could start a distraction, a series of shots sang out from Gordy's hiding place. Splinters of wood flew from the decking and bullets smacked into the gear locker where Lucky Jordan had taken cover.

Taking a quick peak, Lew saw Cole and Sheila running. At the end of the dock, they launched into the water in beautifully stretched racing dives. Behind them, Gordy continued to lay down covering fire.

Gordy was running backward with an awkward gait until he also disappeared off the end of the dock, but with a cannon ball splash.

There was the roar of a powerful engine starting.

"Stay down and hug your ass," Lew yelled at Deke. "Gordy's off the rails again."

LUCKY JORDAN HAD DUCKED down to take cover from Gordy's shots. When he heard a creak of old planking behind him, he whirled to confront Ned Weaver. The agent was poised to throw himself at Lucky, but he hesitated for a split second startled by Lucky turning toward him. The hesitation cost him dearly.

Instinctively, Lucky brought his gun around and fired, catching Weaver in the fleshy part of his left thigh. Weaver crashed to the deck screaming and clutching at his leg.

Lucky saw Deke Rivers and Lew Sutton break cover and sprint toward him.

"Give it up, Jordan," Ned Weaver said from his prostrate position. Pain scrunched up his handsome features. "If you run now, you'll be a bigger rogue than Gordy Fontaine."

"But I'll have an advantage," Lucky said. "Zachary Arceneaux." He pointed his gun at Ned and pulled the trigger again.

WHEN LEW SUTTON jumped for the deck where Lucky

Jordan was making his stand, Joella ran onto the dock. Deke Rivers was behind Lew. He didn't realize Joella was there until she shoved him into the water.

"Freeze!" she yelled at Lew.

Lew looked at her. "You don't know what you're doing."

Joella knew Lew was right, but she also knew she recognized Lucky Jordan. She didn't like Jordan, but she knew he was an FBI agent from dealing with him at the LA office. Lew and Deke could be anybody. She hadn't checked the credentials they flashed at her in the station. Now they were attacking an FBI agent.

Lucky Jordan snapped a shot at her. There was a tug at the sleeve of her blouse. She dropped to one knee, taking cover beside the boat. There was the sound of two more shots and then Lew jumped down beside her.

"This isn't good," she said.

"You don't know the half of it," Lew told her.

There was silence above them. Finally, Lew snuck a look, but he couldn't see Lucky Jordan anywhere. He searched as Joella helped Deke Rivers out of the water. Lew approached the body of Ned Weaver. He felt for a pulse. He found one, but it was weak.

There was a wail of sirens in the distance.

Lucky Jordan had vanished.

———

COLE'S HEAD broke the surface of the murky water. He gasped for breath. Sheila surfaced next to him and grinned. She was as at home in the water as a mermaid.

There was the roar of an engine and the prow of a metallic purple cigarette boat slid beside them before reversing its engine. A ladder splashed over the side. Cole sent Sheila up ahead of him. The head of Gordy Fontaine appeared in the water, and Cole helped him up the ladder as well.

When it was his turn, Cole began to pull himself up then found a strong sunburnt arm reaching out to haul him into the boat. He tumbled over the side. Gordy, who was now at the controls, slammed the throttle forward, pointing the boat for the marina exit. They had to get clear before the Harbor Police or the Coast Guard could be notified.

Cole struggled to catch his breath. Finally, he hauled himself into a sitting position. Sheila was propped against some boat cushions.

"How you doing?" asked the voice belonging to the man with the sunburnt arm.

"I'm okay, I think," said Cole. He took his first good look at the man. He was close to sixty with silver hair getting a little thin on top. He wore wraparound sunglasses nestled on high cheek bones above pouting lips and a chiseled chin. The man was slim but made of wiry muscles. Cole caught a glimpse of the man's profile against the sun.

"Holy cow," said Cole softly.

The man extended his hand. "I'm Elvis Presley."

PART III

WILL THE REAL KING PLEASE STAND UP

CHAPTER 23

THE CABIN AREA OF THE YACHT *HEARTBREAK HOTEL* WAS spacious and warm. Hand rubbed teak paneled the walls and comfortable couches lined the companionway.

"What do you think?" Gordy asked with a proprietary air.

Bewildered by the day's events, Cole looked at his surroundings. "Impressive," he said.

The speedboat ride had been taken at a blistering pace. Gordy had steered them through the marina entrance and out toward the open seas with competent ease. Conversation had been impossible during the trip, which had lasted twenty-five minutes before the outline of a fifty-foot yacht appeared in front of them.

As they came closer, Cole saw the name *Heartbreak Hotel* painted on the transom in foot high script. In smaller lettering below the name was its home port —*Santa Barbara*.

There was a tough-looking young man with a spiky crop of straw colored hair on the deck. When he saw the speed boat approaching, he threw several bumpers over the side of the yacht for protection.

When the two boats snugged together, he helped everyone aboard, except for Gordy. The young man went over the side and landed cat-like on the deck of the speed boat. Gordy handed over the controls then hauled himself up onto the *Heartbreak Hotel* with Cole's help.

Without waiting around for introductions or instructions, the straw-haired young man pushed clear of the larger yacht and hit the speed boat's throttles. He made a wide, wake-spitting turn and raced off in the direction of land.

Gordy and the others acted as if this was an everyday occurrence. Cole quietly bided his time while Gordy launched into a discourse on the yacht's specifications. He was a proud father talking about his child's achievements. "She's got a flat bottom with twin rudders and a winged keel. The hull is steel, and at fifty-feet, she's still manageable for two people. There's a fixed wheel house over a central cockpit and two identical 29-horsepower Perkins Perama diesels for motoring in calm weather."

"Enough," Cole said loudly.

"Enough?" Gordy stopped in full verbal flow, confused by Cole's statement

"Yeah. Enough," Cole said. The flesh wound caused by the bullet from Rex's gun, had stopped bleeding after being submerged in the cold water of the marina. But it still hurt like crazy whenever he moved.

"I have been locked up in a mental institution, chased, threatened, used for target practice, deceived, battered, and half drowned in a wild goose chase over Elvis still being alive," Cole said. "I've tried being a good guy, tried to do the right thing with the options I've been given, but enough is enough. I don't want a tour of your freaking boat. I want answers, and I want them right now."

Gordy assessed Cole then sat on the nearest couch. "Are you really in a position to demand answers?"

"I've earned them," Cole said.

"He might be able to help create the diversion you need when Arceneaux's train comes in." Sheila was speaking to her father, but her eyes were on Cole.

Gordy gave his daughter a quick look. "How so?"

"He's an Elvis impersonator. I'm sure he's friends with a lot of other Elvis impersonators."

Cole didn't get it, but Gordy immediately saw what Sheila had in mind. "And a haystack is the best place to hide a piece of straw. I like it. It has irony."

Cole took a seat on the couch next to Gordy. He was an easy-going personality—too easy going according to his sister—but he wasn't stupid, and he was tiring of being treated as if he were.

Cole spoke. His voice was calm, but his tone was no nonsense. "If this is Elvis Presley," he indicated the man from the speed boat, who Sheila had introduced as the King, "then who did we leave handcuffed at the marina?"

The King himself answered. "He's a second-rate thug out of Detroit named Rex Kincaid. He answers to a first-rate thug named Zachary Arceneaux, who is a big gator in a little pond. Rex Kincaid was a plant. Part of a plan to get Sheila to betray Gordy's whereabouts. You happened to get sucked into the whole deal."

"Are you really Elvis Aron Presley?" Cole interrupted. "How can I be sure you're not another impersonator?"

Elvis grinned. "Because it makes no difference to me if you think I'm Elvis or not. Frankly, it's far better if you don't believe I'm Elvis."

Cole switched his gaze to Gordy.

"I can see you is a might confused," Gordy said in a mock redneck accent. "Let me shine some light."

Cole stayed silent.

"First, tell me what kind of tale Rex Kincaid spun you."

Cole told his story from receiving the April Fool's Day phone call. Elvis brought out fresh brewed coffee and a stack of sandwiches from the galley. Sheila fetched a first aid kit and checked Cole's injury. He winced under her ministrations, breaking the flow of his story, but he told it by the time she was done.

Gordy handed Cole a fresh t-shirt as he mulled over the story. "It's not a bad scam," he said eventually. "I can see how somebody gullible could be taken in if you didn't know all the inside information."

"I wasn't gullible," Cole bristled slightly. "I didn't know what to believe, but it was intriguing enough I wanted to see where it ended up."

"I wasn't putting you down," Gordy said. "I was getting the situation in perspective."

"Tell me the real story and see if I find it more believable."

Gordy paused, looking for a place to start, but Elvis beat him to it.

"Some of what Kincaid told you is true," Elvis said, his voice soft. "When Gordy went on the run, he came to me because he knew I was looking for a way out. My fans have always been loyal, but other factors in my life weren't going well. I wasn't giving value for money anymore. I loved being on stage, but it had become all hype and no substance. I still had my voice—hell, I was singing some of the best songs I'd ever done—but there wasn't much else. My family was apart from me, Momma was dead, and Daddy..." Elvis trailed off and shrugged. "He was being used as much as I was but could never see it."

Cole kept staring at the man who claimed to be Elvis. He didn't look as much like Elvis as Rex Kincaid had, but Rex Kincaid looked more like the Elvis of sixteen years prior. This Elvis looked like an Elvis who, without makeup and stage trimmings, had not aged well. From certain angles there was still a sharp resemblance. And there was the speaking voice. It was soft and hesitant, as if the speaker was shy, choosing his words with care, picking them out one by one before speaking them. Cole was itching to get hold of a guitar or a piano. Maybe a little jam session could clear up the mystery. But first, he wanted more information.

"What about this Operation Fountain Pen caper?" he asked.

Gordy chuckled. "That was the real deal all right. It certainly served our purposes."

"Which were?"

"To get Elvis into the witness protection program."

Gordy sat forward on the edge of the couch. "Kincaid told you about my obsession with Zachary Arceneaux?"

"But he never explained why you were so fired up to catch this guy. Wasn't he just another drug dealer?"

"Man, how times have changed," said Elvis from the other side of the cabin. "So much for the war on drugs. Sixteen years ago, nobody would have said *just another drug dealer*. Sixteen years ago, major drug dealers were shocking monsters."

"They're not shocking any more. But they are monsters," Cole interrupted. "So, what? It doesn't explain the obsession."

"Zachary Arceneaux killed my grandfather," Sheila supplied. "And he's tried to kill my father numerous times, and he's trying again."

CHAPTER 24

"Is this true?" Cole looked hard at Gordy.

"Zachary Arceneaux fed my father inch by inch to the gators, listening to his screams as those freaking reptiles ate my father from the toes up." Gordy's voice was full of feeling. It was a second before he could continue. "After sixteen years, we're getting close to catching up with Arceneaux again." With a wave, Gordy encompassed Elvis, himself, and his daughter. "He is feeling the heat. This mess is a complicated effort on the part of a corrupt FBI agent named Lucky Jordan—who is under Arceneaux's control—to either kill me or get me arrested."

"How did this Lucky Jordan know about me?" Cole asked.

Gordy shrugged. "I don't think he did. He was trying to flush me out by using Rex Kincaid to get to Sheila. When you ended up getting involved it added some credibility to the scheme—an added stimulus to make Sheila reveal my whereabouts."

"If Sheila knew Elvis was alive, why did she play along?"

"To try and turn the tables on Jordan. It was what the phone call she made on the way to the marina was about. We were the center of a lot of attention down at the marina. Attention Kincaid and Jordan are going to have big trouble explaining. Hopefully Jordan will be exposed as the bottom feeding scum he is, or be kept so busy, he'll be worthless to Arceneaux. Either way, it will peel away another layer of Arceneaux's protection. I'm sorry you were put into danger, but there's far more at stake than you know."

There was nothing Cole could say, so he kept his mouth shut.

After a few beats to get his effect across, Gordy continued. "My old DEA partner, Lew Sutton—he was one of those jokers messing with us over at the marina."

"The one who was shooting at us?"

"Nah," Gordy shook his head. "That was Lucky Jordan. I'll get back to him in a minute. Sixteen years ago, Lew and I finally pieced together enough evidence to put Arceneaux away for life."

"What happened?" Cole urged the pace.

"The freaking FBI pulled the rug out from under us. Arceneaux and I had been dancing the two-step for so long he couldn't stand the thought of me taking him down."

"So, he ran to the FBI and turned state's evidence," Cole said, catching on.

Gordy gave a cynical smile. "The FBI used Arceneaux's information to put away a raft of low and mid-level drug dealers, but Arceneaux danced them around the people in his own organization. The FBI then faked Arceneaux's death and put him in the Witness Protection Program.

"He didn't stay there," Cole said.

"Not a chance," this came from Elvis. "I know all about ego, and Arceneaux makes me look shy. He's a megalomaniac. As soon as he established himself in the program, he began filling all the openings his testimony had caused in the drug trade with his own people. His organization continued as if there had never been a glitch."

"Didn't the FBI keep track of him?"

Gordy spoke. "Here's where Lucky Jordan comes in again. He was assigned as Arceneaux's case agent. While they can't see past their wing-tips sometimes, the FBI deserves their reputation. But they aren't immune to bad apples."

"Lucky Jordan was a sour apple?" Cole asked.

"Not at first," Gordy said. "But he hated me. He really believed I shot him. By teaming up with Arceneaux, he thought he could control the situation and get a crack at capturing me. When he realized he was in too deep with Arceneaux, he was bought and paid for."

"But if you had given yourself up, you could have proven yourself innocent?"

Gordy shook his head. "I'd been pushing too hard. The DEA was a fledgling organization compared to the FBI. I would have been handed up as a scapegoat to keep the Witness Protection Program secure. There were also other reasons."

"And they were?"

"I felt the system wasn't working. If Arceneaux was able to manipulate it, then there was something inherently wrong. Plus, after I established myself in the underground, new possibilities opened up. I was no longer confined by the regulations of an organization. I would've had no chance to get Arceneaux following the rules."

"You turned vigilante."

"If you want to stick a label on it," Gordy said. "But I'm finally getting to where I was sixteen years ago."

"Piling up enough evidence to put Arceneaux out of business?"

"For good this time."

"Give me more on how Elvis fits in," Cole said. "Sometimes I've believed as many as six impossible things before breakfast."

Sheila chuckled. "I love that book."

Elvis and Gordy looked at her. "What book?"

"The line about believing six impossible things before breakfast, it's from *Alice In Wonderland*."

"I'll admit he line wasn't original," Cole said. "But I feel I've fallen down the rabbit hole and this is the tea party scene."

As if on cue, Elvis poured more coffee into everyone's cups and then sat back. "Gordy explained the whole Arceneaux situation to me. He knew the FBI was asking me to help them with the Operation Fountain Pen deal with Daddy stuck in the middle. Gordy also knew I was looking for a way to get free of my world. I was forty-two and still trying to rock-n'-roll. Maybe Sinatra looks good singing *My Way* in his seventies but couldn't be doing *Hound Dog* and *Blue Suede Shoes* dancing around with a walker. I wanted more out of life than singing songs. There were death threats against my family, and other terrorist threats. The music didn't count for much by comparison."

"How could you think your music was unimportant?" Cole asked emphatically. "Your influence meant more to music and people than—I don't know—man going to the moon, or any other scientific breakthrough of the last forty years." Cole waved his arms around excitedly.

Elvis held up his hand in a halting motion. "I'm saying, sometimes the music don't accomplish much."

Cole moved to the edge of his seat. "We can't all find a cure for cancer or AIDS. You have to do the best with the talents God gives you. Your voice, your style...man, you were the best there was. Still are!"

"Thank you very much, but at the time I wasn't thinking or feeling important. I'd always tried to do as much as I could to help law enforcement, but this Operation Fountain Pen caper was asking me to give up my career and go into the Witness Protection Program for a while. The people who were running the business side of things for me didn't like the idea. We were worth about ten million, but it was all on paper. The cash flow was tight, and an awful lot of people had quickly become accustomed to the lifestyle we were leading."

"Wasn't Operation Fountain Pen designed to take out con-man named Izod Penzon scamming Panamanian banks?" Cole asked. "Kincaid told me about it."

"Penzon involved Daddy in his schemes then left him to face the consequences. The FBI wanted to use Daddy to take down Penzon. If it had gone right, they would have had tighter control over Noriega in Panama."

"How does Zachary Arceneaux fit in?"

"Arceneaux had major drug ties to Penzon, Noriega, and Panama." Gordy had entered back into the conversation. "He remains connected to them, but at the time, I only wanted to get Elvis into the Witness Protection Program. From inside the program, he could try to find where Arceneaux had gone."

"I owed Gordy," Elvis said. The smile he gave a smile Gordy had Elvis written all over it—half devil, half innocent, and completely disarming. "It went real well at first. The FBI fully bought into my offer of cooperation. But then things started to come apart with Operation Fountain Pen. We went after Penzon with a vengeance, but he was too smooth. A couple of small fish were caught in the net, but the big one got away."

"We found out later," Gordy said, "Arceneaux got word to Penzon the FBI was trying to rope him in."

"From inside the Witness Protection Program?"

"Don't be surprised. Remember, Lucky Jordan was in Arceneaux's pocket. Arceneaux was running the show right from the start."

Cole shook his head in amazement.

"I was stuck," Elvis said. "My death had been faked—something else the FBI couldn't quite do right since there was a witness who saw me being helicoptered away from Graceland several hours after I was supposed to be dead."

"They covered it up pretty well," Gordy put in. "The voice of that one man was lost in the outcry over Elvis' death."

"I couldn't believe the fuss," said Elvis. "But the biggest shock was when it turned out I was worth more dead than alive. The same business people, who hadn't wanted me to help the FBI, now didn't want me to come back. The estate was minting money—cash flow problems had disappeared."

"You stayed dead because of money?"

"Don't be rude," Gordy said. "Elvis stayed dead because he'd agreed to do a job—to expose Zachary Arceneaux and put him behind bars. Izod Penzon was carrying a grudge against Elvis for trying to set him up. He swore to put Elvis in the grave everybody thought he was already in."

"I made some mistakes looking for Arceneaux," Elvis admitted. "I might be a hell of a singer, but I wasn't much of an undercover agent."

"Maybe not then," Gordy said. Cole caught the two men exchanging a glance.

"Cutting to the chase," Elvis said. "Arceneaux found out I was working for Gordy and everything went sideways."

Gordy stood up. He started to pace, as if there was too much energy building up inside him. "Unlike what most people think, the Witness Protection Program is not run by the government. While each person in the program has a federal control agent from the organization who put them under, a private sector contractor called Elysian controls the everyday workings of the program."

"Let me guess," Cole said. "Elvis' control agent was Lucky Jordan. The same FBI agent who was Arceneaux's control, and who was under Arceneaux's thumb."

"A sweet deal, huh?" Gordy said.

"But I can see how it would put Elvis on a knife edge," Cole said. "If he couldn't trust his control, he'd be an easy target."

"If he was killed, the people who ran the program would cover it up," Gordy agreed. "They couldn't risk being exposed for not being able to keep assets safe. Otherwise, it would be impossible to convince anyone it was safe to testify and go into the program."

"What did you do?"

"It took a couple of years for this to transpire. Elvis and I remained in contact through a system we's set up ahead of time. When everything went to hell, I went in and got him out," Gordy said.

"You snatched him from the Witness Protection Program?"

"Was there another choice?"

"But weren't you on the run?"

"The whole federal law enforcement community wasn't trying to track me down. I didn't even make the FBI's Ten Most Wanted list. There weren't all these cops and robbers' reenactment shows they have now. I'd been undercover enough times with the DEA to have many contacts in the fugitive underground. Things weren't bad, except I couldn't spend much time with Sheila." Gordy reached out and took his daughter's hand.

"What we're doing now, Daddy, makes up for those times you couldn't be there."

Cole saw his chance to hone in on loose ends bothering him. "What are you doing now—chasing Arceneaux?"

Elvis chuckled. "And a whole lot more."

"Arceneaux is still an issue," Gordy said. "But I found something far more important."

"Important enough to convince me I did the right thing—staying to help Gordy instead of going back to sing songs for a few more years. What we're doing now is going to make a difference for generations."

Cole looked at the two men expectantly. "I'm hooked. What is this cause?"

Gordy looked at his watch. "We've got to hurry if you're going to make the pickup point, El." Gordy stood and moved toward the wheel house. "Help us get the anchor up," he said to Cole. "If you want the whole story, you're going to have to come along for the ride."

CHAPTER 25

RUNNING THROUGH THE SHADOWS OF THE IMPOSING, ART deco train platforms of Union Station is the oldest thoroughfare in Los Angeles. Olvera Street teems with tourists coming to sample the colorful wares of the Hispanic culture. The area had once been the realm of Chinese immigrants, but time changes all things.

Dressed in traditional costume, performers show off their skills at the Mexican hat dance or the calypso, and Mariachis stroll among the crowds playing songs from past generations encouraging the flow of tourist dollars. Enterprising street hawks turn meat of suspect origin on the grills of temporary food stands, which would send any God-fearing Health Department inspector into shock.

Brightly colored piñatas, huge papier-mâché flowers, and paper lanterns hang from crisscrossed wires above head level. Adding more color and atmosphere are hideous masks of the dead, ornate and gaudy religious paraphernalia, carved effigies of strange animals painted with iridescent colors, and the beautiful weaves of Mexican blankets. Behind the bright colors, however, is the squalor and desperation of a community hanging on to its existence by the sharp edge of a knife.

None of this interested Zachary Arceneaux as his limousine parked in front of the austere facade of the Sanctuary Church of the Black Madonna. What did interest him was the generation prior to the Hispanic invasion—the era when Olvera Street had been home to L.A.'s Chinatown.

It had been a time when opium and gambling dens had to be protected not only from police raids, but also from the vengeance of competing tongs. It had been a time of crooked cops, protection rackets, illegal immigration, and rampant criminality—all things in which Zachary Arceneaux reveled.

Just short of his sixty-fifth birthday, Arceneaux remained a vibrant and virile man. The piercing blue eyes in the dark face had lost none of their ability to psychologically slice through anyone pinned by his gaze. His dark hair was full—worn long to the point of vanity. A slender leather thong secured the hair in a ponytail, which draped down the back of his Armani suit jacket.

With deliberate movements, Arceneaux exited the limo when his bodyguard opened the rear door. Uncurling his tall, slim frame, he checked the drape of his suit before marching to the door of the church and entered without hesitation.

Inside, as his eyes adjusted to the dim light, a huge black Madonna floated above the flickering candles in front of the altar. The effigy appeared to be reaching out to embrace him. It made Arceneaux smile. He always enjoyed the effect. It was as if he had fooled God. If the Madonna held out her arms for him, then all was still right with his world.

There were several parishioners sitting among the pews. Their clothes were of peasant materials, their prayers in the language of their native countries far away. The Madonna above the altar riveted their attention as rosaries slipped through worn fingers. No one turned to acknowledge Arceneaux's arrival.

With brisk movements, he strode down the center aisle between the pews. When he reached the altar, he set flame to a long taper and touched it to a candle nestled in a red glass holder. He snuffed the taper out with the tips of his fingers, lingering over the action and enjoyed the small pain.

After a pause, he moved to the left of the altar and allowed his bodyguard to open the door to the priest's vestry. Inside a slim man, dressed traditionally in black garb and white collar, angrily jumped out of a hard-back chair and approached Arceneaux. He was young with a fanatic's eyes and a clear cause in his heart. The bodyguard moved to intercept the rush, but Arceneaux held him at bay with a casual movement of his left hand.

"Mr. Arceneaux," the priest's voice was full of barely repressed anger, "I will not have you use this church in a manner our Heavenly Father would not approve."

Arceneaux stood casually, striking a relaxed attitude, as the young priest stopped in front of him with a visible quiver. "What are you talking about, Father Romero?" he asked.

"Your men. Two of them, built like this one," he

indicated the bodyguard with a nod of his head, "brought a man into the church obviously against his will. They marched him down the center of the aisle, past the altar, and down through the entrance to the tombs."

"Ahh, yes, the tombs," Arceneaux nodded his head.

"Is that all you have to say?"

"What do you want me to say?"

"Mr. Arceneaux," the young priest sputtered as he fought for words, "You cannot use this church as a prison. The people who come here to seek sanctuary are frightened by such men as you employ. They come from lands where people disappear without a trace. When they see a man dragged through the church and down the stairs, they become frightened. They lose faith in what we are trying to do for them. We appreciate everything you do for us, but this is a house of God. You can not violate its sanctity." Father Romero had become puffed up with self-importance as he spoke, gaining assurance from Arceneaux's casual demeanor.

Arceneaux's hand flashed out with the speed of a striking snake and snatched a handful of hair at the back of Father Romero's neck. The priest grunted as Arceneaux violently pulled his head back, forcing the priest to his knees in one swift movement.

"You dare to tell me what I can and can't do?" Arceneaux's voice had dropped several octaves. Foam spittle appeared at the corners of his mouth as he spoke, his face leaning forward into the priest's. "Your precious church survives by my grace. My money keeps the poor box filled. My money keeps food in the bellies of those ignorant and illegal souls you protect?"

Arceneaux twisted the handful of hair tighter as the priest tried to speak. "Shut up, cretin!" Arceneaux spat the order. "Because of me, your trainload of orphans will arrive safely. Never forget I restored the old Chinatown catacombs under this church. You use them by my blessing alone. If you question me again, you will be disappeared. Your deal is not with God or the devil, it is with me—right here and now. I am far worse than either of those others. Understand?"

"Yes. Yes." The words were a painful whisper.

"Go back to ministering to your pitiful flock and stay out of my business." Arceneaux released his grip with a jerk. Father Romero fell to the floor.

Outside the vestry, Arceneaux moved behind the altar. His bodyguard rolled away a large rug to expose the hidden trapdoor beneath. Under the trapdoor concrete steps lead down to the catacombs. Arceneaux reflected his encounter with Father Romero had been a good warm-up for what was to come.

CHAPTER 26

Lucky Jordan was sweating. He didn't feel lucky. He didn't think too much of the underground accommodations where he'd been brought to meet with Arceneaux. He was trying to convince himself he was going to get out of the catacombs alive. He hadn't even known the tunnels existed until a few hours earlier when Arceneaux's goons had frog marched him through the church and down the trap door opening. He ardently wished he didn't know about their existence.

Lucky knew he'd screwed himself at the marina. Everything had gone wrong, except for the sheriff broad showing up and mistakenly giving him the opportunity to escape. He'd managed to swim back to dry land without being seen. Knowing he couldn't go back for his bureau car, he had no compunction about hot wiring a beat-up red Honda parked unattended on a side street.

For a while he'd driven around aimlessly. Ned Weaver had scared him half to death. He'd had no idea the DEA was running an operation on him. He cursed himself for indulging in the type of overconfidence he knew brought most criminals to justice. When criminals are sure they're untouchable is when they make the mistakes leading to permanent reservations at the Gray Bar Hotel.

There had been too many witnesses at the marina for him to go back to the bureau. But he wouldn't get far on the lam without Arceneaux's help. He didn't have any choice, but to put his head into Arceneaux's mouth.

Pulling the stolen car over next to a gas station pay phone, Lucky dialed the contact number he'd been given. When the line was answered, he asked to speak to Arceneaux.

"Not possible," a disembodied voice had told him.

When Lucky insisted it was an emergency, he was put on hold. When the voice returned, it told Lucky to wait where he was, and he would be picked up.

That was more like it, Lucky thought as he hung up. A little respect for all he had done for Arceneaux over the years. He began to feel everything would work out. A limo parked next to him and two of Arceneaux's goons got out.

"Glad you boys could make it," Lucky said. He felt confident. Lucky.

Without saying anything, the man closest to Lucky struck him across the mouth with an open-handed blow. As Lucky rocked back on his heels, the second man moved in with a series of short hard jabs to the corrupt FBI agent's midsection. Air expelled out of Lucky's lungs in one long whoosh. He flopped to the ground gasping for breath.

The men leaned over Lucky. Each of them grasped

an arm and leg and threw Lucky into the back of the limo. They climbed in after him and slammed the door before the driver sped away from the scene.

Now, in the bowels of catacombs he didn't know existed, Lucky was terrified. Sitting in a wheelchair with his wrists strapped to the padded arms and his ankles strapped to the edge of the foot rest, he watched Arceneaux approach and felt a chill far colder than the air in the tunnels.

"You are a fool," Arceneaux said in a hard, guttural voice. "I could have made you rich, but your blundering has made you a liability."

"Please—" Lucky's voice came out higher than normal. He swallowed visibly and tried again. "I've done so much for you. I placed my career on the line. You wanted Gordy Fontaine dead. I tried to kill him for you."

Arceneaux slapped Lucky across the face with such force the wheelchair rolled back several feet. "But you failed!" Arceneaux's rage was instantaneous, a boiling over of anger and venom.

Lucky gasped for breath. "I can still kill him," he whimpered. "But I need to know you'll get me clear when it's done. I can't go back to the bureau, but I can still get Gordy. I can still kill him."

"I don't have time for your paper-thin promises," Arceneaux said. "I have tired of waiting for you to take care of Fontaine and his supporters. Other plans have been made to eliminate them. You are not part of those plans." Arceneaux stroked his chin with a weathered hand.

"I can no longer risk bumbling or interference," he

said. "Tomorrow night, the largest shipment of drugs I've ever imported will arrive. Coming with the drugs is a special bonus—fifty boys and girls who the good padre thinks I'm saving from the ravages of their impoverished countries. I have other plans for them with special interest buyers lined up."

"You're going to sell kids?" Lucky sounded shocked.

Arceneaux laughed. "What do you care? They would die if they were left in their own country." Arceneaux paused for effect. "Here, their fate won't be worse than death."

Lucky was silent. Even he drew the line somewhere. He didn't know how to respond. Then he realized the implication of Arceneaux sharing this information.

When the dawn of realization showed in Lucky's expression, Arceneaux smiled wide

"I can still help you," Lucky said quietly.

"I can live without your help."

"But—Fontaine."

"I will deal with Fontaine. His time is rapidly running out."

Arceneaux nodded at the man standing behind Lucky.

"Wait!" Lucky yelled when his wheelchair began being pushed forward. This time Lucky's plea clear.

"Yell loud," Arceneaux told him. "You're already in Hell and the Devil won't care."

Arceneaux walked ahead of the wheelchair as it was pushed farther down the catacomb corridors. A side passage emitted a musty reptilian odor, which heavily overlaid the dank and damp natural smell of the catacombs.

Lucky's eyes were popping with terror. His voice was lost to fear. He'd heard how Arceneaux dealt with enemies and informants. He felt the nerves along his spine scream with anticipation.

A barred grating blocking the corridor was opened by the other henchmen who had grabbed Lucky at the gas station. Beyond the grate, the catacomb slid steeply down into darkness. The fetid smell was overwhelming.

Lucky whimpered, straining at the bonds holding him to the wheelchair. His bladder involuntarily voided, soaking his clothing and dripping onto the hard-packed dirt flooring.

"Calm yourself," Arceneaux said, moving behind the wheelchair. "I was raised to believe FBI agents were brave and fearless. What would good old J. Edgar think?"

There was a shuffling beyond the grate as several gators made their way toward the light like Pavlov's dogs at feeding time.

"Be kind to my pets," Arceneaux said as he gave the wheelchair a shove starting it freewheeling down the incline beyond the grate.

Lucky's screams reverberated off the walls.

The henchman closed and locked the grate.

Arceneaux stood listening. A gentle smile played across the angular rock of his features as if he were absorbing the strains of a sweet symphony.

CHAPTER 27

COLE LOOKED AT ELVIS' PROFILE. THE WHOLE SITUATION was farfetched, but then here he was seeing with his own eyes and hearing with his own ears. If he tried to explain the situation to anyone else, they would think he was out of his tree—and perhaps he was. He kept expecting to hear Rod Serling's voice at any second; "Elvis impersonator Cole Ramsey never expected to meet the King until he took a wrong turn and found himself on a journey into the *Twilight Zone*."

The trip aboard the *Heartbreak Hotel* had deposited Cole, Elvis, and Sheila at a marina in Redondo Beach. Elvis led the way to a plain-color, late model Ford with unexpected power. Gordy stayed with the yacht, taking her back out to sea when everyone else was on shore.

"Where are we going?" Cole asked from the front passenger seat. He'd asked the question several times while still aboard the *Heartbreak Hotel*, but the noise of their passage had drowned out any reasonable answer.

"Underground," Elvis replied, flicking his eyes to check the rear-view mirror.

"What does that mean?" Cole asked.

"It means you're going to find out what it's like to live as a fugitive, scared of your own shadow, with nowhere to turn, and no one to trust. We're taking you for a trip on the new underground railroad."

Cole thought. "The old Underground Railroad would be the pipeline taking slaves to freedom during the Civil War?"

"The man knows his history," Sheila said from the back seat.

Elvis checked the rear-view mirror again.

Cole shifted in his seat, trying not to turn and look out the rear window. Elvis was making him nervous. "What does this new underground railroad save? Whales? Manatees? Dead rock stars?"

"Kids," Elvis said quietly. "Kids."

"Kids?" Cole was perplexed. "What do you mean?"

"What do you know about sexually or physically abused children?" Sheila asked him.

Cole reflected. "I'm aware it goes on, but I've never experienced it personally."

"Then you're one of the lucky ones," Sheila told him.

"Aren't there courts to handle those problems when they're discovered?"

"There's the problem," Elvis said. "Justice is not perfect. The courts don't necessarily make the right decisions."

"You've lost me again," Cole said.

Elvis sighed. He cut a quick glance at Cole and then returned his eyes to the road. "There are places in this country where money speaks louder than the rights of children. Places where women are considered hysterical simpletons if they dare to accuse their husbands of molest or abuse. There are court cases where young children have been returned to their abusive fathers—even after fully documented evidence from doctors and psychologists prove they were being raped and abused. There's even a case where a video was shown of a father forcing his eight-year-old daughter to have sex with him, yet he was given unsupervised visitation rights because—even after the child's tearful testimony—the video was declared not in focus enough to prove it was indeed the child's father on the screen."

"You have to be kidding," Cole said in shock.

"He's not," said Sheila. "Right now, there are about 400 families who have entered the Underground Railroad, and there are more coming every day. Scared parents and their children running from obsessive, abusive, and dangerous spouses who have the whole weight of the law behind them—including the FBI and federal task forces.

"Mostly it's mothers and their children," Elvis said. "But there are also fathers who need the underground. We have several cases where, after a divorce in which the mother gets custody, the mother's new boyfriend has abused the child or children. When all legal venues have been exhausted, and these bastards continue to enjoy the same sickening and abusive habits, the fathers have nowhere to turn but the underground."

"How do you determine these people you're helping are telling the truth? Maybe they're the abusers. Maybe they're just over protective—obsessive mothers with a psychotic fixation against their ex-husbands."

"It's not easy to get into the underground," Sheila said, shaking her head vehemently. "The underground has a cadre of volunteer lawyers and mental-health professionals on call. They screen everyone who gets in contact with us for help. The screening is demanding. They examine all the documentation in the cases, all the available information. They interview and access the victims and the parents who are on the run with them. They review all the evidence before advising us if someone is right for the underground. We know how to test these people. If a molesting parent is trying to run a scam, they don't get past the first checks. We then turn them in to the proper authorities."

"A civilian run version of the Federal Witness Protection Program," Cole said.

"Close," Elvis agreed. "But it's not an easy life. Those who enter must be prepared to withstand great hardship. We have to be careful not to allow inductees to have information endangering to the program if they are caught."

"You've had people turn on you?"

"Twice," Elvis said. "We've had inductees back out and give up the names of the people who helped them. We won those cases in court, but we learned to be careful. We know even the people we're trying to help can hurt us."

"Is it worth it?"

"When you spend time with the children, hearing their stories, seen the looks on their faces, examined the medical and court reports of their ordeals, there is never a doubt all the effort is worth it."

"But it has cost you so much," Cole said.

Cole watched Elvis shrug. "What has it cost me? A career rapidly going in the dumper? A lifestyle going to kill me before long? Those can't compare with the satisfaction helping Gordy with the underground has given me. My life counts for something. I'm finally able to give something back for all the blessings I've been given. This is what Momma and Jesse Garon would want me to be doing."

"What about your music and your fans?"

"The music is always there for my old fans. I have a whole new generation of fans. They are younger and defenseless, and they need me more than my other fans ever did."

"You think the fans of your music would feel betrayed if they found out you were alive?"

Elvis gave a short laugh. "My true fans know I would never betray them. Let me tell you something— there are Elvis fans all over this great country, all over the world, who are there when I need them. They are good people who have stepped in to help the underground when they've been asked."

"Some fans know you're not dead?"

"A few know, a few suspect, and others don't care, but help anyway."

"What about the people who run your estate?"

"The same can be said of them."

"Isn't this Underground Railroad gig illegal?"

"Perhaps. You're need to decide for yourself if it's wrong." Elvis brought out a pair of wrap-around, blackout glasses and handed them to Cole. "Put these on."

"Why?"

"Because we're going to take you to an underground safe-house. We have to protect ourselves."

Cole put on the glasses. They effectively closed off his sight.

"Here's a new twist," Cole said. "The dead leading the blind."

CHAPTER 28

THE INTERIOR OF THE HOUSE WHERE COLE HAD BEEN taken was large and comfortably furnished. The wall between the living room and family room had been knocked down to form one big communal room with a plush dark tan carpet, a large entertainment center, and several plump couches covered with hard-wearing fabrics. There was a piano in one corner and several bean bag chairs scattered around. The slatted, rose colored, mini-blinds covering the windows were closed, but light flooded into the room through two skylights.

Sheila led Cole on the grand tour. Along with the big communal room downstairs there was a large kitchen, a dining area, a bathroom, and an office. Through a sliding glass door, he saw a huge patio leading to a grassy backyard filled with swings and other active toys. An eight-foot-tall block wall enclosed the yard. There were no neighbor's close enough to overlook grounds.

On the second story were six bedrooms and two bathrooms. One of the bedroom doors was open to reveal more tan carpet, two twin beds with fresh sheets and old-fashioned quilts, a small dresser, and a lamp on a night stand.

"It might not look like much," Sheila told him when Cole didn't comment. "But for some people it's considered a paradise. It's a safe haven. Nobody gets hurt or molested here. People can breathe and have a chance to think and make rational decisions."

"I'd say it looks like a lot. This place must have cost a fortune to buy, let alone run."

"We have a lot of supporters, not the least of which is that guy downstairs who used to wear long sideburns and wiggle his butt for a living. He's given many parents and their children the gift of escape from a life of hell. You revere the man for his music. I revere him because he's put everything on the line to help others."

"Quite a testimony," Cole said. He took another look around the bedroom. "How long does a family stay here?"

"Usually no more than a few days. Long enough for us to finish checking out their stories and find them more permanent housing."

Cole had been introduced to Candice, the tall willowy woman who ran the safe house, when he arrived. Along with Candice there were three other women, two white and one black, staying at the house along with six children—two boys and four girls. The children ranged in ages from a baby to a fifteen-year-old girl. They had been downstairs when Cole and the others had arrived and had greeted Elvis like a long-lost uncle. They called him Jon and were oblivious to his resemblance to a dead legend.

From downstairs came the tinkling of the piano. Cole looked at Sheila.

"He plays sometimes," she said. "It helps to ease the tension and uncertainty. Gets everyone to forget the stress for a while."

Cole and Sheila walked back to the communal room to find everyone gathered around the piano. The kids sat in bean bag chairs while the women chose the couches.

A little girl sat next to Elvis on the piano stool. She was around eight with long straight blond hair. She was obviously a musical prodigy, pounding out complicated riffs on the keys, spreading a huge smile over Elvis' face.

"Ain't you something," Elvis said, his voice dripping with Southern Comfort. "You sure play pretty, Sally." He went to give the little girl a hug, but she burst into tears and ran across the room to her mother.

Everyone was silent as the reality of Sally's reaction vibrated around the room like a shockwave. Elvis recovered first and turned the pain in his face back to the piano where he picked out a few melancholy keys.

"Do you have a guitar here?" Cole asked, forcing the words past the lump in his throat.

"What?" Candice asked, bringing her thoughts back into the present.

"A guitar?" Cole asked again.

Candice stood up from the couch and walked to a hall coat closet. From inside she pulled out a battered folk guitar. "It's not much," she said, handing it to Cole.

"It's enough," he replied. He strummed the strings and tried to tune the worn instrument. When the sound was close to in-tune, Cole sat down on the piano bench next to Elvis but facing the room. "Do you want to play some, Jon?" he asked. The name sounded odd, but he knew Elvis had used the name Jon Burrows a lot when he was officially alive.

"Sure."

"How about this one?" With a smile, Cole hit the first notes of the Holly's *Bridge over Troubled Water*.

Elvis picked up the melody on the piano, and the two men's voices immediately blended as they caressed the words. The sound soothed the audience and the children scooted closer. Even Sally pulled her face away from the security of her mother's chest to face the source of the music.

When the last note of the song faded away, Elvis blasted into the Jerry Lee Lewis standard *Great Balls Of Fire*, his voice filled with an imitation of Lewis' gravel. Cole followed on the guitar, then took over with Chuck Berry's, *School Daze*.

Everyone in the room was feeling the power of the beat. The kids were dancing, the women bouncing together on the couch. Sheila stood to one side, leaning against a wall with a happy grin, her toes tapping.

This cat can cook, Cole thought, jamming to his new musical partner. *He may be Elvis after all.* Cole decided to try something and ran from the end of *School Daze* right into the opening of *Blue Suede Shoes*. Elvis kept pounding the piano keys, but he didn't sing along when Cole started the vocal.

Cole took this as a cue. He put all his natural talent into his voice blending in everything he'd learned from years of listening to the King. He stood up from the piano bench as if filled with electricity. His left leg started jumping and his pelvis swiveled with a life of its own. He moved through all the kids, getting them wound up, and finally finished up with a flair bringing a big round of applause from the audience.

"You we're great," said one of the women. "You sounded just like Elvis."

"Thanks," said Cole. Sweat trickled down the back of his neck.

"Who's Elvis?" asked the woman's young daughter, and all the adults laughed.

The little girl looked hurt. "I don't care. I think he's better than Donnie."

"Donnie?" Elvis looked bewildered. "As in Osmond?"

The girl's mother laughed. "No. Donnie as in the latest teen idol. Donnie is all she talks about, so I guess you can take it as a compliment."

"If you say so."

Sheila approached the piano and sat next to Elvis. She put her hands on the keys and moved easily into *I Can't Stop Loving You*. The two men backed off and let her play, her clear voice filling the room with the rich quality of every note.

When she finished there was more applause. Candice, the housemother brought brownies, milk, and coffee in from the kitchen. She set them on the big dining table for everyone.

"You're good, kid," Elvis told Cole.

"You ain't no slacker yourself. How come you didn't join in on *Blue Suede Shoes*?"

"Playing the music from the early days is bad enough, but singing my own stuff is real tough."

"You were the best, man."

"Not anymore."

"Baloney—you could walk back on stage any time anywhere and knock them off their feet."

Elvis shook his head and looked down with an *aw-shucks* grin.

"You boys better get moving," Sheila interrupted, holding out her watch.

"Where are we going?" Cole asked.

"We've got a pick-up," Elvis said. "Are you in or out? How much are you willing to risk getting involved?"

"You're trusting me with an awful lot," Cole said. "Why?"

"Gut instinct," said Elvis. "You've come this far on faith...how about all the way?"

"Does all the way include going after this Arceneaux character?"

Elvis shrugged. "Sheila has a great idea about how to use you."

"Like a staked goat probably," Cole said.

"You complaining?"

Cole stared at Elvis. Elvis stared back. Cole move his gaze to look at the kids happily chomping around the table.

Then he remembered little Sally's scream.

Quietly, he said, "I'm in."

CHAPTER 29

"WHERE'S GORDY?" COLE ASKED FROM HIS SIDE OF the car.

Elvis shrugged. "He was supposed to be on this pick-up, but he got an emergency message to meet the snitch he has inside Arceneaux's organization. We know Arceneaux is gearing up for a major caper, but we don't know the details. The snitch has the info, but he'll only give it up face-to-face."

"Sounds dangerous."

Elvis shrugged again. "Could be worth dying for."

"What exactly are we supposed to be doing?"

Elvis drove casually with the driver's window rolled down and his elbow sticking out. "We're picking up a young mother named Judy Hudson and her five-year-old daughter, Stella. Judy was six months short of completing law school when she went on the run."

Darkness had fallen. The night was sultry with the promise of heat and rain. Elvis stopped for a red light and looked over at Cole.

Before leaving the safe house, Cole had called John

Peel at Copper's. Peel agreed to use Cole's spare key to retrieve the Pink Madam from the marina. Cole hoped he would be around after this adventure to drive it again.

"Why did Judy and her daughter split?" Cole asked.

Elvis turned his eyes back to the road as the light changed. "Judy discovered her husband Max was sexually abusing Stella. Judy told Max she was going to divorce him and take Stella. Good old Max beat the hell out of Judy and told her he'd kill her if she ever tried to take his daughter away, or if she went to the cops. He's a high priced and powerful Chicago lawyer. Judy believed every word he said.

"Judy tried to protect Stella by never letting her be alone with Max. Max decided he was going to file for divorce. He schemed to get sole custody of Stella by trumping up evidence to prove Judy was an unfit mother."

Cole shook his head. "Max used his connections to get the law on his side."

"Without question," Elvis agreed. "Judy dropped about $200,000 in legal fees, but the outcome was never in doubt. Max was awarded full custody of Stella."

"Did she try the police despite her husband's threats?"

"She tried, but she had no proof beyond what Stella had told her and a pediatrician's statement Stella had been sexually abused. Max brought in a tame doctor of his own who refuted the findings of Stella's doctor. Since Stella wouldn't talk about what happened to anyone but Judy, the case didn't hold up."

"How did Judy take the edict?" Cole asked.

"Judy is tough. She broke into her old house, and bonked Max on the head with a lamp when she caught him in the act with Stella. She then packed a few things for her daughter and they took it on the lam."

"How can you be sure she's telling the truth?"

"Not difficult," Elvis said. "The people who prey on young children are called pedophiles. They have usually been victims of abuse themselves and tend to molest children of the same age from when they were molested. Some of them are pretty sophisticated. They have their own underground. They publish magazines and newsletters as well as make arrangements to move kids from one pedophile to another. Our intelligence system established Max Hudson is on several of the mailing lists for these perverted publications. We couldn't prove it, but it was clear he'd participate in the sharing of other children."

"Tell me this is a bad joke." Cole was horrified. He'd known these problems existed, but he didn't know the extent. It was not a subject he'd chosen to think a lot about.

"It's the horror of real life," Elvis said. "Do you see why I feel it's more important to work with the underground than to play rock-n'-roll?"

"I do," said Cole. "But couldn't you do more with the money you made as a superstar than what you're doing now?"

"I've got more money now than I ever had when I was performing. My estate is worth millions more with me dead than with me alive. When I was performing, there was always a precarious balance between overhead and income. As things are now, I have ways of tapping into the estate's income, and it all goes toward helping the cause."

"Don't you miss it?"

"The performing?"

"Yeah. The rush? The energy?"

A rueful grin worked its way across Elvis' lips like a wave. "Every damn day, man. Every damn day." When he spoke, his voice came out low and calm, but every word was filled with the anguish of his sacrifice.

"Is it why you didn't play any of your old stuff when we were jammin' at the safe house."

Elvis gave the little shrug of the shoulders again, it was a movement part embarrassment and part cool. "Maybe. It's not the same playing the stuff without the hope of ever being on stage again."

The two men drove in silence for several minutes after Elvis' pronouncement. Eventually, Cole stirred and asked, "Where are we going to contact Judy?"

"There's a hotel in a couple of miles where she should be waiting. We have to be careful. Judy and Stella are hot. Not only is the FBI actively looking for them, but Max Hudson has hired a slime ball private eye named MacAlister to track them. According to Gordy, MacAlister is major bad news."

CHAPTER 30

"YES," ZACHARY ARCENEAUX SAID INTO THE RECEIVER OF the cellular phone his bodyguard handed him.

"They haven't shown yet."

"Is the woman there with her daughter?"

"Yes."

"Don't mess this up. I want Gordy Fontaine to be shaking hands with the devil before this night is over."

"Everything is under control."

"You've taken a big chunk of my money, MacAlister. You better prove to be worth it."

"I've brought you this far, Arceneaux. And I always deliver."

Arceneaux hung up the phone without further conversation. He would have to do something about MacAlister's lack of respect. Then again, MacAlister was like the alligators still feasting on the remains of Lucky Jordan. You left them alone to do their job. If you tried to tame them, you ran a high risk of getting chomped.

MacAlister was a big man. His six-foot six inches

frame carried two hundred and eighty pounds of muscle and bone. He wore size fifteen shoes and had hands so large they made phone books tremble with fear. Someone had once described his face as enough to scare the devil.

The big man wore a black t-shirt stretched taut across his pectoral muscles and down over his flat stomach to a tapered waist. Huge biceps bulged from the short sleeves. His lower half was encased in tight black jeans outlining the muscles of his legs. Specially ordered black high-tops covered his humongous feet.

MacAlister liked his clothing tight, as if it were a second skin. It gave him a feeling of barely contained power waiting to explode and tear the clothing to shreds. As a kid, his favorite comic book character was The Incredible Hulk. The steroids and growth hormones he'd taken since high school helped him to emulate his childhood hero. Their side effects often sent him into bouts of dark depressions.

With unnatural gentleness, he placed his car phone on the console of his black Aerostar van. With his left hand, he caressed the pistol stock of the sawn-off shotgun resting across his lap. The double barrels had been cut down to eighteen inches and contained high density, hand loaded shot. The kick from firing both barrels at once could near tear the arm off a normal man. MacAlister was far from normal.

He had waited a long time for a score this big. He made a good living picking up stubborn bail jumpers but tracking kids who had been snatched by one parent or another had turned into a profitable sideline. He enjoyed it most when the women took the kids because they were nearly always ready to offer him anything not to take their kids back. He enjoyed their favors and then took their kids anyway.

He didn't care about the kids. What their parents did to them could never be half as bad as what the bastard who'd sired him had done. MacAlister's attitude was to let the little jerks learn to fend for themselves. He'd had to do it, and he'd turned out all right.

When he'd heard the rumors Arceneaux was looking for a pipeline to the underground organization protecting abused kids, MacAlister smelled money. He knew there had to be a big payoff to interest someone like Arceneaux.

The whole story came out when MacAlister contacted the drug czar. Arceneaux wasn't interested in the kids except as a possible source of income. What really interested Arceneaux was the destruction of some cowboy named Fontaine who helped run the underground. Arceneaux promised a million-dollar payoff if MacAlister could deliver Gordy Fontaine's ears on a string.

MacAlister knew about the underground but hadn't dealt with it. Any contracts he took for missing kids were cleared up with ruthless efficiency before they got to the underground. But when Arceneaux named a price for delivering Fontaine, MacAlister actively hunted for leads to the underground and to Gordy. The Hudson case had been perfect.

It was easy to get Hudson to hire him. MacAlister was happy to earn a double fee—Hudson paying for the return of his kid, and Arceneaux for the head of the cowboy. All MacAlister needed to do was track Judy

Hudson and her daughter, make sure she got nudged in the direction of the underground, then sit back and wait.

A simple scenario, thought MacAlister. He was calmly watching the hotel across the street where Judy Hudson and her daughter were waiting. He'd been following the woman for two weeks. She had finally contacted the underground after MacAlister had placed several people in her path to point her in the right direction.

Using illicit technical skills developed over the years, MacAlister tapped the phone lines of the hotels and motels where Judy and Stella stayed. He'd listened to the conversations she'd had with the underground and the plans they made. He knew Gordy was coming for the pickup tonight. He'd heard Gordy tell Judy so himself. Gordy and another guy named Burrows.

No problem, MacAlister smirked. The two guys would go down easy. Then he'd dump the woman, take the kid home to daddy, and pick up his fee. The fee from daddy, and a million from Arceneaux.

A brown Ford passed in front of the hotel. MacAlister saw the profiles of two men. Fontaine and Burrows?

No problem, MacAlister thought again. He hefted the shotgun in his lap and waited for the Ford's next pass. Sometimes life was almost too good.

————

INSIDE THE MOTEL, Judy Hudson stared through the lobby window into the darkness of the evening. She felt as if she were a sitting target—lit up and on display—but she would have felt more vulnerable outside. For the hundredth time, she cupped her hands to the window and anxiously glanced up and down the street. There was no sign of the brown sedan she had been told to expect.

Sitting beside her mother, Stella happily flipped the pages of an oversized picture book. The young girl's once long blond locks had been sacrificed in favor of a little boy's haircut with a precise part down the right side. Blue jeans, Keds, and a boy's plaid flannel shirt completed the disguise. Stella thought the game was neat. She even liked her mom calling her Josh. Make-believe was a lot more fun with mommy than with daddy. It never hurt with mommy.

If someone had a photo of Judy Hudson in their hand, they wouldn't have recognized her either. Her own blond hair had been dyed black. The curls she usually fought to keep tight had been straightened, falling across her forehead in lank strands. Her cheeks were hollow from loss of weight, and a pair of large clear glasses could not hide the heavy purple stress bags beneath her eyes. A worn and faded fabric coat hung from her shoulders, buttoned across a small pillow to make her look pregnant.

Judy hated the make-believe, but she knew her husband and refused to underestimate the risk she was running. If playing dress-up could give her any edge at all, she'd continue to do it until Max Hudson dropped dead.

She cupped her hands to the glass again and was rewarded with a glance of a brown sedan as it passed under a street light. Judy felt her chest tighten as if the air was being squeezed out of her lungs. She prayed the car was the right one. She prayed the waiting was over. She closed her eyes and mumbled under her breath, praying the nightmare would end.

"Mommy?" Stella sensed her mother's disquiet.

Judy opened her eyes and bent down beside her daughter. "Everything is fine, honey." She hugged her daughter. "I'm just a little tired."

"Are we waiting for daddy?" the child asked, then added with a child's bluntness, "I don't want to see daddy."

Judy felt a blunt knife sawing through her heart. She hugged her daughter again. "Don't worry, darling, you won't have to see daddy again." Standing up, she returned her cupped hands to the window and stared out.

From across the street, she saw the dome light of a parked van come on and a huge man step out. Over his right arm, concealing his hand, was a folded raincoat. Judy's mind clicked onto the words of a song claiming it never rained in California. She took a closer look at the man and realized she'd seen him before—twice since she'd been on the run, but it hadn't registered before.

As Judy watched the man, the brown sedan pulled into the motel entrance and stopped in front of the lobby. The man from the van was blocked from her sight, but Judy knew what he was doing, and she knew what she had to do.

———

COLE LOOKED out of the passenger window as Elvis parked in front of the motel lobby. Through the lobby window, he could see a pregnant woman and a boy.

"That's her," Elvis said.

Cole looked at the child seated near the woman. "I thought you said she had a daughter. And she's pregnant."

"Misdirection and disguise," Elvis said. "The FBI and her powerful ex-husband are after her. We told her what she needed to do, and she's followed our instructions."

The woman moved away from the window and burst out the lobby door. Her obvious agitation alarmed Cole.

"What's going on?" he asked.

Judy Hudson was pointing across the street and yelling something.

Cole and Elvis turned to look. They saw a huge man running toward them. His left hand was tossing away the raincoat draped over his right arm and hand. Underneath the raincoat was an ugly, sawn-off shotgun pointing directly at them.

CHAPTER 31

GORDY LEANED ONE SHOULDER AGAINST THE ENTRANCE wall of Union Station. A newly arrived Amtrak train was disgorging its passengers into the terminal like so many ants abandoning a corpse. Outside in the night, cars slipped through the area like frightened horses. Citizens walked quickly, afraid to linger for fear of predators who prowled the squalid area surrounding the once magnificent terminal.

Arriving passengers avoided making any eye contact as they walked by Gordy. Part of the reason was a natural inclination to avoid strangers, but mostly it was the air of controlled danger emanating from Gordy's bantam rooster physique. Even the aggressive vagrants kept their distance from the small man with the hard eyes.

Unlike most people on the run, Gordy thrived on life in the underground. The adversity of it all suited his David and Goliath complex. Within the boundaries of the life he'd taken upon himself, he was free to make or break rules as he saw fit.

This freedom, this ability to play fast and loose with the strictures of society, became Gordy's reason for living. He loved his daughter, and he knew his lifestyle had originally caused her much grief, but now she was as committed as he was to the cause of the children's underground.

Sheila had grown to accept those things he could not be changed and loved him unconditionally. In many ways her acceptance made her a more mature person than her father, because Gordy refused to accept there were things he could not change.

He saw himself as judge and jury of the situations into which he was thrust. On occasion, he had no qualms about being executioner as well. In his mind there was something wrong when the law protected a madman like Zachary Arceneaux. The law was wrong when it allowed children to be the pawns of sick desires or unbridled rage.

As an upholder of *The Law*, he had been forced to stand by in frustration while others determined the best course of action based on *the big picture*. Gordy had found he didn't care about *the big picture*. He was much more concerned with *the little picture*—the individual— the actual concept of right and wrong.

Gordy knew other people saw the concept of right and wrong differently than he did. But this did not sway him from his convictions. For Gordy, the truth was simple—if someone was doing something to hurt another individual, then they were wrong and needed to be stopped. If they wouldn't stop, they needed to be punished. If they still refused to stop, they needed to be removed from the equation. Gordy believed you were part of the solution or part of the problem and should be dealt with accordingly.

Gordy didn't worry about the ethics of his philosophy. Life was generally unfair. It was Gordy's calling to make life fair more often.

The kids in the underground needed life to be more fair. Zachary Arceneaux was another situation where the fairness of life needed to be tweaked. In one situation, Gordy was a savior. In the other, he would either be destroyer or the destroyed.

With the animalistic sixth sense developed from years of being hunted, Gordy heard soft footsteps approaching from behind. Without urgency, he turned to find Father Romero standing behind him with worry woven across his features.

"Hello, Father," Gordy said, returning the other's weak smile with his own sardonic version. "It's good to see you."

"It is good to be seen, amigo," Father Romero held out his hand and Gordy shook it. "Days like today I despair of ever seeing another sunrise."

"A hard line for someone so young."

"I may be young in age," Father Romero said, "but I am old in spirit."

Gordy nodded. His eyes swept the area for potential dangers. "When you have an animal like Arceneaux in your world, a long life is never assured."

Romero agreed. "I think his madness will soon drive him to his own destruction, but not before he has done a great deal more damage."

The relationship between Gordy and Father Romero went back many years to before Father Romero was ordained. As a teenage refugee from the death squads in El Salvador, Romero had become involved with the sanctuary movement. His church calling came as part and parcel of the cause. His priest's collar gave him a legitimate base to pursue his life's work—saving other refugees from the hell holes that had taken the lives of his parents, his two brothers, and his three sisters.

Gordy and the Father had been sympathetic adversaries when Gordy was with the DEA. Their respect and trust grew when Gordy investigated a drug ring using the sanctuary movement's refugee routes to smuggle product into the United States.

The sanctuary movement was a political hot potato. Gordy could have scored big points using heavy-handed methods to destroy the drug ring by disrupting the entire sanctuary movement. Instead, Gordy followed his instincts and acted like a scalpel—cutting out only the cancer of the drug runners from the body of the controversial political movement. Father Romero had never forgotten Gordy's restraint.

When Gordy had gone on the run, he turned to the sanctuary movement for help. He had received it without question as Father Romero returned the long-owed favor. Later, when Gordy became involved with the children's underground, Father Romero became an invaluable ally, providing contacts and tradecraft.

Now, Father Romero needed Gordy again. Father Romero mistakenly received Zachary Arceneaux into the movement as a monetary savior. He had no idea of the high price he would have to pay for taking Arceneaux's six pieces of silver. Consequently, he found not only himself, but his whole movement in jeopardy. Once again, the system of smuggling routes used to rescue refugees seeking political asylum were being used for criminal purposes.

"Arceneaux is a rogue elephant destroying everything in his path. He does not care about jeopardizing the movement. All he is interested in is power and profit."

Gordy couldn't help saying a variation of *I told you so*. "You should have recognized him for what he was when he first came to you. Nobody does anything for free."

Father Romero's temper flared briefly. "You know as well as anyone there are people who support our cause without wishing for anything in return. We didn't know who Arceneaux was when he first came to us. We needed his support and money. It saved many lives."

Gordy kept his voice low, but he was also mad. "And now it is costing many. Are the handful of refugees you were able to save worth the thousands of lives ruined by the drugs Arceneaux smuggled into this country using your organization?"

"Would I be risking my life to help you stop him if they were?"

Gordy was quiet, giving both parties time to calm down. Finally, he gave Father Romero a rueful grin and fumbled a stick of gum out of its wrapper. "I'm sorry, Father. I'm letting my own eagerness to destroy Arceneaux get the better of me." He popped the gum in his mouth and waited.

Father Romero watched him then took a deep breath. "There is something I must show you," he said. Turning, he began to walk slowly away from the terminal entrance.

CHAPTER 32

"What was so important we had to meet right away?" Gordy asked as they walked.

"I found out Arceneaux is ready to make his largest shipment of drugs ever. He is vulnerable right now. He is over committed to his suppliers, and if he doesn't deliver, his power base will shatter. He is playing with the biggest of the big boys, and if he disappoints them they will squash him like a cockroach."

Gordy couldn't keep the anxiety out of his voice. "How did you learn this?"

Father Romero shrugged. "Arceneaux thinks I am nothing but a weak sheep. He believes he can intimidate me into submission, but I did not survive the death squads in my own country by being weak. I watch, I listen, I learn, and I survive."

"There's something more?"

Father Romero nodded. "This time he is not only bringing drugs, but children—orphans from countries all over Central America. He has told me the children will be turned over to the sanctuary movement, but he lies. He is planning on selling them to the highest bidder for whatever perverted practices satisfy their desires. To him, the children are nothing more than another cash crop."

Gordy was on a slow burn. "How many children?"

"Fifty."

"How is he bringing them in?"

"Big bribes have cleared border crossing. Once across, the children and the drugs will be sealed into an enclosed freight car attached to an Amtrak train coming up from San Diego."

"Arceneaux plans on taking delivery at Union Station," Gordy said, jumping ahead in the scenario. "Then what does he do with them?"

"I'll show you," Father Romero said.

The Priest led the way along the side of the terminal building. He pulled aside a length of chain-link fence, stepping through onto a concrete plateau at the far end of the station platform.

In the darkness, Gordy followed the priest without question.

They jumped down onto the tracks. At a grated sewer opening, Father Romero pushed aside the heavy metal bars and ushered Gordy through.

"I always wondered how you managed to come up behind me whenever we met at the train station," Gordy said. The factor had always bothered him.

"You never asked."

"I didn't think you'd tell me."

"Everyone needs a few secrets."

Father Romero turned into a dark opening, which was hidden from view unless you knew it was there.

The two men had to turn sideways to get through it. On the other side there was complete darkness until Father Romero turned on the flashlight he had brought with him.

"Where the hell are we?" Gordy asked.

"These old catacombs were built by the Chinese who ran the opium dens when Union Station was located in what was the original Chinatown section of Los Angeles."

"Catacombs? You mean like tunnels set up to escape from police raids?"

"And competing tongs."

"I thought catacombs were something out of old B-grade movies with Charlie Chan or something."

"These catacombs are very real. There is a Chinese heritage museum not far from Union Station with a display memorializing the system. It was how I learned about their existence. Most are less than a quarter of a mile long, while some can go for a mile. Even if your enemies found the entrance to the catacombs, there were so many tunnels they would quickly be lost in the maze. If you knew your way, you could get to safety. If you didn't, you could wander for hours without finding an exit."

"How did you get into them?"

"Through the museum. There was an entrance to the catacombs at the back. From there it needed only hard work and dedication to extend them to the church, and to map them for use by the sanctuary movement. My people are not afraid of hard work."

Gordy looked around in the dim light. If either man had been any taller they would need to stoop to avoid the rounded roof. "Doesn't look safe to me," he said.

Father Romero laughed. "Safe is a relative concept, my friend. No, they are not safe. There are occasional cave-ins, and a few tunnels have filled with methane gas. Whatever you do, don't strike a match."

Gordy thought about the catacombs. "Arceneaux found out about these tunnels and has been using them to smuggle his dope into town."

"And he will be using these tunnels again tomorrow night to bring in his human cargo."

"Tomorrow?" Gordy again felt the rising anxiety within him.

"Yes. The train arrives at ten p.m. These tunnels have ears. Arceneaux thinks I am a lamb, but I am really a wolf. He thinks he is safe here to plot and plan, but I know the tunnels better than he ever will. I know where to go to listen. Now you know what I have heard, I know you will stop him."

Gordy shrugged. As he did so he felt the bulk of his .9mm Berretta rub against his chest in its shoulder holster. "Where is Arceneaux?"

"In the tunnels. He has been feeding his beasts."

"I don't understand."

"He has established an alligator den in one of the tunnels. If Arceneaux is upset enough with you he feeds you to his pets."

Gordy felt sick. His mind filled with the memory of his father's remains after Arceneaux had fed him to the alligators in New Orleans. Bile fought its way up his throat. When he spoke, his voice was a croak. "Can you get me to Arceneaux right now?"

"Yes, but I won't."

"Why not? It would be safer for your orphans if I take care of the problem immediately."

"I am still a priest above all other things. I will not have the blood on your hands on my conscience."

"But tomorrow it will be okay? You're playing semantics."

"Semantics is what religion is all about, my friend. Tomorrow you will have your chance and your choice. I have done all I can for now."

"And if I go through the catacombs myself?"

Father Romero turned off the flashlight. "Be my guest," he said into the complete darkness.

"I could come back with a light of my own," Gordy said without moving.

There was no answer.

"Father?"

Silence.

"Romero!"

The priest's disembodied voice came from a great distance. "Turn around and take eight or nine steps. You will find the exit."

"Wait!" Gordy yelled.

This time there was no reply from the darkness.

CHAPTER 33

MacAlister was ticked off. Somehow the woman had spotted him. He wasn't used to his plans being disrupted—and being spotted by the woman was definitely classified as a disruption. Somewhere, he'd been sloppy.

This was supposed to be an easy kill. Knock off Fontaine and his partner for Arceneaux, take out the woman, and grab the kid. Boom. One, two, three. Hit quick and dirty and be gone before the straights knew anything was happening. Another example of gang violence catching some fine, upstanding, innocent folks in the crossfire.

He could pull it off, but he was going to have to rush things. He ran toward the brown sedan as the woman ran out of the lobby and started yelling. Pulling the raincoat off his arm to reveal the sawn-off shotgun, he saw the passenger in the sedan turn toward him.

It wasn't Fontaine.

MacAlister swore loudly. He'd been told Fontaine would be in the pick-up vehicle. He'd been sure the passenger had to be Fontaine. The whole caper was going sour.

He'd been tripped up by his own over confidence. The rage inside him grew as he watched a million dollars slipping away. MacAlister was angry. Angry with himself. Angry with the world. Anger made him dangerous.

MacAlister realized he could still salvage something. Taking out the woman and snatching the kid back were on the agenda. If he could get hold of one of the guys from the sedan, maybe they could lead him to Fontaine. He only needed one guy from the sedan. He could waste the other to keep things simple.

MacAlister picked up the pace of his sprint toward the motel entrance. As he did so, he leveled his ugly weapon at the driver's side window of the sedan and pulled one trigger.

———

THE BUCKSHOT BLEW out the car window. Brilliant crystals of safety glass showered across the horizontal bodies of Elvis and Cole.

"Move!" Elvis shouted at Cole, but Cole was already sliding out the passenger door to the ground in front of the motel. Cole rolled to his feet, shot one quick glance backward to be sure Elvis was following, and made a mad dash for Judy Hudson. He wrapped his arms around the woman's waist and carried her slim form back through the motel doors.

"What are you doing?" Judy screamed.

"Mommy! Mommy!" Stella yelled her alarm when she saw Cole carrying her mother.

"Come on, Stella," Cole said to the little girl, realizing she was dressed to look like a boy as a disguise.

"Are you from Daddy?" the little girl asked as she shied away from Cole.

There was a second retort from MacAlister's shotgun. One of the lobby doors exploded and glass shards rained down like diamonds. Elvis ducked through the doors a second later. "Run while he's reloading!" As he moved past Cole and Judy, he scooped Stella up into his arms and ran toward the emergency exit at the back of the lobby.

"Mommy!" Stella screamed again, as she wriggled in Elvis' tight embrace.

"It's all right, darling," Judy called back, trying to reassure her daughter. With Cole now dragging her by the hand, she stumbled and almost fell. Cole steadied her and kept moving after Elvis. He risked a glance backward, seeing MacAlister in pursuit shoving shells into the sawn-off weapon as he ran.

Somewhere a woman was screaming in the lobby, and as Elvis hit the panic bar on the emergency exit the *whoop-whoop* of an alarm was activated.

Cole pushed Judy through the door after Elvis. Looking around wildly, he spotted a wooden wedge the motel janitor used to hold the fire door open when emptying the trash. Cole grabbed it and stuffed the wedge under the outward opening door, effectively wedging it shut. He heard MacAlister slam into the panic bar on the other side and then curse as the door sprang open an inch and then refused to open farther.

Cole didn't know how long the wedge would hold, but he wasn't about to hang around to find out. He saw Elvis holding open the door to a beat up pick-up truck in the motel's rear parking lot.

"Come on," Elvis called as he slid into the driver's seat.

Stella and Judy were already in the cab. Cole sprinted toward them. As he ran he saw Elvis fiddling under the truck's dashboard and the engine roared into life. Behind him, he heard MacAlister still battering at the fire exit. The door was coming open an inch at a time as the wedge was forced backward.

With an athletic leap, Cole swung himself into the bed of the pick-up as Elvis threw the stick-shift into gear and put his foot down. There was a small sliding panel in the middle of the truck's rear window. It was open, and Cole crouched by it to speak. "Where did you learn to hot wire cars?"

"Product of a misspent youth," Elvis replied.

Cole grabbed the side of the truck bed as Elvis turned out of the motel's rear parking lot and sped toward the street. Passing the front entrance to the motel, Cole realized they weren't clear yet as a blast of shotgun pellets peppered the truck's tailgate.

Cole ducked instinctively, but he risked another look. The truck was out of range of MacAlister's close-work weapon, but the assassin wasn't wasting time capping off ineffective rounds. Instead, MacAlister was running across the street in the direction of his black van. He had never blown a hit this badly before, and he was determined not to let his quarry escape.

Cole saw the black van pull out to give chase.

"Any bright ideas about how to give this guy the slip?" he asked, as he put his head back to the opening in the rear window. "Unless you're planning on dying again tonight, we gotta do something fast."

"This is your town, kid." Elvis passed the obligation of decision back to Cole.

Cole glanced at Judy, who had Stella wrapped tightly in her arms.

"What time is it?" he asked Elvis.

"What difference does it make?"

"Maybe life or death. Humor me."

Judy gave him an answer after a quick look at her watch. "Eight o'clock."

"Take a left at the next corner," Cole told Elvis decisively. "Pick up the freeway north and head for the Sunset Boulevard off-ramp."

"What have you got in mind?" Elvis asked.

"It's time you made your long-awaited return to the stage."

"What are you talking about?"

Cole looked back as the truck raced onto the freeway on-ramp. The black van blew through a red light to chase them, closing fast.

"Let me put it another way, El. It's show time!"

CHAPTER 34

THE PALADIN CLUB WAS A KNOWN ICON ALONG THE sunset strip. Originally converted from an early Hollywood movie theater, the club had weathered the storms of time, trends, and fashion to take its place in Hollywood history alongside Universal Studios, the Hollywood sign, the Capitol Records building, and the Walk of Fame.

The Paladin had become a mainstay on the club circuit. It was *the* place for up-and-coming bands, but it often ran special events to bring in revenue on the non-prime party nights of the week.

Tonight, banners proclaiming *Elvis Night* were strung across the front of the club. People were lined up at the entrance wearing fifties style outfits or imitation Elvis jumpsuits from later in his career. Everyone's collars were turned up, and gaudy costume jewelry glittered in the bright lights of the club's facade. *Elvis Night* was a weekly ritual at the Paladin. It consistently brought in a respectable house crowd of regulars and tourists.

Because he knew where the club was, Cole spotted the marquee while they were still a couple of blocks away. He pointed it out to Elvis and told him to pull the truck around the back. "As soon as you get this rattle trap stopped, everyone bail out and follow me."

Traffic on the freeway and on Sunset Boulevard was heavy enough to work to Cole and Elvis' advantage. MacAlister's black van was behind them, but there was a number of cars in between. On the freeway, Elvis had the luck to pull in front of a Highway Patrol car for a distance. This had effectively stopped MacAlister from taking any drastic action.

Cole and Elvis briefly considered stopping the Highway Patrol officer and requesting help, but they nixed this approach for two reasons. First, the officer was safe while he was moving in his patrol vehicle as a blocking entity. If Cole and Elvis stopped the patrol officer, MacAlister probably wouldn't worry about killing him along with them. Second, Judy and Stella were fugitives—neither they nor Elvis could stand up to official scrutiny without disastrous results. Once off the freeway, Elvis used the traffic on Sunset Boulevard to keep MacAlister at bay.

Approaching the Paladin Club, Elvis slowed his pace to time catching a traffic light before it turned red. The two cars behind the pick-up were forced to stop for the light, pinning MacAlister behind them.

"Nice move," Cole said through the open rear window. "Should buy us a few seconds."

"But only a few," Elvis said. "I hope you know what you're doing."

"I never know what I'm doing," Cole told him. "But

this is as good a chance as we're going to get. You're sure the guy chasing us is the MacAlister character Gordy warned you about?"

"Who else could it be?"

"We've been lucky so far, but there's no way we're going to outrun him in this tub. The Paladin is the only chance I can think of."

"Let's do it then," Elvis said. He turned into the short alley leading to the back parking lot of the club. As the truck jerked to a stop in the only empty parking space in the lot, Cole jumped out to help Judy and Stella from the cab.

Stella had calmed down since her scare in the motel. She remained quiet when Cole picked her up. Judy, however, was wound tight as a drum skin. She pulled the pillow out from under her coat and dropped it on the ground. The coat hung in a shapeless mass from her thin shoulders.

Cole smiled at her. "Don't give up. We're the good guys. Somehow, we'll get you through this."

Judy nodded as Cole hurried them to the performer's entrance at the back of the club. There was a bouncer standing in the open door. He put his hand up to stop them until he recognized Cole.

"Hey, Jerome," Cole said to the big man. "Is Benny around?"

"Yeah. He'll be real glad to see you Cole. He's got a big problem."

"I'll see what I can do to help," Cole said, as he made a show of putting Stella on his shoulder.

"What's with the kid? You can't bring anyone in here under twenty-one."

"Special circumstances," Cole said. He pushed inside. "Jerome, can you keep the door shut behind us. We've got a fanatical fan chasing us, and I need to keep these people safe."

Jerome looked surprised. "Fanatical fan? Who are you trying to kid? You ain't that big."

Cole was getting exasperated. He knew they were running out of time. "Jerome! Keep the damn door shut. I don't have time to explain."

Jerome looked hard at the little group then nodded. "I read you. How big is this problem?"

"The biggest. The guy chasing us talks in lead."

"No cops?"

"No cops," Cole said.

"I'll tell the others." Jerome swung the stage door closed and dropped the security bar across it.

Cole felt better knowing the big man and his compatriots were on their side. They say home is where they have to take you in, but actually home is where you're taken in because people want you.

The Paladin was only another club, but to Cole it was home. It was where he'd done his first Elvis gig. He had a lot of personal history invested in the Paladin.

"Where's Benny?"

Jerome pointed toward a closed door. "In his office."

"Thanks," Cole said, moving his group to the door and knocking once before entering.

Benny Kravitz, the owner of the Paladin, was a substitute father to everyone who came through either as customer, worker, or performer. His mercenary bluster was a cover for his big Jewish heart. Even if you screwed him, Benny would let you back into his good graces, but the key was you had to earn your way back.

Benny was sitting behind his desk yelling into the phone as the group entered. "I don't give a pit bull's testicle if he's got laryngitis. He's got a contract to perform here tonight and I've got a club full of customers who have paid to see Elstein do his shtick." Benny stood up still yelling. "If he ain't here in ten minutes, the Jewish Elvis can forget doing his act in this town again." He slammed down the phone and looked up at his visitors. The expression change on his face was comical as Benny saw Cole. He couldn't have been more surprised if Cole had been the Queen of Sheba.

"Cole! Baby! You is exactly what the doctor ordered! How did you know I needed you? How quickly can you get ready to go on stage?"

Cole put his hands up in a placating gesture. "Slow down, man. First things first."

"You worried about your fee? Have I ever stiffed you? You wound me."

"Calm down, Benny. It's nothing like that."

"Then what? The amateur hour can only keep the customers happy for so long. Come on, Cole, baby. I got a whole club full of Elvis wanna-bees who are expecting a professional Elvis impersonator. That schmo Elstein crapped out on me. The Jewish Elvis, my left butt cheek. He can play and jiggle while wearing a yarmulke, but if he knew about Jewish guilt he wouldn't do this to me. Ask me. I know all about Jewish guilt. Didn't I marry the first girl whose breast I touched? Try to give a guy a break and look what happens."

Cole had his hand up in the air again. "Benny, shut up and listen for a minute!"

Benny looked slightly shocked, but he realized something important was going on. For the first time, he took in the sight of the other trio with Cole. Judy was hugging Stella and Elvis was standing by the door, nervously looking behind them. Benny almost did a double take when he saw Elvis, and then he looked at Cole. "You got troubles, boychick?"

"Big time, Benny." Cole's tone was decisive. "My friend Jon and I will take care of your problem, but we need your help with ours."

"Anything." Benny was sincere. His mouth tended to run on and on through most occasions, but Cole knew he could count on the man. Benny had come up the hard way and had respect for others, like Cole who followed their own star. When he became a friend, he stood by you—always. "What can I do?"

"This is guns, blood, and bullets trouble, Benny. It's also no police type trouble."

"You think I'm gonna turn tail and run?"

"No way. I'm only letting you know the situation."

"Boychick, I seen more trouble in my life than you'll see in a hundred life times. Oy, the stories I could tell you."

"Another time, Benny? Right now, we need a little less talk and a little more action."

"No cops, huh?" Benny looked hard at Elvis. "I never known you to stray from the straight and narrow, boychick," he said to Cole. "I gotta believe you is on the up and up."

"Never straighter, Benny."

"Good enough for me," Benny said. He came around from behind his desk and squatted down to Stella's level. "Uncle Benny's going to make everything okay, little boychick."

"I'm not a boy?" Stella said, and Benny laughed at his mistake.

"You're involved in a doozy this time, Cole," he said. He ruffled Stella's hair and turned his attention to Judy. "I don't know who is after you or why, but if Cole says you're kosher, who am I to doubt him? He's a good boy. He can't help it if he's not Jewish."

Stella giggled, and Benny looked at her. "Now you think I'm a funny guy. Comedians I got. A dime a dozen. A good Elvis impersonator—there you have me."

Elvis, who had been nonchalantly leaning in the doorway, rolled his shoulders to loosen the tension. "Cole, what exactly is the plan here?"

Everyone, Benny included, looked at Cole.

"When you first built the Paladin Club, Benny, didn't you have a special exit put in for all the big name acts who never turned up?"

"Cole, you wound me."

"This is serious, Benny. I know you make a mint out of this place, but it ain't the Hollywood Bowl."

Benny sniffed and shrugged his shoulders. "I make a living. Is that a crime?"

"About the exit, Benny."

"Yeah. Yeah. The door in the back of my office leads into the next building. From there you go to the roof and get access to the building on the corner. It lets out onto a side street on the next block."

"Great," Cole said. "While Jon and I are taking care of business on your stage can you get Stella and Judy out of here without anyone knowing?"

"No problem," Benny said. "I got a car parked over there every night. You never know what might come up. But what about whoever is chasing you?"

"I think he'll hang around waiting for us to come out. If he comes in, he'll see the situation is against him with so many people around. He's using a close-up weapon. With us on stage surrounded by the crowd, the odds are too short to get away clean. I don't think he'll risk it.

Cole nodded toward Stella and Judy. "They're the prize he's really after. He won't do anything to us until we lead him to them. Hopefully, you'll have them clear of here before that happens."

"I'll guard them with my life," Benny said. His voice was clear and hard without any of the characterization he usually threw in for effect. The change made Cole look at Benny in a different light. He'd known Benny was a hard but fair business man, but there was an aura of cool confidence about him now. Cole wondered if half the wild stories Benny told about his colorful past might be partially true. "Where do I take them?" Benny asked.

Elvis took a piece of paper off Benny's desk and wrote the address of the safe house. He looked at Cole before handing over the paper to Benny.

"The man's a mensch," Cole said, realizing what Elvis was asking. "I wouldn't trust him with my sister, but I'd trust him with my life."

"I wouldn't trust the Pope with your sister," Benny

said, slipping back into his accustomed patter. "She's a woman to keep the cold away at night."

Elvis handed Benny the paper. As Benny took it, he also took Elvis' hand and held it. He stared hard into Elvis' face. Elvis stared back unperturbed. "Are my eyes getting as old as the rest of me?" he asked after a second. "You can't possibly be—" He trailed off.

Elvis didn't respond. Benny continued to stare into his face, then he shrugged and sighed again. "I got a good eye for the changes made by age. It comes from looking under rocks for Nazi war criminals." Cole knew Benny made big contributions to the Simon Wiesenthal Center. "I don't know where you been, or what you been doing all these years," Benny said, finally releasing Elvis' hand. "But I'm honored to have you in my club. I never thought I'd live to see the day."

"Don't let your imagination run wild," Elvis said with a gentle smile. "You said yourself good imitators are hard to come by."

Benny laughed. "Have it your way. Get on stage before the paying guests tear the walls down." He turned away and put his arm around Judy and took Stella's hand. "Don't worry," he told them. "You are safe as a house with Uncle Benny."

CHAPTER 35

"I DON'T KNOW IF THIS IS A GOOD IDEA," ELVIS SAID. HE and Cole were in the dressing room reserved for the evening's main attraction. The jumpsuits used by Elstein in his act hung from several hooks except for one Cole had practically forced Elvis into wearing. Elvis was a little larger in stature than Elstein, but the white stretch material and rhinestones didn't mind the difference. "It's been too long. I don't know if I can do this again."

"There'll be nothing to it when the music starts," Cole said.

Jerome stuck his head through the dressing room door. "Five minutes."

"Thanks," Cole said. "You got MacAlister spotted?"

"Yeah," said Jerome. "Ted let him in through the front door like you said. He's sitting at the bar watching the last of the amateur Elvis acts go through the motions. Dalton and Chantry are shadowing him."

"Not too close," Cole put in quickly. "The guy is dangerous."

267

"Dalton and Chantry are pros."

Cole nodded. Good bouncers were rare. Dalton and Chantry were great. "How about the black van?"

"Parked across the street. Wiseman will have it ready for you when you want it."

"Dalton and Chantry will run interference to get us clear?"

"With help from me and Ted. You know Dalton and Chantry. Whatever Benny tells them is gospel. They'll get you clear."

Cole took a deep breath and let it out. "We'll be there on cue."

Jerome closed the dressing room door.

"Let me put this another way," Elvis said, picking up where he'd left off, verbally digging his heels in. "I don't know if I *want* to do this." Elvis' mouth creased into the lopsided grin Cole would have recognized anywhere. The man might not look the same at first glance, but the more you were around him, the more you recognized the traits the world had come to love. "I used to read a lot of comic books when I was a kid," Elvis said. "My favorite was always Captain Marvel, Jr. I wanted to be him. I wanted to save the world every day of the week. I never thought it would work out like this."

"You do save the world every day of the week. If they blasted *That's All Right* through the U.N., all the national representatives would be so busy getting down, they couldn't go to war."

Elvis laughed softly. "You think so, huh?"

"You betcha."

Elvis didn't say anything else.

"Do you want to get out of this mess alive?" Cole asked.

"Yes, but—"

"No buts! MacAlister isn't going to give up easily. Who knows why he wants to kill us—except maybe so he can get to Judy and Stella. But he knows we can't go to the cops. He'll keep coming after us. He expects us to run and hide. He won't be prepared for us to appear on stage. If we can get him contained in the club, not knowing what to expect, maybe we can outsmart him using Jerome and the other bodyguards. Then we can become magicians and pull a disappearing act."

Elvis laughed again. "Will your friend Benny ever forgive us for deserting the stage?"

"He's your friend, too. He'll forgive us as long as we go out there and knock the crowd off their feet."

Cole and Elvis both caught the strains of the band's intro music coming from the stage. Elvis seemed to pale behind his quickly applied stage make up. Cole reached over and straightened Elstein's wig, which now covered Elvis' close-cropped locks. The wig unfortunately had a Yarmulke glued on to the crown.

Elvis turned to look at himself in the mirror. "Elstein the Jewish Elvis. What is going on in this life?"

Cole patted his friend on the back. "Elstein isn't the only one. There's Elvez the Mexican Elvis, Wally Chan the Chinese Elvis, and Janner Singh the turban wearing Hindu Elvis. There are women Elvis impersonators, and I even saw a dog Elvis once who barked his way through *You Ain't Nothing But A Hound Dog*.

"You're a whole cultural phenomenon all by your little lonesome tonight. Your music and your image has done more for world peace and harmony than all the politicians and religious leaders put together. You bring the whole world together through a mutual snapping of fingers and shaking of legs. Man, you are a way of life for millions of fans. You're their god."

"I'm not a god!" Elvis said with some fierceness. "I'm just a singer."

"When was the last time you heard of a singer being raised from the dead?"

PART IV

LONG LIVE THE KING

CHAPTER 36

LAWRENCE *FATS* MCCORKLE HAD COME A LONG WAY since the infamous day in August 1977, when he'd first stood in front of a television camera and spoke about the death of Elvis Presley. The Voice of Memphis had come west and found fame and fortune in the La-La-Land fast lane.

Network TV had been good to Fats McCorkle. It made his face recognized by millions and parlayed his comfortable persona into dependable ratings. However, Fats wasn't fat anymore. A hundred and fifty pounds had been sweated and dieted away until he was a svelte shadow of his former self. The flat stomach and trim inverted A-line of his torso made him the envy of his network peers, while his gray tinged hair gave him an air of experienced responsibility.

The pounds had stayed off over the years by sheer dint of effort and the routine expense of a personal nutritionist and trainer. The *TV Guide* cover story from the previous season told the tale. But the story never latched on to the rumors concerning liposuction farms, or the face lifts making it necessary for Fats to shave behind his ears. Nobody wanted the Pandora's Box of Hollywood's *nip, tuck, and suck* set spilled into the open.

Fats started out in LA as a clowning TV weatherman. In a relatively short time, he made the move to an on-camera reporter, and then to a late-night news anchor spot. His easygoing style made his TV persona a welcome nightly guest in millions of homes, and his deep, distinctive voice was heard on hundreds of radio commercial voice-overs.

His true fame came as the host of *Ragtop*, a Saturday evening dance and music show permanently stuck in a time warp ranging from the roots of fifties rockabilly through the early sixties beach and soul music. *Ragtop* was syndicated on television stations nationwide. For eight years, *Ragtop* flew in the face of the odds before *MTV* and others of the same ilk sent it into oblivion.

Still, *Ragtop* established Fats as a public personality. The show, and judicious investments, had relieved him of financial worries and made it possible for him to pursue other interests. Currently, Fats hosted a late-night radio show on a popular FM station and a music nostalgia show, which aired in the no-man's land of Sunday afternoon. Both activities kept him happy and close to the roots of the music he cared about.

Through it all, Fats remained loyal to Elvis Presley. He had produced numerous Elvis radio specials, and the King was always an integral part of his Sunday afternoon nostalgia show. Having been there when it happened, Fats found himself constantly fascinated by the rumors and controversy surrounding the death of the King. He didn't believe any of the tabloid bluster, but there was a seed of doubt because of all the unanswered questions.

Because of his ties to the King, Fats always made himself available to talk to Elvis fan clubs, or to be the Master of Ceremonies for any kind of Elvis event—especially those involving charities. Tonight, as he had done before, he was hosting *Elvis Night* at the Paladin Club. In return, Benny Kravitz agreed to donate a portion of the evening's take to The Elvis Presley Memorial Trauma Center in Memphis, Tennessee.

The early part of the evening had been filled with Elvis music Fats spun from the club's DJ platform. The crowd swelled, and everyone had a good time be-bopping to old vinyls while the club musicians set up on the small stage. The band's job was to play back-up for the entrants in the Elvis impersonator contest, but also to back the pro impersonator Benny had hired to round out the activities.

When the impersonator contest started, Fats worked the crowd in his inimitable fashion, and they responded in kind. He was having a good time and the audience tuned into those vibes. They rocked-n'-rolled with him as he put the impersonators through their paces, and subtly guided the panel of celebrity judges into awarding first prize to the crowd favorite. It was all in the tricks of the trade. If you give an audience what they want, they'll want more and more.

And more and more was what tonight's audience wanted. The club band was tubed. Normally, they were an above average collection of session musicians picking up an extra buck, but tonight they were jamming. There was something in the air and the band and the audience were flying on the same frequency.

Fats smile widely. He knew what was happening. He'd seen it before. He'd done Elvis gigs all over the country and every blue moon or so, the presence of Elvis would invade the room. Fats knew if he looked into the night sky, the moon would be a milky blue. Elvis was in the Paladin Club tonight, and Fats could feel him. Everyone could feel him.

Fats had seen Elstein, the Jewish Elvis, perform on several occasions and he liked the act. There was a lot of humor in the guy's gig, but along the way he did a pretty credible Elvis. But Fats couldn't see Elstein giving the type of performance the evening promised. Tonight, demanded an act that would go beyond impersonation into possession.

While the band members continued their warm up numbers, Fats saw Jerome coming toward him. When he was close enough, he handed Fats a folded piece of paper, then bent over and whispered in Fats' ear.

A silly grin too genuine for network TV spread across Fats' face. Elstein was out and Cole Ramsey and some guy named Jon Burrows were in. Fats unfolded the piece of paper. It was a note from Cole. Fats had been friends with Cole for a long time and they trusted each other. The short missive told Fats to hype Jon Burrows for all he was worth.

Elstein was good, but Fats had seen Cole perform on many occasions and knew he was one of the best. Cole Ramsey would knock this crowd on his ass. If this Jon Burrows guy was half as good, then tonight was going to be dynamite. It was a cliché for the guy to be using one of Elvis' old pseudonyms, but Cole's word was good enough for Fats to put his doubts aside.

With confidence, Fats stepped to the main stage microphone. Behind him the band went pianissimo. In front, the crowd surged forward in anticipation. There was electricity in the air. Fats could feel the excitement —he could feel the spirit of Elvis in the building.

"Cats and gals listen up. I have some news that's going to put you in orbit!" Fat's voice spilled out of the large speakers. It was full of deep resonance and soft southern culture. It was a voice that held you, a voice that promised everything, a late-night voice coming out of your radio on a cold, black, stormy night when you were all alone.

"The Paladin Club is proud to bring you two of the top Elvis impersonators to ever put on a white rhinestone jumpsuit." Fats was really into the flow of the evening. He knew Cole never wore a jumpsuit in his act, but hype was everything. "First up, I'd like you to give a big hand to one of my favorites—fresh from his act with *Legends Alive*—Cole Ramsey!"

Fats stepped back as the band, who had been given a hand-written song list, swung into *Mystery Train*. Cole bopped onto the stage with a swagger and a snarl that rocked the crowd back on their heels. He played the borrowed guitar slung around his neck as if it were an extension of his body, his voice filling the club with his trademark soul of the early Elvis. During the early part of the song, Cole tried to pierce the glare of the spotlights and pick out MacAlister's position at the bar. It was an impossible. The club was filled with swaying bodies hungry for the greatest music of all time. The relentless beat soon had Cole in its grip.

He didn't give the audience a chance to catch their breath. Without missing a note, he led the band into *Suspicious Minds* and then *Kentucky Rain*. The songs weren't part of his normal repertoire, but then nothing this evening had been normal.

Moving into *When My Blue Moon Turns To Gold Again* and then into *Blue Suede Shoes*, Cole put every ounce of effort into his performance. The sweat flowed down his face. His left leg danced out of control, sending the women in the crowd into a frenzy. He ended the set on a hard note and the crowd cheered and applauded explosively.

With barely a pause to acknowledge the tribute, Cole grabbed the microphone. "Ladies and gentlemen —Jon Burrows!" He extended his hand to the stage wings and the band went into the introduction of *One Night*. There was a pregnant pause, and for a second, Cole thought Elvis had disappeared on him.

Then the man himself walked out onto the stage.

Elvis, impersonating Jon Burrows impersonating Elvis, pulled the Elstein wig off his head and dropped it dramatically on the stage. He took off the heavy gold framed glasses he'd borrowed from Elstein's props and cast them aside. There was the noise of the entire audience taking in a collective gulp of air.

Elvis shucked his shoulders and strode to the edge of the stage. The band was in the groove, continuing the musical buildup. Glaring at the audience, Elvis dared anyone to question his right to the spotlight.

Sexual heat rolled off him as if an interior switch had been thrown.

Cole couldn't believe what he was seeing. This fifty-nine-year-old man with hollowed out cheeks and a funky haircut, who looked like Elvis only because he was wearing a borrowed white jumpsuit, had taken over control of the crowd in seconds.

Elvis' leg started to tremble.

A female voice yelled out, "I love you, Elvis!"

And suddenly the floodgates opened.

A woman screamed. Another one joined her. There was a collective rush of bodies toward the stage, and every female in the house was caught up in the act. Their screams drowned out the band. Every time Elvis twitched, another fresh wave of frenzy crashed across the crowd.

The King grabbed the microphone instinctively on cue with the music, began to slowly sing, "One...night... with you..."

Cole felt his heart racing. This was the voice. This was the power. If there had been any doubt the man in front of him was really the King come back to life, it was banished forever. There was one man in the history of the world who had that sound—Elvis Presley.

Elvis pulled a red scarf from around his neck, wiped his brow, and let the thin material flutter into the audience. Pandemonium broke out in front of the stage. Several of the club bouncers stopped a woman from climbing onto the stage.

Cole was fascinated, riveted by the spectacle. As Elvis picked up the beat with *Jailhouse Rock*, Cole realized there had never been an impersonator who could successfully captured the essence of the man. The art of impersonation was all caricature—give the audience an impression, a look, a move, a sound, and they will provide the rest through their imagination.

But to capture the essence of a king was impossible.

Elvis cooled the band out with his hand and came to rest in front of the microphone as the audience clapped and cheered the end of the song. He waited the audience out. Staring at them, his guitar slung behind his back, legs astride, brooding eyes filled with sexual threat, his mere presence acted as a pressure cooker.

With impeccable timing, in an instant of perfect quiet, Elvis began to sing. The band remained frozen as the King's a-cappella voice rang out through the club in a rendition of *Don't Cry Daddy*—a tear jerker written by Mac Davis in which a divorced father's children console him as he spins his tale of single parent misery.

The King held everyone in the club in thrall. Even MacAlister, still sitting at the bar, was unconsciously enraptured by the voice and presence of the man on stage. He could feel something inside of him bring tears to his eyes. He swore under his breath, but he couldn't break the spell.

On either side of MacAlister, bouncers Dalton and Chantry halted their devious progress toward the man they had been assigned to neutralize. Years of hard living, hard drinking, and walking the hard side of life had inured these men to anything resembling emotional reactions. But as the music welled up inside them, each man individually resolved to do whatever he could to stop the threat toward this man whose voice moved them so.

With an incredible ear and perfect pitch, Elvis rolled from *Don't Cry Daddy* straight into Paul Anka's *My Way*. He moved his borrowed guitar into position and began to accompany himself. Gradually, the band began to fill in the background. Even Cole found himself playing his own instrument as Elvis motioned for him to join him on stage.

The man known as the King of Rock n' Roll had taken them to a place where the energies of every musician, and every member of the audience, were totally in sync.

Fats stared open mouthed at the man standing at center stage. The magic the evening promised had exploded through the club the moment *Jon Burrows* had stepped into the spotlight. Fats knew the King's voice, style, and movements as well as he knew his own. If anyone had asked him who was center stage at the Paladin Club, he knew there was only one answer.

As the song ended, the crowd went wild, but Elvis didn't give them time to recover.

"Thank you. Thank you very much," he said into the microphone. He put one hand on Cole's arm to keep him close, then turned his head to speak quickly to the band. The musicians never questioned him. He was absolutely in charge.

Keeping Cole with him for a duet, Elvis led the way into *The Wonder of You*. The song had ample opportunities for vocal pyrotechnics, and the two men knocked hell out of it as they wrung it dry of every emotional possibility. The crowd ate it up and threw their own emotions into the performance to fuel the two singers and the band.

Together, Cole and Elvis jumped into *If I Can Dream* with the same complete dedication and conviction Elvis originally used to turn the song into his own version of soul. The song sealed and validated Elvis' 1968 comeback, and this night's version sealed a comeback of another type.

As the last notes faded away, Elvis grabbed Cole's hand and raised it over their heads. The crowd loved it and wrapped the pair in wave after wave of adulation. Fats stood applauding so hard his hands would sting for two days.

Elvis turned and cued the band. Immediately, he swung into his trademark finale—*You Don't Have To Say You Love Me*. His voice was strong and clear, unchanged by age or lack of use. Cole rode with him on the song, getting an instant education in the intangibles that made Elvis great. It was a humbling experience, and as the song ended he felt tears streaming down his face. He turned away in embarrassment, but Elvis grabbed him in a bear hug and squeezed him tight.

"Thank you," Elvis whispered into Cole's ear over the roar of the crowd. "Thank you."

The crowd continued their applause as the band continued to play back-up music. Elvis held Cole's hand up over their heads again. The crowd cheered louder than ever. Fats bounded onto the stage continuing to clap his hands with stinging results. He hugged Cole and then turned to the man who called himself Jon Burrows.

"You're looking a hell of a lot slimmer, Fats," Elvis said, his mouth coming across with his naturally crooked grin. Fats stared at him in dumbfounded recognition. Elvis wrapped his old friend in a bear hug.

When he released Fats, Elvis shucked his guitar and grabbed Cole's hand. "Let's go," he said, and the two men jumped into the crowd.

CHAPTER 37

WHEN MACALISTER SAW COLE AND ELVIS JUMP OFF THE stage, he felt the spell he was under shatter. He was sitting on a high stool with his back to the bar. His elbows were supporting him on the brass railing that ran around the bar top behind him, and his feet were propped on the lowest rung of the stool. When he saw his targets disappear into the crowd, he lurched forward on the stool and tried to get to his feet. Instead, he felt himself slammed backward his arms pulled behind him.

There was a pain around both of his wrists and he heard a ratcheting noise even over the din of the crowd's cheering. Like an enraged bull he struggled to free himself, but the handcuffs Dalton and Chantry had sprung around his wrists had been secured by another set of cuffs to the bar railing. The ratchets around his wrists bit tighter into his skin.

"What kind of crap is this!" he yelled at the two men standing calmly next to him. He had been concentrating so hard on attempting to locate Elvis and Cole, he hadn't seen the bouncers approaching.

"Calm down, cowboy," Dalton said. "We don't like drug pushers in the Paladin Club. But we won't have to get rough unless you make us."

"Drug pusher?" MacAlister was livid. "What are you talking about? Drug Pusher?" He struggled with the handcuffs again. Chantry responded by hitting him in the stomach. Air whooshed out of MacAlister's lungs and a thin stream of bile escaped over his lip and ran down his chin.

When he managed to get a little air back, he spat on the floor and then looked at Chantry. "I'll remember you," he said. The tough as iron Chantry felt a cold sweat flow over him.

Dalton said, "There's no need to be unneighborly, cowboy. We're only doing our job."

MacAlister switched his gaze over to him. "What job?"

Chantry replied, "Making sure dope pushing scum don't bother the nice folk who come to our club."

MacAlister was confused and pissed off. He figured Burrows and his partner, the guy introduced as Cole Ramsey, were in the club with the woman and the kid, but if he was held to long, he could lose them. He didn't know if this pair of idiots really thought he was a dope pusher, or if it was a scam to let the others escape.

MacAlister didn't understand how he had become overwhelmed by seeing Cole and Burrows on stage. When the pair had appeared in the spotlight, MacAlister had experienced a rare moment of indecision. He didn't know what to do other than wait them out. He'd decided the duo had to finish their act at some point, and he would deal with the situation then. But *then* had become *now*, and he was handcuffed to a brass bar rail being set-up for a phony drug charge.

"I'm not a drug pusher, you idiots," MacAlister was fuming.

"You are now," said Chantry. He reached into a pocket of his jeans and pulled out several packets of white powder. He casually stuffed them into the pockets of MacAlister's light overcoat.

MacAlister had put the coat on before coming into the club to help conceal the sawn-off shotgun on a sling underneath his left arm. If he could have reached the weapon at that moment, he would have started blasting away despite the consequences.

MacAlister saw Jerome and several other bouncers forging a wedge through the crowd to help Cole and Elvis reach the club's front door of the club. He was wondering where the woman and the kid were, when two uniformed police officers entered the club. When Dalton signaled the cops over, MacAlister understood what the game was all about.

"There will be another time," he said in a low voice to the two bouncers.

"Maybe in ten years when you get out of jail for possession of cocaine with intent to sell," Chantry said. "You'd be amazed at how sincere Dalton and I can be on the witness stand."

"You forget I'll probably be out on bail before you've finished your shift here tonight."

Chantry shook his head. "Nice try, but we have

friends in low places. Bail ain't going to figure anywhere in your future."

As the police officers arrived, MacAlister saw Dalton wave in the direction of the front door. He looked over and saw Cole wave back. Cole shifted his gaze to lock eyes with MacAlister. Raising up a hand, fingers pointed like a gun barrel in MacAlister's direction, Cole popped his thumb down in a firing motion. He then laughed as he was swept out the door.

MacAlister slammed a cap on his emotions. He heard Chantry telling the cops how they had caught MacAlister trying to sell drugs to the club's patrons. He also heard Fats McCorkle's voice over the P.A. system.

"Ladies and Gentlemen, Elvis has left the building."

————

OUTSIDE THE CLUB, Cole and Elvis made straight for MacAlister's black van. The vehicle had been located and hotwired by another of the club's employees and parked at the front curb. Cole took the driver's seat this time, and Elvis clambered in on the passenger side.

Cole rolled down the window. "Thanks for everything," he said to Jerome, who was standing beside the van.

"Anyone who can rock the house like you two did tonight deserves the red-carpet treatment."

"Tell Benny we appreciate him."

"You got it. But I think he'll be thanking you."

Cole threw the van into gear.

"Where to?" he asked Elvis.

"Head for the safe house. We'll make sure Judy and

Stella arrived, then we need to hook up with Gordy and decide what to do next. We may have to close down part of the underground pipeline until we can know how much we've been compromised."

Cole heard a tremor in Elvis' voice. When he looked over at his companion, he could see Elvis' hands were shaking.

"You okay?" he asked.

"Adrenaline reaction, man. It's been a long time since I was on stage doing the old songs. I'd almost forgotten the high it gives you—how much I love performing for a big audience."

"Did you know Fats, the announcer guy?"

Elvis laughed. "He and I go way back. Bet we gave him a shock."

Cole turned serious. "You were unbelievable out there tonight."

"You weren't too bad yourself."

"No, I'm serious. You were incredible. I've never seen anything like it. You have something I've never seen before in a performer. You have an incredible presence, and unmatchable timing. But it's more—" his voice trailed off. "I don't know how to explain it."

"Don't try," Elvis said, shrugging it off. "Performance is all about the moment."

Cole turned the van onto a freeway on-ramp. "The King lives," he said quietly.

———

INSIDE THE PALADIN CLUB, the crowd had thinned. The two uniformed police officers had searched MacAlister while he was handcuffed. They removed the planted cocaine from his coat pocket, which hadn't surprised them. They also located the sawn-off shotgun in its sling under MacAlister's left arm, which did surprise them. The discovery also surprised Dalton and Chantry.

As the officers bent to remove and exchange the bouncer's handcuffs for theirs, MacAlister made his move. As the cuffs came free, the big man whipped his arms forward and slammed the heads of the two officers together. He then pushed them apart and into the startled paths of Dalton and Chantry.

Using the handcuffs as weapons, he slashed the sharp ratchets of the open ends across the faces of the two bouncers. As blood spurted, MacAlister whirled and kicked Dalton's exposed midsection. He then smashed a fist into Dalton's throat, dropping the big bouncer to the floor in pain.

"I told you I'd remember," MacAlister said.

Wasting no further time, he turned to the bar. Laying where it had been placed by the policeman was his sawn-off shotgun. Grabbing up the ugly, short barreled gun, MacAlister fired one chamber into the ceiling of the club. Instantly the remaining customers began screaming and cleared out of his way.

Without looking back, MacAlister moved quickly toward the club entrance. Outside, he reloaded with the extra rounds he kept looped under the back of his belt. A quick glance told him his van was gone, but he didn't waste any time worrying about how to procure new transportation.

Running to the closest tri-light controlled intersection, he waited for the red light to stop a line of oncoming cars. Walking up to the driver's door of a white Saab Turbo, he pulled open the door and pointed his weapon at the woman driver.

"Get out," he said.

The woman looked at him and screamed. MacAlister reached in and grabbed her roughly. He pulled her out and threw her on the roadway.

The two cops came running out of the Paladin Club with their guns drawn. "Freeze! Police!" they yelled when they spotted him.

Who do they think they were kidding, MacAlister wondered as he jumped into the Saab and pulled it out of traffic and onto the sidewalk. With little regard for the car's shocks, he rocketed forward off the curb, through the red light, and back onto the street again.

The *freeze police* could kiss his butt. He had been made a fool, and somebody was going to pay.

CHAPTER 38

WHEN COLE AND ELVIS ARRIVED AT THE SAFE HOUSE, Sheila Fontaine ran out to greet them.

"Thank goodness you're safe," she said, hugging first Elvis then Cole.

Cole was surprised by the embrace but enjoyed it. The hug made him see Sheila differently in the light switched on in the romantic impulse part of his brain.

Sheila saw his look. It was clear the same confusion of unexpected feeling was messing with her own emotional makeup.

Elvis caught what was going on and laughed softly.

Sheila snapped out of it and turned on him. "What are you laughing about? We've been worried sick."

"Did Judy and Stella arrive safely?" Cole asked, getting priorities back on track.

"Yes. Candice was initially upset because she thought the integrity of the safe house was compromised by having Benny bring her straight here."

"We didn't have much choice," Elvis tried to explain.

Sheila shook her head. "Don't worry. Your friend Benny has charmed Candice silly. He's promised to make monetary contributions and secure further contacts for the underground. He could be a big help."

"Is your father back?" asked Elvis.

Sheila rolled her eyes. "He's been pacing around in the house like a crazy person. You better go calm him down. He's sure this thing with Arceneaux is coming to a head."

MacAlister's hotwired black van was still running. "This hunk of machinery is as hot as a Van Halen guitar riff," Cole said. "Can we stash it somewhere before it gets spotted."

Sheila said. "You go inside and talk to Dad. I'll hide the van in the garage." She hugged Cole again. "I'm really glad you're okay."

"Me too," said Cole, hugging her back.

Inside the house there were more hugs and handshakes. Gordy kept slapping them on the back. Candice and Judy hugged them. Judy kept saying, "Thank you," over and over again.

"You're welcome," Elvis reassured her. "Is Stella okay?"

Judy said, "She's sleeping sweetly in one of the bedrooms."

Elvis looked at Candice. "Is there a plan to get Judy and Stella moved on?" he asked. "This situation is more dangerous than normal. We're going to have to bury them deep."

"I'm on top of it," Candice replied. "They'll be clear of here within the hour." She put a hand on Judy's arm. "We'll keep you safe."

"Hey, hey!" said Benny, coming in from another room carrying a sandwich. "I called the club. You guys brought the roof down. Fats said he ain't seen nothing like it before. Any time you guys want a gig, you come see Uncle Benny. I'll take care of you."

"What about MacAlister?" Cole asked.

"Oy vey," Benny said, with a huge arm gesture. "There the news ain't so good. He managed to get away from Dalton and Chantry when the cops took the cuffs off him."

Elvis was immediately concerned. "Was anyone hurt?"

"A little hurt," Benny said with a shrug. "But nobody was killed, so we can count our blessings."

"How much is a little hurt?"

Benny gave his patented shrug again. "Let's say I got two employees who are going to be a lot more careful in the future."

"I hate to break this up," said Gordy interrupting. "But we have some major problems to deal with before tomorrow night."

"MacAlister is a major problem," Cole said.

"Maybe," Gordy said. "But right now, there's an even bigger one."

"Arceneaux?" Elvis said the dreaded name.

"Give the man a prize," replied Gordy.

"What have you learned?"

Rapidly, Gordy shared the information given to him by Father Romero.

After letting it sink in, Elvis asked, "You've seen these catacombs?"

"I've been in one of them."

"How safe are they?" Cole asked.

Gordy shrugged. "Father Romero says most are okay. But they've had several cave-ins and some of the tunnels have filled with methane sewer gases."

"One spark could blow those sky high."

"Be thankful you're a non-smoker."

The three men were sitting in the living room of the safe house with Sheila.

Candice and Benny—fitting together like pieces of a jigsaw puzzle—were off making arrangements for the safe onward passage of Judy and Stella.

"Kids and dope," Elvis said. "We should bring the cops in on this."

Gordy jumped up. "We don't know who we can trust on the cops. Lucky Jordan was FBI, and he couldn't be trusted. I've earned the right to take Arceneaux down myself. Most importantly, we have to protect both the underground and Father Romero's sanctuary movement. We want to save those fifty kids, not send them back where they came from to suffer further—which is what will happen if they get taken by the cops."

"What about Lew Sutton—hasn't he earned the right to be in on this?"

Gordy calmed down for a second. "Lew's okay."

"I know another cop we can trust," said Cole.

"Who?"

"My sister is an investigator with the Sheriff's department. She got me involved in this in the first place. She's probably worried sick."

"Will she go along with our plan?" Gordy asked.

"We have a plan?" Cole asked.

"You betcha." Gordy's grin was something to behold. "Something I've had in mind since I first laid eyes on you."

CHAPTER 39

IN THE BLACKNESS OF THE NIGHT, HARSH GOLDEN LIGHT flooded out of Union Station as if the structure was the last glowing ember in an otherwise cold fire. It was nine o'clock and the parking lot of the station was almost empty after the arrival of the 8:45 Amtrak from San Diego. No other arrivals were scheduled until the ten o'clock special arrived from the Mexican border via San Diego, San Clemente, and Oceanside.

Inside a large motor home, which had been rented with false identification especially for the evening, Gordy, Elvis, and Cole waited with ever increasing anxiety. Cole figured they might have made use of the van they'd stolen from MacAlister the night before. Gordy, however, had already seen to the disposal of the van through a chop-shop. Gordy, who'd got a thousand dollars for delivering the van, said, "After all the grief MacAlister and others like him have caused us, it's not nearly payback enough."

The waiting in the dark was getting to all of them.

"Where are all your buddies?" Gordy asked Cole. He made no effort to hide the agitation in his voice.

Cole said, "It's only nine o'clock. You said not to have them arrive before nine-thirty. These guys are okay. They'll be here."

Gordy was not mollified. "They better be."

"Have we arranged enough transportation?" Elvis asked.

Gordy grunted. "It's not the transportation I'm worried about—Sheila and Candice should be here soon with the station wagons—I'm more worried about where we're going to find temporary homes for all these kids."

"Do you think Father Romero can help?" Cole asked. He squirmed in his seat to observe the entrances to the parking lot.

Gordy unwrapped a piece of gum and stuck it in his mouth. He threw the wrapper on the motor home floor. "Probably, but I haven't been able to contact him since I spoke with him last night."

"Is his information reliable?"

"There aren't a lot of people I trust in this world. This whole thing could be a set-up to take us out. But I trust the padre. He'd die before he turned against us." Gordy chewed his gum noisily. "I want to take Arceneaux down, but those fifty kids—if they do exist—are more important than anything else."

Elvis said, "Having the chance to do something about situations like this makes the personal sacrifices worthwhile." He looked at Cole. "Do you understand why I've stayed dead? There is nothing more important than helping the kids involved with the underground."

"If Gordy and you don't do this, nobody will?"

Elvis shrugged. "I guess."

"No guessing about it," Gordy jumped into the conversation. "If it wasn't for Elvis, the children's underground wouldn't exist. I have contacts and trade-craft, but Elvis is the driving force. His inspiration keeps us all going through the rough parts. He keeps doing the best we can in a rotten situation."

"What about MacAlister?" Cole asked.

Gordy produced a wicked smile. "What's life without a loose cannon to keep things interesting?"

Cole looked at his watch.

9:15

A two door, pink, Chevy Impala pulled up next to the barrier to the parking lot. A hand reached through the driver's window to snatch a ticket from the auto-matic machine. The barrier raised, and the big car drove in and parked near the station's main entrance.

Two men climbed out of the car.

Both of them were Elvis Presley.

CHAPTER 40

INSIDE THE SANCTUARY CHURCH OF THE BLACK Madonna, Zachary Arceneaux paced back and forth beneath the effigy that gave the church its name. In front of him, in the deserted chapel, his bodyguard and two other henchmen sat on a hard wooden pew.

This was a big operation. Arceneaux believed the fewer people involved the safer you were. The men were silent, knowing anything they said would be interpreted wrong by Arceneaux and cause them grief.

Arceneaux had spent many years putting himself back into a position to again become a major player in the drug world. After Gordy Fontaine's pursuit had forced him to abdicate his lifestyle by turning informer, he had worked night and day to retrieve all he had lost. The difference this time was he was doing it in plain sight of the federal investigators who thought they had him under their thumb.

People he gained control over—such as Lucky Jordan—made his task easier. He felt bad about what he'd been forced to do to Jordan, but not from empathy. He felt bad because Jordan had been a good tool. But when a tool breaks, you don't keep it around. You throw it away and buy another one. It shouldn't be too hard, he thought. Cops like Jordan were always available.

Tonight's delivery of five hundred kilos of cocaine represented the largest shipment he'd received since he'd been back in the business. It represented millions of dollars in cash he'd already been paid by several big-time players. Arceneaux was committed to deliver the product. If he didn't, he would rapidly find himself the next dinner for his own pets.

The importance of the delivery to his future was the main reason Arceneaux was taking personal control. The other reason was the fifty, snot-nosed, little brats who were along for the ride. The kids had not been Arceneaux's idea. If he had a choice, he would have refused them. However, his Central American contacts waited until he was financially committed before they threw the children into the pot. Either the kids came or there would be no delivery of the narcotics. It was the price he had to pay for using the Sanctuary movements smuggling routes.

Arceneaux had looked for an angle he could play. He knew how pedophiles preyed on young children. He had made use of them before, by blackmailing those from whom he needed *favors*.

He was not going to allow himself to be used. If the kids had to come, then he would make a profit from them. The good padre and his holy crusade could go to hell after this shipment of drugs was delivered. When he had fulfilled his obligations to his buyers, he would be able to use the standardized drug routes of the major players.

Arceneaux would be free to dispose of the children at a major profit. It had taken time to make the arrangements, but in Arceneaux's deranged world anything was possible. A man who fed other men to gators for his own enjoyment did not worry about the fate of fifty children he did not know.

Arceneaux turned his wrist like a nervous twitch and checked his watch for near the hundredth time in the last hour.

9:20

Arceneaux was a control freak. Everything had to be done to his design and carried out on his schedule. Time, however, was refusing to cooperate. The laws of nature were something Arceneaux could not feed to the gators. It upset him, because he hated what he could not control. If he could not control something, he sought to destroy it—like Gordy Fontaine.

Arceneaux's rages were one of the reason his men remained silent and unmoving on the wooden pew. They didn't want to replace Gordy in the gator pit.

Arceneaux wondered about MacAlister. He'd checked the man out personally. He was supposed to be the best in the business. But, he hadn't heard from the hitman since their phone conversation the night before when MacAlister was outside the woman's motel. This was not a good sign.

"You're sure MacAlister never called to report?" Arceneaux demanded as he stopped in front of his

PAUL BISHOP

bodyguard. It was the tenth time he'd asked the question. The question was only a useless explosion of energy.

"I'm sure, Mr. Arceneaux." The bodyguard's answer did not betray his own frustrations. He'd keep answering as long as Arceneaux kept asking. It was his job. He'd seen what happened to people working for Arceneaux who did not do their job.

"Where's the padre?"

"In the vestibule."

"Bring him here."

The bodyguard rose and walked the few steps to the vestibule door. He opened it and looked inside. Father Romero was kneeling before a small cross affixed to the wall, praying. A set of silver worry beads made their way rapidly through his fingers.

"Mr. Arceneaux wants to see you."

Father Romero did not move.

The bodyguard moved into the room. He put his hand on Father Romero's shoulder.

Romero looked up at him. "Just a moment, Anthony," he said, using the bodyguard's first name. "I must finish my last contemplation."

Being a good Catholic in his own right, Anthony *Knuckles* Franks was uncomfortable disturbing the priest's prayers. He was more uncomfortable not responding quickly to Zachary Arceneaux's demands. Fortunately, Father Romero finished quickly.

Father Romero noticed the bodyguard's obvious distress. "You're a good boy, Anthony. I won't make trouble for you."

"Ain't me you got to worry about," Tony told him, leading the way back into the chapel.

Without preamble, Arceneaux began tossing questions. "Do you have the rooms set up for the children as you were told?"

"Of course," said Father Romero. Several of the shorter catacomb tunnels near the entrance to the church had been set aside and furnished as basic dormitories.

"You've laid in the food you're going to need to feed the brats?" Arceneaux was only concerned because he didn't want to be hassled by his human crop before he could get rid of them the following day.

"Everything is in readiness," Father Romero assured him.

Arceneaux reached out a hand and patted the priest on the face. Somehow the movement was nowhere near as benevolent as when the priest had used it on Tony Franks. "You've done well, padre."

Arceneaux checked his watch again.

9:30

"I can't wait any longer," he said. "It's time, padre. Take us through your precious tunnels to the station."

Tony Franks moved forward and pulled open the trapdoor behind the altar. Father Romero led the way down the steep steps. He was followed by Arceneaux, Tony Franks, and finally Big Timmy and Ollie Dale— Arceneaux's other two thugs.

In the tunnels, Father Romero turned on the lights illuminating the first part of the tunnels. He led the way past the dank smelling entrance to the tunnel housing Arceneaux's gators. When the electricity ran out, Father

Romero turned on his flashlight and continued ahead at a rapid pace.

The good Father took comfort from several things —his faith in God, his faith in Gordy Fontaine, and his faith in the razor-sharp switchblade taped to the small of his back.

CHAPTER 41

MacALISTER HAD NO FAITH IN ANYTHING. HE HAD LONG ago given up the concept of God as a losing proposition for weaklings and sheep. In MacAlister's vision of the world, death was final. There was nothing beyond— you had to take everything you could on the first go round.

In MacAlister's world a man lived or died by his reputation. Without a rep you were nothing. The best things in life passed you by without a backward glance. If word got out some young punk and an over-the-hill Elvis impersonator tied him up in knots and walked away laughing, he would never again be trusted with anything beyond nickel and dime keyhole peeping.

It only took one screw-up and you were no longer in the loop. He had to get to the punk and the Burrows guy before word got out. If Arceneaux gave him a bad time about payment, he might have to take the big man out as well.

The image of Cole Ramsey pointing his fingers at

him like a gun and dropping his thumb hammer was burned into MacAlister's brain. He saw it happen over and over in slow motion. He knew he'd be haunted by the image forever unless he could splatter the kid's brains across the landscape.

He wanted the punk, he wanted Burrows, he wanted the woman and her daughter, but most of all he wanted Gordy Fontaine. Because Fontaine's failure to show up had set the whole screw-up in motion. MacAlister was determined to get them all. MacAlister had his own sources who had told him what Arceneaux had planned for the evening and where. If his sources knew what Arceneaux was doing, Gordy Fontaine would certainly know. Fontaine was as hot to trot to get Arceneaux as MacAlister was to get Fontaine.

MacAlister parked on a dark street on the perimeter of Union Station and waited not-so-patiently. He was in a new black vehicle, a Nissan SX he'd stolen from the airport's long-term parking lot after he dumped the white Saab. He had seen the motor home he knew held Gordy, Cole, and Burrows pull in. He fingered his weapon and touched the extra rounds in the pocket of his black windbreaker.

He checked his watch.

9:45.

He looked at the parking lot. Six more cars pulled in.

He watched in amazement as Elvis Presley got out of every one of them.

———

SOPHIA UNGARTE LOOKED at the cheap watch pinned to her worn madras skirt.

9:50.

They should be pulling into the Union Station in five more minutes. Then they could get free of the hell-hole the freight car had become. Fifty children and five adults in the enclosed space, with no toilet facilities and no windows. The freight car had become an oven of oppression before the train pulled away from the station where they were smuggled on board. After the five-hour trip, they would be lucky to find nobody had suffocated when they finally were let out.

She looked at the children around her. Most were between the ages of seven and ten. A few were older and a few younger, but they all shared the haunted look of small, wild animals. The look came from not knowing where your next meal would be, or if the shadow you saw was a predator waiting to strike. Life had to be better in Los Angeles. It couldn't be any worse than in the rotting jungles of Nicaragua, or El Salvador, or Guatemala, or any of the other Central American countries from where the orphans had been gathered.

The lives they left behind were filled with death squads—who murdered parents before the terrorized eyes of their children. Their lives had been filled with pestilence, famine, brutality, depravity, and despair. Sophia believed any life would be better than those the children were leaving behind. She had no idea what a monster named Zachary Arceneaux planned for their ultimate fate.

Sophia felt the change in the speed of the train and realized they must be slowing down for the scheduled stop at Union Station.

She checked her watch again.

9:55.

———

Neither Joella nor Lew Sutton were happy. From their separate back-up positions around the perimeter of Union Station, they fumed about the roles they had agreed to play in the plans hatched by Cole and Gordy.

They saw their sibling and best friend as their own personal burden. Conversely, both felt the weight of their own guilt for putting Gordy and Cole into their situation. They knew they would always stand with them. If they had talked about it, they would agree the most amazing thing happening was the stream of cars pulling into the Union Station parking lot. The cars weren't amazing, but watching Elvis Presley, the King of Rock-n'-Roll, get out of every car was amazing. Some cars had one Elvis, some cars had two, and several had three or four.

Elvis Presley was supposed to be dead and spinning in his grave in Graceland.

He was supposed to be tapping his blue suede shoes all over Rock-n'-Roll Heaven.

He was supposed to be buying Twinkies at 7-11 stores in Kalamazoo, Michigan.

Instead, here he was—cloned and cloned again—walking into Union Station.

If Lew or Joella could have stopped staring at the parking lot to check their watches, they would have seen the digital displays kick over to the hour.

10:00.

CHAPTER 42

10:00.

As the scheduled Amtrak train pulled into the station, Cole, Gordy, and Elvis clambered out of the motor home and sprinted toward the10:00.

As the scheduled Amtrak train pulled into the station, Cole, Gordy, and Elvis clambered out of the motor home and sprinted toward the crowd gathered at the entrance to the huge terminal. All three were wearing white jumpsuits with wide, turned up collars, wide belts with wider belt buckles, and an assortment of rhinestones dripping from their shoulders to their toes. They wore jet black wigs, complete with long side-burns and big hair pompadour styling.

In a normal setting, they would have stood out like pimples on a debutante's chin, but when they reached the stairs to the terminal, they blended into the crowd like albinos in a snow storm. It wasn't difficult. They were surrounded by fifty other carbon copy versions of Elvis Presley. There were enough white jumpsuits to choke a drycleaner's, and enough rhinestones and sequins to outfit a dowager's ball.

There were tall Elvis's and short pelvises. Fat Elvis's and emaciated ones. There was an Oriental Elvis and three or four black pelvises. There was a Mexican Elvis, and even an Eskimo version complete with a harpoon shaped guitar. Three female Elvis impersonators, who had all arrived together in a pink limousine, waved when they saw Cole jogging up the steps toward them.

Everyone within the group knew everyone else from Elvis impersonator contests and gigs all over California. Many had competed together in nationwide competitions, while others simply enjoyed playing dress-up at Elvis conventions and functions. All of them knew Cole Ramsey through friendship or reputation, and they had come running when Cole or Benny Kravitz had called and said their help was needed.

Cole and Benny had worn out their dialing fingers trying to reach everybody in time, but they had managed the task. What was most gratifying was the effort had paid off. Everyone they contacted was willing to drop what they were doing to help. Like Elvis fans, the impersonators were genuinely caring individuals whose fascination and love for the King of Rock-n'-Roll shaped and influenced their lives for the better.

Somebody in the parking lot had opened up the hatchback of their car to reveal two huge speakers. Within a few seconds the sounds of *Mystery Train* were blasting through the night air. A party atmosphere was quickly generating. Following Cole's lead, the whole group began moving into the Union Station terminal— an army of Elvis clone warriors. Searching for one Elvis amounted to trying to spot a specific Dalmatian in a dog run containing a hundred other running and jumping Dalmatians.

MacAlister exited his vehicle with his weapon concealed again on a sling under his unzipped windbreaker. He was moving forward, but he felt disoriented by what he was watching. Again, he was not sure how to handle the situation. He had planned to take out Cole, Burrows, and Gordy as soon as they got out of the motor home, but he hadn't planned for this mass confusion.

He couldn't shoot down every single Elvis look-a-like until he got to the three he wanted. It wasn't a moral decision, but a logistical one—he didn't have enough time or enough bullets. He also discarded the idea of running through the crowd, pulling off wigs and phony glasses. He had to hit quick and get out. This kind of crowd was going to attract a lot of attention including cops and witnesses—the two last things MacAlister wanted.

While this was running through his head, MacAlister's survival instinct picked up movement on his right side. He also heard the scuffing of a shoe on the pavement behind him. He whirled, attempting to bring the sawn-off shotgun out from the folds of his windbreaker.

"Drug Enforcement!" Lew Sutton shouted, as his tall, impossibly awkward body dropped into a shooting crouch. "Don't move!" His hands came together in front of him with a 9mm Berretta clasped between them.

MacAlister wasn't impressed. He kept his body moving, swinging his weapon out from under his arm. Before he could get a firm grip on it, however, he was hit from behind with the force of a Mack Truck. Sprawling, he instinctively threw his hands out to break his fall. Gravel bit into his palms, and the knees tore out of his tight jeans as they dragged across the ground.

Behind MacAlister, Cole's sister, Joella Garner, got to her feet after delivering the flying kick that knocked MacAlister to the ground. The fight was far from over, but she felt vindicated by getting in the first blow. Knowing MacAlister wouldn't go down easy, she'd moved fast. Her 9mm Smith & Wesson was holstered on the wide leather belt looped through her jeans, and the twenty-four-inch length of her Sheriff's side handle baton was grasped in her right hand. Also, on her belt were mace and handcuffs.

Steroids made MacAlister big and tough, but they had also made him slow. As MacAlister tried to get to his feet, Lew Sutton introduced one of his G-man style wingtips to MacAlister's nose. The big man rolled with the blow, trying to get at the sawn-off shotgun hopelessly tangled up in its sling.

When Cole called Joella she had been by turns angry, concerned, stubborn, and finally willing to go along. She didn't think her brother lived up to his potential, but she did trust him to make good choices. If he said the guy this Elvis guy was on the level, then she believed him.

Lew Sutton didn't go through the same process when Gordy contacted him. Lew had been following up on Gordy's wild goose chases for so long, he never argued anymore. When Gordy told him this was the big payoff, the ghost they had been chasing for years was going down, Lew simply asked what he could do to help.

MacAlister escaping from the trap laid for him at the Paladin Club bothered both Cole and Gordy. They knew MacAlister was going to turn up at the worst possible moment. To handle the situation, they asked Joella and Lew to cover their back door, allowing them to take down Arceneaux and rescue the children.

Joella and Lew were not used to being kept out of the main action, but as they fought the big man between them, they realized how important their role actually was. Joella jumped into the air and came down with both her knees slamming into the small of MacAlister's back. The big man roared in pain and lashed back with an elbow and knocked Joella back. She yelled as she bounced on the pavement and felt a bolt of agony zap up her tail bone.

Lew darted in and screwed his gun in MacAlister's ear. "Give it up!" he yelled

MacAlister ignored him as he rolled away from the pressure of the gun. He reached out with a huge hand and tore the gun out of Lew's grip. With a contemptuous gesture, he climbed to his feet and flung the gun away from him. Lew was too shocked to react, which gave MacAlister time to reach out and grab him by the throat.

A squawk was all Lew could force out of his voice box before MacAlister's hand constricted. The big man lifted Lew off the ground and shook him like a dog with a rat. With both his hands wrapped around MacAlister's huge wrist, Lew fought to get free, but he was rapidly losing the battle to remain conscious.

Lew felt his eyes were being squeezed out of his head. Held off the ground, he was forced to look directly into MacAlister's malevolent stare. He saw a flicker of something deep in the pupils of those eyes. He thought it was his imagination, then he saw it again.

The grip on his throat loosened then let go completely. He dropped to the ground in a heap and stared in amazement at Joella. She was standing directly behind MacAlister driving her police baton straight up between the big man's legs into his groin.

Once, twice, three times more, she repeated her movement with all the force her body could muster. Finally, MacAlister groaned, dropped to his knees with his hands between his legs and rolled into a fetal position. Joella was taking no chances. With her left hand, she pulled the can of mace out of its holder on her belt and sprayed it into the big man's face.

In unbelievable pain, MacAlister didn't know whether to hold his groin or claw at his eyes. He didn't have a chance to do either, as Lew and Joella roughly pulled his arms behind his back and handcuffed him. Joella also used a braided leg restraint to hog tie him and attach his ankles to the handcuffs around his wrists.

Lew looked at Joella. "Thanks," he croaked through his sore throat. "I couldn't have taken him alone. You've got a hell of a way with a baton and a can of mace, lady."

Joella's laugh was jittery as adrenaline continued to race through her body. "I think this hairball would probably agree with you." She nodded her head toward

MacAlister. "Except for the part about me being a lady."

Standing up together, they looked toward the main entrance of the train station and wondered how the main event was shaping up. crowd gathered at the entrance to the huge terminal. All three were wearing white jumpsuits with wide, turned up collars, wide belts with wider belt buckles, and an assortment of rhinestones dripping from their shoulders to their toes. They wore jet black wigs, complete with long sideburns and big hair pompadour styling.

In a normal setting, they would have stood out like pimples on a debutante's chin, but when they reached the stairs to the terminal, they blended into the crowd like albinos in a snow storm. It wasn't difficult. They were surrounded by fifty other carbon copy versions of Elvis Presley. There were enough white jumpsuits to choke a dry-cleaner's, and enough rhinestones and sequins to outfit a dowager's ball.

There were tall Elvis's and short Elvis's. Fat Elvis's and emaciated ones. There was an Oriental Elvis and three or four black Elvis's. There was a Mexican Elvis, and even an Eskimo version complete with a harpoon shaped guitar. Three female Elvis impersonators, who had all arrived together in a pink limousine, waved when they saw Cole jogging up the steps toward them.

Everyone within the group knew everyone else from Elvis impersonator contests and gigs all over California. Many had competed together in nationwide competitions, while others simply enjoyed playing dress-up at Elvis conventions and functions. All of them knew Cole Ramsey through friendship or reputation, and they had come running when Cole or Benny Kravitz had called and said their help was needed.

Cole and Benny had worn out their dialing fingers trying to reach everybody in time, but they had managed the task. What was most gratifying was the effort had paid off. Everyone they contacted was willing to drop what they were doing to help. Like Elvis fans, the impersonators were genuinely caring individuals whose fascination and love for the King of Rock-n'-Roll shaped and influenced their lives for the better.

Somebody in the parking lot had opened up the hatchback of their car to reveal two huge speakers. Within a few seconds the sounds of *Mystery Train* were blasting through the night air. A party atmosphere was quickly generating. Following Cole's lead, the whole group began moving into the Union Station terminal—an army of Elvis clone warriors. Searching for one Elvis amounted to trying to spot a specific Dalmatian in a dog run containing a hundred-other running and jumping Dalmatians.

MacAlister exited his vehicle with his weapon concealed again on a sling under his unzipped windbreaker. He was moving forward, but he felt disoriented by what he was watching. Again, he was not sure how to handle the situation. He had planned to take out Cole, Burrows, and Gordy as soon as they got out of the motor home, but he hadn't planned for this mass confusion.

He couldn't shoot down every single Elvis look-a-like until he got to the three he wanted. It wasn't a moral decision, but a logistical one—he didn't have enough time or enough bullets. He also discarded the idea of running through the crowd, pulling off wigs and phony glasses. He had to hit quick and get out. This kind of crowd was going to attract a lot of attention including cops and witnesses—the two last things MacAlister wanted.

While this was running through his head, a MacAlister's survival instinct picked up movement on his right side. He also heard the scuffing of a shoe on the pavement behind him. He whirled, attempting to bring the sawn-off shotgun out from the folds of his windbreaker.

"Drug Enforcement!" Lew Sutton shouted, as his tall, impossibly awkward body dropped into a shooting crouch. "Don't move!" His hands came together in front of him with a 9mm Berretta clasped between them.

MacAlister wasn't impressed. He kept his body moving, swinging his weapon out from under his arm. Before he could get a firm grip on it, however, he was hit from behind with the force of a Mac Truck. Sprawling, he instinctively threw his hands out to break his fall. Gravel bit into his palms, and the knees tore out of his tight jeans as they dragged across the ground.

Behind MacAlister, Cole's sister, Joella Garner, got to her feet after delivering the flying kick that knocked MacAlister to the ground. The fight was far from over, but she felt vindicated by getting in the first blow. Knowing MacAlister wouldn't go down easy, she'd moved fast. Her 9mm Smith & Wesson was holstered on the wide leather belt looped through her jeans, and the twenty-four-inch length of her Sheriff's side handle baton was grasped in her right hand. Also, on her belt were mace and handcuffs.

Steroids made MacAlister big and tough, but they had also made him slow. As MacAlister tried to get to his feet, Lew Sutton introduced one of his G-man style wingtips to MacAlister's nose. The big man rolled with the blow, trying to get at the sawn-off shotgun hopelessly tangled up in its sling.

When Cole called Joella she had been by turns angry, concerned, stubborn, and finally willing to go along. She didn't think her brother lived up to his potential, but she did trust him to make good choices. If he said the guy this Elvis guy was on the level, then she believed him.

Lew Sutton didn't go through the same process when Gordy contacted him. Lew had been following up on Gordy's wild goose chases for so long, he never argued anymore. When Gordy told him this was the big payoff, the ghost they had been chasing for years was going down, Lew simply asked what he could do to help.

MacAlister escaping from the trap laid for him at the Paladin Club bothered both Cole and Gordy. They knew MacAlister was going to turn up at the worst possible moment. To handle the situation, they asked Joella and Lew to cover their back door, allowing them to take down Arceneaux and rescue the children.

Joella and Lew were not used to being kept out of the main action, but as they fought the big man between them, they realized how important their role actually was. Joella jumped into the air and came down with both her knees slamming into the small of MacAlister's back. The big man roared in pain and lashed back with an elbow and knocked Joella back. She yelled as she bounced on the pavement and felt a bolt of agony zap up her tail bone.

Lew darted in and screwed his gun in MacAlister's ear. "Give it up!" he yelled

MacAlister ignored him as he rolled away from the pressure of the gun. He reached out with a huge hand and tore the gun out of Lew's grip. With a contemptuous gesture, he climbed to his feet and flung the gun away from him. Lew was too shocked to react, which gave MacAlister time to reach out and grab him by the throat.

A squawk was all Lew could force out of his voice box before MacAlister's hand constricted. The big man lifted Lew off the ground and shook him like a dog with a rat. With both his hands wrapped around MacAlister's huge wrist, Lew fought to get free, but he was rapidly losing the battle to remain conscious.

Lew felt his eyes were being squeezed out of his head. Held off the ground, he was forced to look directly into MacAlister's malevolent stare. He saw a flicker of something deep in the pupils of those eyes. He thought it was his imagination, then he saw it again.

The grip on his throat loosened then let go completely. He dropped to the ground in a heap and stared in amazement at Joella. She was standing directly behind MacAlister driving her police baton straight up between the big man's legs into his groin.

One, twice, three times more, she repeated her movement with all the force her body could muster. Finally, MacAlister groaned, dropped to his knees with his hands between his legs and trolled into a fetal position. Joella was taking no chances. With her left hand, she pulled the can of mace out of its holder on her belt and sprayed it into the big man's face.

In unbelievable pain, MacAlister didn't know whether to hold his groin or claw at his eyes. He didn't have a chance to do either, as Lew and Joella roughly pulled his arms behind his back and handcuffed him. Joella also used a braided leg restraint to hog tie him and attach his ankles to the handcuffs around his wrists.

Lew looked at Joella. "Thanks," he croaked through his sore throat. "I couldn't have taken him alone. You've got a hell of a way with a baton and a can of mace, lady."

Joella's laugh was jittery as adrenaline continued to race through her body. "I think this hairball would probably agree with you," she nodded her head toward MacAlister. "Except for the part about me being a lady."

Standing up together, they looked toward the main entrance of the train station and wondered how the main event was shaping up.

CHAPTER 43

THE STAFF OF UNION STATION HAD NEVER SEEN anything like the invasion of Elvis Presleys flooding the huge art deco waiting room. The late-night ticket agents and baggage handlers stood open-mouthed.

Several of the Elvis's had brought their guitars in with them. Taking up positions on the red leather covered waiting chairs, they began to rip into a medley of the early songs. Their voices rang out strong and echoed wonderfully around the magnificent acoustics of the terminal.

The other impersonators, who obviously knew all the words, joined in the singing as they made their way out onto the platform. Some of them jumped and jittered around, striking poses from their acts, getting into the spirit of the evening.

The ten o'clock Amtrak special pulled to a stop next to the main platform. It was longer than the commuter trains on the non-stop run between L.A. and San Diego during the morning and evening rush hours. Unlike those trains, it ran on an infrequent schedule, usually two or three nights a week, making stops at every nook-and-cranny station between the Mexican border and San Francisco. The entire run took close to twenty-four hours pulling both passenger and freight cars.

The trip was long and exhausting, and the passengers getting off the train showed signs of fatigue and irritability. At first, they were not amused by the huge gaggle of strangely dressed singers that greeted their arrival. But there has always been—and always will be—something about Elvis' music that lifts the spirits. Before long, the disembarking passengers were smiling and dancing around their luggage.

Elvis, Cole and Gordy were the only people on the platform not involved or engrossed in the performance. Making their way toward the back of the train, Cole and Elvis were trailing behind Gordy, who was half a step away from running. Cole figured Gordy was the shortest and weirdest looking Elvis impersonator he had ever seen—a strutting rooster in a glittering white suit.

The train's three freight cars were in front of the caboose at the end of the train. Because of the length of the train, they extended beyond the platform. They were made from the same shiny silver siding as the passenger cars and were decorated with the same red white and blue Amtrak logos. The biggest exterior difference between the two types of cars was the lack of windows and the large sliding doors featured on the freight haulers.

Following Gordy's lead, Cole and Elvis jumped off the platform onto the gravel paths running alongside the track. Gordy, who was wearing a heavy white cape two sizes too large for him, brought a huge pair of bolt cutters out from under its voluminous folds. The cloak fluttered making Gordy look like a grounded white bat.

The train guard stepped out of the caboose as the trio approached. His uniform was neat and trim. It was clear he was expecting somebody to approach the freight cars, but three versions of Elvis Presley were definitely not what he'd anticipated.

"Where is Father Romero?" he asked. The guard was of Latin descent, and Gordy figured him for part of the Sanctuary movement—aware of the human cargo in the freight car, but totally unaware of the plans Zachary Arceneaux had in mind for it.

"He'll be here," Gordy said. He spoke with such confidence the guard didn't question him further.

"Which car?" Gordy asked.

The guard pointed to the container car directly in front of the caboose. "That one."

"Do you have the key?"

The guard began to dig through the pockets of his uniform, but Gordy didn't wait for him. With deliberation, he stepped to the sliding door of the car, brought the bolt cutters to bear on the securing padlock, and sliced through the U-shaped shank. The lock dropped down to the tracks with a clank.

Wasting no time, Gordy pushed up the restraining bar and slid open the heavy door.

The power of the odor billowing out was slightly less shocking than the sight of the small bodies crowded silently into the cramped space. Several of the children took one look at the strangely dressed men outside of the box car and began to cry from fear complicated by exhaustion, dehydration, and hunger.

"Time to die, Fontaine!"

The three men whirled around at the sound of the harsh voice that had shouted Gordy's name. They had been so intent on their mission, so shocked by the state of the children, thoughts of Arceneaux had been forgotten.

Their defenses were lowered, and trouble caught them unprepared.

CHAPTER 44

GORDY'S REACTION TO ARCENEAUX'S SHOUT WAS LIKE something out of an old super hero television show. With one hand he caught the leading edge of his white cape and pulled it across in front of him. He ducked his head behind his arm and crouched down so the bottom of the cape touched the ground. His movements had the effect of completely hiding his small body behind the cape.

The 44 magnum in Arceneaux's hand roared, blasting death toward Gordy's huddled form. The bullet impacted the cape and elicited a muffled "Ooof!" from Gordy, but nothing more.

Before Arceneaux could fire again, Father Romero flashed into action. Breaking away from where he was standing with Tony Franks and Arceneaux's two other goons, the priest reached under his shirt and pulled out his knife. It had been secured to the small of his back with adhesive tape and came away easily. Tony Franks reached out to grab him, but the wiry padre slipped through his grasp.

The switchblade in his hand snapped out to its full length, and Father Romero drove the tip of it into Arceneaux's gun hand.

The crime kingpin screamed in outrage as the gun dropped from his numbed fingers. He lashed out with his other hand and knocked the priest back into the arms of Tony Franks.

The gunshot had mobilized everyone on the platform. Commuters began to scream and run for cover. Mingled in with the commuters, the Elvis impersonators realized Cole's mission was for real and began to run assist him.

Gordy emerged from under his cape with his own gun in his hand. The cape was one of two stage props Elvis had ordered years before at Gordy's suggestion. Inside its flashy white covering, the cape was made from bulletproof Kevlar designed to save Elvis in the case of threatened assassination attempts coming true.

"Take them!" Arceneaux screamed at Tony Franks and the other men standing with them. As in past encounters, Arceneaux's megalomania caused him to underestimate his adversary. In his arrogance, he didn't believe he could be stopped. Arceneaux had purposely kept his inner circle as small as possible to handle this important drug shipment. He couldn't afford leaks within his organization. This meant he did not have the number of men needed to deal with Gordy's assault, or for the totally unpredictable appearance of fifty Elvis impersonators.

MacAlister was supposed to have taken Gordy out of the scenario long before it reached this point.

MacAlister was supposed to be the best. How could he have failed?

So close! Arceneaux agonized in the split second it took for him to turn away from the freight car. He knew the cocaine was inside hidden behind the frightened faces of the children he had planned to enslave. He was so close, but so far away.

Tony Franks was struggling with the scrapping form of Father Romero, but Big Timmy and Ollie Dale both pulled guns from shoulder rigs.

Gordy removed the heavy, cumbersome cape from around his neck and threw it at the two heavies. Behind Gordy, Elvis reacted on instinct and slid closed the door of the freight car to protect the children from gunfire.

Gordy fired, and Ollie Dale crashed over backward. Big Timmy returned Gordy's fire. Cole heard Gordy grunt as the bullet took him high in the left shoulder and spun him around.

"Freeze, police!" Joella and Lew yelled in unison as they came running up the platform toward the action. They had locked an angry MacAlister in the trunk of the Pink Madam—which Joella had driven to the scene —and ran into the terminal to help. Seeing the guns pointing at him, Big Timmy immediately dropped his. He wasn't a coward, but he was a realist, and he could see this whole situation was rapidly going to hell.

Arceneaux wasn't going to give up so easily. From the gambler's holster hidden up his left sleeve, he slid a two-shot derringer into his palm. He fired once in the direction of Joella and Lew and then ducked down to roll under the train.

Not wanting to be left holding the bag, Tony Franks

picked Father Romero up and used him as a shield. Taking three quick steps, he threw the priest toward Joella and Lew then dove under the stopped train to follow his boss.

Gordy grunted in pain as he pulled himself to a sitting position. "Get him!" he begged. Elvis and Cole were closest to where Arceneaux and Tony Franks had disappeared. Before Lew or Joella could stop them, they were off in pursuit.

Joella yelled at Cole to stop, but it did no good. Joella went in pursuit of her little brother. Lew still had Big Timmy covered. With professional speed, he hand-cuffed the goon to an attachment on the caboose. When he was done, he quickly went to check on the condition of his ex-partner.

"I told you he wasn't dead," Gordy said, as Lew bent down next to him to look at his wound.

"Who? Elvis?"

"No!" Gordy said in frustration. "Arceneaux! You saw him with your own eyes."

"I never doubted you for a minute," Lew said.

Several of the Elvis impersonators reopened the freight car. Father Romero was with them. He helped Sophia Ungarte down to solid ground and began organizing the unloading. The children were calmed by his presence, and soon they were holding hands with the Elvis clones, being guided away to a brighter future.

"The local cops will be here soon," Lew said. He pulled out a handkerchief and put it over the bullet entry wound in Gordy's shoulder. "How am I going to explain this?" he asked rhetorically. Turning to one of the Elvis impersonators, he grabbed a scarf from around his neck and used it to plug the exit wound.

"You'll think of something," Gordy told his old friend. "You always been creative."

"Let's hope they don't find out about the warrant for your arrest."

"I'm simply another citizen who got caught in the crossfire. My new ID is good enough to hold up under local scrutiny."

"How are you going to explain being down here with fifty other Elvis look-alikes?"

"Karma?"

Lew laughed. "This is L.A. It's an acceptable excuse."

"How's the bullet hole look?" Gordy asked. He winced as he moved.

"Like somebody tried to wire you for cable. You need a doctor."

"Am I going to die?"

"Eventually, but not from this bullet wound."

"I'm going to want to be dead if Arceneaux gets away again."

"Who were the two guys chasing him?"

"You wouldn't believe me if I told you?"

"What else is new?"

———

ELVIS AND COLE rolled out from under the train in time to see Tony Franks follow Arceneaux into the opening to the catacombs. Gordy had told them about the tunnels and they had come prepared with flashlights.

Following quickly, Cole entered the tunnel first. A fist smashed into his face as Tony Franks burst out of ambush. Cole grabbed Tony as he was falling, letting his flashlight drop to the ground.

"Get Arceneaux!" Cole yelled.

Elvis didn't argue. He scrambled past the two grappling men and ran in pursuit of Arceneaux's echoing footsteps.

Cole and Tony wrestled and gouged at each other like two kids fighting on a playground. It wasn't pretty, and it wasn't clean. The darkness was only slightly diffused by the beam from the fallen flashlight.

A third body joined the fray as Joella stumbled into the tunnel. Chasing after Cole and Elvis, she had seen them duck into the hidden tunnel entrance and followed the sounds of the fight until she caught up with them.

Tony Franks wasn't on the psychopathic level as MacAlister. When Joella jammed her gun under his chin, the fight went completely out of him. With practiced movements, Joella rolled him over and cuffed him.

Cole picked up his flashlight and started to hustle deeper into the catacombs.

"Cole! Where the hell are you going?" Joella yelled at him.

"I've got to help him."

"Who?"

"Elvis! Isn't that what this is all about?" He began to run.

"Cole! Stop!" Joella went after him.

CHAPTER 45

EVEN THOUGH THE TUNNELS WERE DESIGNED TO THROW off pursuit, Elvis was still able to track Arceneaux. The crime czar was not in good physical shape and the pain from his stab wound was weakening him further. He made a lot of noise as he ran, constantly bumping into walls, and stumbling on occasion.

Elvis heard Cole calling his name and he yelled back.

Hearing the closing sounds of pursuit, Arceneaux looked behind him and saw the beam of Elvis' flashlight. Looking around for an escape, he turned into one of the smaller offshoot tunnels. He had one bullet left in the derringer and he planned to make it count.

Elvis saw the shadow in front of him turn into the side tunnel and went after it. He knew Cole was on his heels and he felt confident of his back-up. As he entered the smaller tunnel he caught a whiff of something bad, something sickening. The smell was suddenly stronger, and Elvis realized what it was.

He brought his flashlight up and caught Arceneaux

full in its beam. Arceneaux was backed against a tunnel wall. He had the derringer at full extension and a death's head grin on his face.

"Don't—" was all Elvis could get out of his mouth before he clearly saw Arceneaux's finger tightening on the trigger.

Elvis dove to the side, toward a deep blackness as Arceneaux fired and flame flashed from the derringer's barrel.

The methane gas in the tunnel exploded with a huge roar and the walls collapsed in on themselves.

In the main tunnel, Cole and Joella saw flame belch out of the smaller tunnel entrance. The blast knocked them to the ground and showered them with debris. There was a horrible rumbling as the smaller tunnel collapsed.

"Cole!" Joella called out.

Cole picked himself up and rushed to his sister's side. "Are you okay?"

"Twisted my knee."

From somewhere there was a deeper rumbling.

Cole looked around. Dirt was falling from the tunnel roof.

"Elvis!" Cole screamed at the top of his lungs.

There was no reply.

More dirt fell.

"Cole, the tunnel—"

"I know," he said. He pulled Joella to her feet and picked her up in a fireman's carry. He started back the way they had come.

"Elvis!" he screamed again.

There was a crackling from overhead and Cole ran as fast as he could with Joella on his back.

As they hit the opening to the catacombs there was a deeper rumbling, as if a monster were dying, and the main tunnel collapsed behind them.

EPILOGUE

COLE RAMSEY LEANED AGAINST THE END OF THE SANTA Monica Pier and stared out at the cold black/green waves of the ocean. He'd been doing that a lot over the past month. He felt he was searching for a part of himself that had been lost, torn out of his soul, and cast away on the winds. The overcast skies and thin drizzle of the late afternoon fitted his mood.

Turning away from the sea, Cole sighed deeply, filled with a great melancholia. The three lone fishermen who shared the pier had their backs turned to him. They were too engrossed in their own worlds to pay any attention to Cole. Two seagulls landed on the wooden walkway and began to squabble over a piece of rotting bait.

Cole shoved his hands in the pockets of his worn pea coat, hunched his shoulders, and began walking back to the parking lot. As he passed them, the gaudy facades of the closed pier stores took on the appearance of cheap props from a long-abandoned carnival.

"I've got to snap out of this," Cole said quietly, to no

one in particular. He knew his sister was worrying more and more about him. Even his parents had voiced more than their usual concern.

His job with *Legends Alive* was in jeopardy. He'd taken a leave of absence and his understudy was getting rave reviews. But somehow, he couldn't get back in the groove. He hadn't even picked up his guitar since the night Elvis had done his Big John act deep in the hidden catacombs.

Cole's memories of the night were a jumbled nightmare.

Father Romero had taken charge of Gordy, relieving Lew Sutton of any responsibility. With his contacts, the priest was able to get Gordy to a doctor who wouldn't ask any questions about gunshot wounds.

The cops arrived, and half of the Elvis impersonators had stuck around to give impossibly conflicting stories of what happened. The other half had disappeared to help transport the smuggled children to temporary Sanctuary safe houses. Since then, Father Romero, Sheila, Candice, and others connected with the Sanctuary movement had worked tirelessly to find more permanent homes.

Joella had taken great pleasure out of booking MacAlister for possession of his illegal sawn-off shotgun. The charge wouldn't have held him for long, but fortunately, Lew Sutton came up with several federal no-bail warrants against MacAlister from other states.

After being filled in by Cole, Joella and Lew had worked quickly to arrange for Judy Hudson to give a protected deposition against MacAlister. Through her videotaped testimony a grand jury indictment had been brought against the big man for attempted murder and kidnapping.

Under intense federal pressure, brought to bear by Lew Sutton, MacAlister had struck a bargain. In return for considerations at time of sentencing, MacAlister agreed to testify Max Hudson had hired him to kill Judy and bring back Stella.

Judy's husband was arrested and held without bail. The decision giving him custody of Stella was immediately reversed. Judy and Stella were no longer fugitives but were being given new identities and lives through the witness protection program.

With the recovery of the narcotics from the freight car being tied to one of their *clients*, the witness protection program was put under scrutiny. Steps were immediately taken so another situation, like the one involving Arceneaux's second rise to power, could not occur again.

Teams of city workers excavated part of the collapsed catacomb tunnels. The burned and crushed body of Zachary Arceneaux was recovered and positively identified through dental records. Arceneaux's gator pit was located and the gators shipped off to several local zoos. The mangled remains of the wheelchair, to which Lucky Jordan had been strapped, was recovered. Lucky's fingerprints were found on the metal parts of the wheelchair, and slowly the depth of his involvement with Arceneaux was revealed.

The catacombs were eventually filled in properly to protect the streets overhead.

The federal warrants against Gordy Fontaine were dropped with a minimum of fanfare. Gordy could have been hailed as a hero, but he had been on the run so long it had become a way of life. Ever the stubborn idealist, he preferred to return to his efforts with the children's underground. His quest to avenge the death of his father was over, but there were other wrongs to right.

Of Elvis there was no sign.

Not all of the collapsed tunnels had been cleared, and his body was never recovered. This was the factor at the root of Cole's unrest. His time with Elvis seemed unreal now. He had so many questions, so much to learn from the man.

On stage at the Paladin Club, Cole had seen the power of the man. It had been a humbling lesson. He felt no matter how far he went with his own music, he would never have the talent Elvis possessed in one shaking leg. It hurt him and discouraged him. He felt deflated and without direction.

Cole loved the music of Elvis. He revered the legend Elvis became. He'd revolved his life around a man he had never met and never seen perform live.

And then a dead man had called him.

Through Sheila and Gordy, Cole came to know Jon Burrows. A man who Cole was convinced was the still living King of Rock-n'-Roll. When the catacombs beneath Union Station had fallen to entomb him, Cole felt the life go out of his own existence.

Don MacLean had written a song called *American Pie* in which he referred to the death of Buddy Holly being *The Day The Music Died*. Buddy Holly had been known as *The Music*, but Elvis Presley was *The King*.

And when *The King* had been crushed by a ton of falling rock, Cole felt the music in his world die.

The Pink Madam was the only car in the beach parking lot. The drizzle had stopped, but even though it was cold, Cole put the rag top down before starting her up. He pushed in a cassette of Elvis' gospel songs and sat looking out at the ocean again. The opening strains of Elvis' favorite, *How Great Thou Art*, poured into the air. Cole put the car into gear and began to drive slowly home.

Cruising down Santa Monica Boulevard, he began thinking about Sheila Fontaine. She had never been far from his thoughts during these past weeks. He knew if he could shake off this mood of gloom, he would call her. There had been the starting sparks between them of something special.

At Santa Monica and Third something caught his eye...

Cole swiveled his head.

There—on the opposite side of the street—sitting in the empty patio of a restaurant, a familiar figure grinned and waved a newspaper at him.

A bus pulled in front of the restaurant and the figure was hidden from view.

Cole slammed on the Pink Madam's brakes and turned the wheels toward the curb.

There was nowhere to park!

Traffic was backing up behind the Pink Madam. Horns started to blare. Cole looked desperately around for a parking space, saw one on the other side of the street and pulled and illegal U-turn.

An old Camaro beat him to the spot.

Cole looked for a fire hydrant.

Somebody was already illegally parked next to the closest one.

In front of the restaurant, where Cole had seen the figure, there was a police only parking spot. Cole grabbed it. He was related to a deputy sheriff.

He hoisted himself over the door of the Pink Madam and raced for the patio.

It was deserted.

Cole looked around desperately.

A waitress came out onto the patio.

"Can I help you? Our patio is closed today because of the weather."

Cole was confused. "I know this sounds silly, but did you see a man out here a few seconds ago who looked like Elvis Presley?"

The waitress gave Cole an odd look and began to back away. "I'm sorry, sir, but the patio is closed. There's been nobody out here."

"But I saw him sitting here. He waved at me with a newspaper."

"Elvis Presley?"

"Yes!" Cole craned his neck to look around the area again.

"Are you okay, sir? Is there someone I can call for you?"

Cole looked at the waitress again. "What are you talking about?"

"Elvis Presley is dead. Has been for a lot of years."

"Shows how much you know."

The restaurant's bartender stepped outside. "What's

up?" he asked the waitress. "This guy giving you a problem?"

She shrugged.

He gave Cole a glare. "Either come inside and order something or clear off."

Cole saw a folded newspaper on top of a patio chair.

"No problem," he said to the bartender. "I'm sorry," he said to the waitress. "I haven't been sleeping well lately."

As casually as he could, he reached over and snagged the newspaper before walking away. The bartender and the waitress went back inside.

Third Street at Santa Monica had been turned into a pedestrian walkway, part of the Third Street Mall. The restaurant patio had been on one side of Third Street. Cole crossed over to the other. Leaning up against a wall, he looked down at the newspaper. It was the latest issue of *The Celebrity Tattler*. It was folded to highlight a familiar column:

THE CELEBRITY TATTLER

Volume 28 Number 24
May 1991

MOONE AND THE STARS

By
Celebrity Tattler Columnist
Linda Moone

THE EL-VIRUS RUNS RAMPANT

This columnist has been kicking around celebrity gossip circles for longer than it takes a big-name actress to wear out three face lifts, but I have never come across the likes of the following. Reports from Elvis Night at the Paladin Club have been pouring in. People are convinced a mysterious performer by the name of Jon Burrows is actually the King of Rock n' Roll in disguise. His performance was so hot it practically burned the place down. When it was over, he blew out of the place like a hot wind. The consensus is if Jon Burrows isn't Elvis Presley, he should be. But the information coming in from the Paladin Club can't compare with the mother of all Elvis sightings from Union Station in Los Angeles. From all reports, every Elvis impersonator and look-a-like decided to take the A-train at the same time. I have heard from hundreds of people who saw Elvis's guiding little children by the hand, being shot at, or chasing bad guys down ancient sewer tunnels. The El-Virus seems to have turned into an epidemic infecting everyone in its path. Authorities are being closed mouthed about what happened. The reason for this is probably because they don't know what is going on either...

The column went on for a dozen or more paragraphs, but Cole didn't read further. He was more interested in the additions made to the page in red pen. The handwriting was somewhat spidery, but Cole had no trouble reading it through a veil of happy tears.

Thanks for giving me back a part of my life I thought was gone forever, read the scribbled words across the top of the column. Below the column was more red ink; *You have the music in you, the special talent it takes to be great. Never give up.*

And there was a final line; *If you ever need me, all you have to do is call.*

The message was simply signed; *El.*

Cole shouted for joy and threw the paper up into the evening sky.

He had to call his sister! He had to let Gordy know! He had to find Sheila and tell her he'd fallen in love at first sight with her!

His heart was suddenly filled with singing. The music was back!

The King lives!

Long live The King!

A LOOK AT FIGHTCARD:
FELONY FISTS

Los Angeles 1954

Patrick "Felony" Flynn has been fighting all his life. Learning the "sweet science" from Father Tim the fighting priest at St. Vincent's, the Chicago orphanage where Pat and his older brother Mickey were raised, Pat has battled his way around the world – first with the Navy and now with the Los Angeles Police Department.

Legendary LAPD chief William Parker is on a rampage to clean up both the department and the city. His elite crew of detectives known as The Hat Squad is his blunt instrument – dedicated, honest, and fearless. Promotion from patrol to detective is Pat's goal, but he also yearns to be one of the elite.

And his fists are going to give him the chance.

Gangster Mickey Cohen runs LA's rackets, and murderous heavyweight Solomon King is Cohen's key to taking over the fight game. Chief Parker wants wants Patrick "Felony" Flynn to stop him – a tall order for middleweight ship's champion with no professional record.

Leading with his chin, and with his partner, LA's first black detective Tombstone Jones, covering his back, Patrick Flynn and his Felony Fists are about to fight for his future, the future of the department, and the future of Los Angeles.

AVAILABLE NOW FROM PAUL BISHOP AND WOLFPACK PUBLISHING

BOOKS BY PAUL BISHOP

Fey Croaker Series

Croaker: Kill Me Again

Croaker: Grave Sins

Croaker: Tequila Mockingbird

Croaker: Chalk Whispers

———

Hot Pursuit

Deep Water

A Bucketful of Bullets

Lie Catchers

Nothing But The Truth (Almost)

Fightcard: Felony Fists

Fightcard: Swamp Walloper

ABOUT THE AUTHOR

Novelist, screenwriter, and television personality, Paul Bishop is a nationally recognized behaviorist and deception detection expert. A 35-year veteran of the LAPD, his high profile Special Assault Units produced the top crime clearance rates in the city. Twice honored as LAPD's *Detective of the Year*, he currently conducts law enforcement training seminars across the country.

As a deception detection consultant, his unique skills make him a valuable resource for private companies faced with potentially damaging in-house data breaches, industrial espionage, or corporate sabotage. His low-key, non-invasive, approach to these challenges has proven consistently successful.

Paul is the author of fifteen novels—including five books in his LAPD Detective Fey Croaker series—and has written numerous scripts for episodic television and feature films. He starred as the lead interrogator and driving force behind the ABC TV reality show *Take the Money and Run* from producer Jerry Bruckheimer.

A regular speaker at writing conferences, he is also an adjunct professor at the University of California Channel Islands, where he lectures on criminal investigation. He regularly presents his popular seminar, *Six-Gun Justice—Western Novels, Movies, and TV Shows*, at libraries and other community functions.

He is the co-writer/editor of the acclaimed *52 Weeks • 52 Western Novels—A Guide To Six-Gun Favorites And New Discoveries*. Three follow-up volumes (*52 Weeks • 52 Western Movies, 52 Weeks • 52 Western TV Shows*, and *52 Weeks • 52 More Western Novels*) will be published in 2018. His latest book, *Lie Catchers*, is the first in a new series featuring top LAPD interrogators Ray Pagan and Calamity Jane Randall. The sequel, *Admit Nothing*, is due in 2018.

ON THE WEB

www.bishsbeat.blogspot.com
www.elementrixconsulting.com
Twitter @BishsBeat